P9-DFL-511

BRIGHT BEFORE US

A NOVEL

KATIE ARNOLD-RATLIFF

Tin House Books
Portland, Oregon & New York, New York

Powell's Books is proud to present this exclusive hardcover edition of *Bright Before Us* to Indiespensable subscribers.

Published by Tin House Books, Portland, Oregon,
and New York, New York

Distributed to the trade by Publishers Group West,
1700 Fourth St., Berkeley, CA 94710, www.pgw.com

ISBN 978-1-935639-19-0

First U.S. edition 2011
Printed in Canada
Interior design: Diane Chonette
www.tinhouse.com

the face of love . . .
is the face turning away.

—LOUISE GLÜCK, "LOVER OF FLOWERS"

1

We hadn't expected it; the sky had been clear. But as the afternoon waned, clouds converged above the beach, and then the first shocks of rain came down stinging. Soon the wind picked up, and the drops collected in pools. Most of the kids were in short sleeves. I hadn't thought to bring umbrellas. I crouched in the downpour, waiting out the clock, watching the two men in the stranded boat.

They were thirty feet away in a deep and narrow cove, edged by the sand on one side and a rock wall on the other. Their boat bobbed gently, their fishing rods shimmying in the wind. They had just set off for deeper waters, but hadn't gotten far before the motor cut out. As the older man stood with an appraising scowl, his puffed vest darkening with water, the younger man ripped at the pull-cord. Nothing happened. They would have to wade ashore.

It was, on warm weekends, a popular beach. On past trips I had seen teenagers negotiate the jagged rocks in flip-flops, lifting starfish from suctioned slumber to chuck them into the surf. But it was a Friday afternoon, so there was just me, the two parents who had come to help, and my two dozen second graders. For a listless hour, as we moved incrementally down the beach, my students inspected the kelp-littered dunes with clipboards in hand, making tick marks on their flora observation lists and rubbing their noses with their palms. Now, I wiped the water from my wristwatch and folded my soggy newspaper, ready to call it a day and begin the weekend. It was close enough, I reasoned, to when we had planned to leave.

One of the parents walked over—Mr. Noel, a burly, hulking creature built like a linebacker. *Mr. Mason,* he barked, *I'm getting my umbrella. Then we'll line them up?*

I scanned the beach for the other chaperone. *Where's Mrs. Stone?*

She went to get her daughter's coat, he said. *You'll be okay alone for a minute?*

I nodded—I'm alone with them every day, I thought—and he took off at a jog toward the bus; with his jacket pulled high above him he looked headless. As I watched him, one of my students approached me. Since the beginning of the year, eight months earlier, I had worried about her—Emma was thin to the point of frailty, and when I spoke, her eyes remained unfocused, as though she were blindly aiming her face toward the sound. I would call her house to arrange conferences or check up on unreturned permission slips, and listen to the phone ring and ring. Her mother hadn't dressed her for the weather. She was shivering.

Can I please go to the bus? She pointed to Mr. Noel, who was halfway to the parking lot. *Caleb's dad is going.*

You have to line up like everybody else, I said, shoving the newspaper into my backpack. *I'm blowing the whistle in three minutes.*

She began the tantrum dance, her clipboard against her chest.

Consult some classmates until departure time, I said. *Scientists collaborate, remember? Go share your findings.*

I didn't find nothing, Mr. Mason, Emma said. *I don't even see what's here to find.*

I hesitated, then unzipped my jacket and gave it to her. In seconds the rain had pasted my shirt to my back. I glanced at the men in the boat, and then, in the foreground, the children. I felt myself tense.

They had gathered into one still group.

I heard shouting. The men in the boat were now both standing, their vessel rocking as they waved their arms. I took a step forward. The children—nearly every one— turned around, several mouths open in alarm. A few of them broke away and ran in my direction, their feet failing beneath them in little stumbles. *Mr. Mason,* they said in chorus. I could see Jacob panting, and as they reached me I heard the characteristic rasp, the beginnings of an asthma attack curling around his chest. *Mr. Mason, Mr. Mason.*

I took off at a run, waving to the men in the boat and shouting, *I've got it,* not knowing what that meant. I hollered for the children to go immediately to the bus, my voice shrill, unmistakably panicked. The rest of the children at the water's edge mostly dispersed, starting toward the parking lot, but a few remained, still looking down at whatever was there. I called up the beach for Mr. Noel and Mrs. Stone. They were out of earshot. I barked at Emma, behind me now, *Go get them*, and as she ran up the beach in my jacket the sleeves grazed the sand. I paused midrun, remembering Jacob. *Someone go in my backpack!* I yelled. *Inhaler, get his inhaler.* I didn't wait to make sure someone did as I asked.

One of them is hurt, I thought. Somebody's head is cracked open. A tableau unfurled—the sound of sirens, the arrival of an ambulance. The things I had learned in first aid returned to me: *Assess responsiveness. Press firmly on the wound.*

I squinted at the water; my feet moved slowly in the sand. The boat was now empty. Then I spotted the two men, wading ashore, chest-deep in the gray inlet. One of the kids fell in, I thought. He's filling with water. *Tilt the head with two fingers under the chin. Breathe for him until help arrives.* Sharp points pressed into the soles of my sneakers as I stepped over the rocks at the cove's mouth. The gaze of the four remaining children—Jeffrey, Marcus, Edmund, and Benjamin—remained fixed on the place where the water met the sand. *Go,* I said, and though I was in motion, I saw it plain as anything: they hesitated. I snapped, *Get over there*, and watched them move toward the dunes. I stepped forward, headlong and terrified.

First I saw the flies. They were giddy, drunk on what they had found, big and overfed. They were indifferent to my presence, letting me step into them. I no longer remember the smell, only what it did to me. I doubled over. The tableau evaporated. There would be no CPR, no wound to staunch. I knew what I would find. I looked back, delaying. Most of the kids were going to the bus, but others stood where I had been sitting, staring back at me. Jacob was coughing frantically, inhaler in hand. He doubled over, desperate for air. I took another step and saw an outcropping of damp wood half-buried in the sand, surrounded by tiny footprints. Bunches of yellow grass wavered in the wind. And a few feet away, beside a slick tangle of brown kelp, was the body.

I see myself as the children must have seen me: a young man stepping cautiously forward, rocks and reeds obscuring his bottom half. His face distorts as he bends at the waist, his palm goes to his open mouth, and then the back of that same hand moves to his nose. The children are afraid. Unexpected events frighten them. But they look at the man and they are, in a small way, put at ease. They look at him and think, He's our teacher.

And then they hear him scream. And as two men emerge dripping from the water and pull him away, the children drop their clipboards. They do what their teacher has commanded them to do whenever they feel they are in danger: they run.

. . .

Roughly one year earlier, I had received my teaching certificate in a quiet ceremony at a local state college. I secured a job in the struggling district with unsettling ease, and began looking for holes in the prescribed curriculum that I could fill with art, the People's History, the teaching of tolerance. At home, I practiced finger painting, free-association writing, explosive science experiments, a segment on cooking. I swore I would take my students outside no matter the season; we would do a unit on international sports, like jai alai and cricket. I would teach them the silly camp songs of my youth—*Fish and chips and vinegar, vinegar, vinegar.* I stood in front of the medicine cabinet mirror and practiced my enthusiastic lectures, my voice low so Greta wouldn't hear me from the bedroom. I perfected faces to use when they spoke, so they would know that I was really, truly listening to them.

I could see the San Francisco Bay from the roof of the school building, the dividing line between gray sky and gray water nearly indistinguishable. I occasionally left Greta in our bed before dawn to drink my coffee up there in a lawn chair, staring down the sun as it rose over the playground. Sometimes I went up there to grade homework as the evening wind kicked up, watching stragglers play foursquare while waiting for their parents. I knew I could be seen from the apartments nearby, and that I wasn't hard to peg: a young guy just starting out as a teacher, his wrinkled clothes flecked with last week's tempera paint, crumbling sneakers stained with soccer-field mud. With my conspicuous glasses and purple-rimmed eyes, I looked the part.

Large-scale additions had been made to Hawthorne Elementary in the fifties, accommodating the bulge of children born after their fathers returned en masse from the war. The dismal chunky-block design betrayed its quick, utilitarian construction: it was all cement and stucco, later accompanied by a sea of prefab portable classrooms huddled on the former kickball diamond. But I was lucky enough to be placed in the older wing. Tall dark-wood pillars anchored my classroom, their proximity to adjoining walls creating odd nooks—one I used for a storage area, another for a small study lab. The interior was paneled in that same dark wood, like a saloon.

On my first day, I was surprised by my confidence; nervousness had always been my default setting, but that morning I couldn't wait to get started. I arrived long before the children did, and sat staring up at the posters I had chosen: Martin Luther King Jr., a lesser known Matisse, Einstein with his tongue out. I realized, too tired to fix it, that they were hung crookedly. I had put them up hastily days earlier, preparing like mad but slowed by the unrelenting heat. Though outside it was a mild September, the room was stuck at eighty degrees, and the oscillating fan I had brought barely moved the air. But the lessons were planned, the books were on the shelves, and I marveled: whatever happened in there would happen because of me.

My students sat in small blue chairs at tables rather than individual desks, each of the six tables named for a state. I was the president, and they voted on things like where to go for field trips, whether we should play dodgeball or softball in afternoon gym, chalkboards versus whiteboards. The thrill they experienced when given a choice was immense. Their wonder, too, came easily, and was wholly uncomplicated. They cried when I read them *Charlotte's Web*, viewed repro impressionist paintings with pious reverence. When we made buffalo stew for the unit on California's Native Americans, they leaned over the pot like we were cooking up magic. Those first months, I swelled with something unfamiliar: a secure knowledge of the good I was doing.

I took them on field trips as often as possible. The first, in early October, was to the Rockland Hiking Trail, an hour north of the city, on the long, parched stretch to Sacramento. The children mostly slept on the ride up, the Indian summer heat wafting in through the open bus windows. Once we arrived, they started a game of soccer in the grassy field near the parking lot. I always brought a ball on trips, and had memorized easy diversions— Telephone, or the Alphabet Game: *A, my name is Adam and I live in Antarctica*—in case there was time to kill. I watched as Edmund, invoking Class Foundation #2 (*We can always pass if we feel uncomfortable or need some time alone*), stayed out of the game, tossing the ball back in if it went out of bounds and dutifully pointing out players who went offside. Ed was a squat, tow-headed boy with a strong jaw and watery green eyes. When we played sports he was always among the first chosen. The kids liked him, and I liked him too. When I told Greta stories about school, she would ask after him: *How's your pet?*

After the soccer game, we began our hike: a two-mile jaunt up and then around a small hill, a green lake curving around the last half where the trail hit level ground. We passed a small quarry where ribbons of rust ran down the sloped limestone. I kept an eye on Edmund, who lagged a few paces behind.

Ed, everything okay? A moment passed, as though he hadn't heard me. A bird called out in the quarry, the echo rising. The air was herbal, an acrid scent that registered in the throat. *How come you didn't want to play soccer today? You love soccer.*

He knelt in the weeds.

Hey, what'd you find? I bent down, my voice gentle. *Let's see it.*

His eyes glimmered. *I never saw one like this before.* He held up a striped pebble. *I didn't feel like playing soccer today,* he said. He put the stone in his pocket and ran to catch up with the others.

I found the rock on my desk at school the next morning, on top of the homework I had nearly finished grading. That afternoon, soccer came up in our normal rotation and Ed asked to be a team captain, high-fiving each kid he picked. I watched, relieved, from a nearby goalpost.

I never did figure out what caused their moods to sink or lift. They were each little mysteries, improvising in a world they didn't comprehend. They remained mostly unreachable. I could teach them how to add, or to enjoy a Monet, or to understand the basic tenets of baseball, but I would never know what they thought about, what they worried about. And as soon as I thought I had a handle on it, they stopped loving the things they had loved, stopped listening to the stories they had often requested, stopped wanting to play soccer when they always played soccer. As soon as I figured them out, they weren't them anymore. For a while, I was content with that, thinking it added to the charm of the work I had chosen: helping them learn how to be people.

. . .

I was guided toward the bus, flanked by the wet fishermen. I watched the blurred ground pass as I took heavy, deliberate steps through the sand. *Easy does it,* the older man kept saying. My mouth seemed disconnected from my body. I tried to say, *I'm fine, really. I'm okay, I just . . .* but I didn't know what words came next. I was soaked, rainwater dripping from my chin. I could hear whimpering. Oh no, I thought, one of the kids is crying. Then I felt a dull pulling at my eyes: the sound was coming from me.

We walked as a threesome, the men holding my arms. I saw the younger man turn toward the older—I guessed then that they were father and son—and give him a look. *What the fuck?* the look said. We reached the parking lot. The younger man patted one of the kids on the head, and though I didn't know why, it angered me. The men sat on a bench opposite me and stared blankly, openly, like I was a television.

I tried to parse it out, but the whole thing was nonsensical. We had gone to Steinhart Aquarium on a field trip, and then we had come here, to the beach, and this had happened. These children, my charges, had witnessed something far worse than the things routinely kept from them: the R-rated movies, the content of encoded conversations. And they had seen it on my watch. Everything that had happened here had happened because of me. The extent of the situation started to become clear: I would need to call parents, organize conferences, send home a letter. I would need to explain. Wisps of weariness for all I would have to do surfaced and, for a moment, clouded everything. And then the image of the body came back: nude, torn into, and without—*my God*—its limbs, color, or breath. I repeated the story to myself, trying to understand, and feeling for the life of me like there was something more, something else—something that was humming beneath my consciousness, not yet ready to be examined.

Everyone was milling, their words like insects. I saw Mrs. Stone dialing her cell phone. Emma broke from the crowd and walked over.

Why are you sad, Mr. Mason? she asked. She had tossed the arms of my coat around her neck like two scarves, and she looked bound, straight-jacketed.

The older man whispered to his son, *I don't think we should leave yet.*

Mr. Noel did his gruff best to corral the children, clumsily getting them onto the bus. After a while, they ate whatever portions of their lunches they hadn't finished at the aquarium. Mrs. Stone began calling the parents to explain why we were already a half hour late. When her cell phone couldn't get reception, she paced the parking lot, holding the phone aloft like a torch. She perfected her recitation, shuffling through the yellow emergency cards. *There's been an incident.* My insides crawled, sure that to the parents' ears this statement was too cryptic, that her skirting of the subject implied guilt. My guilt. Her fucking euphemism: it let the imagination run to judgment for entire seconds before she elaborated, saying simply, *The children came upon a crime scene.*

Officer Buckingham found me sitting at the edge of the parking lot. He was bigger than me, with streaked silver hair and eyes creased at the outer edges, and he smelled like a sweet cigar.

Mr. Mason, he said. He loomed above me; to see his face, I had to look up. *The U.S. Park Police intends to do everything possible to make sure the family of the decedent finds some peace.*

Slowly, my ability to speak returned. *You can call me Francis,* I said carefully, aware of my swollen eyes. I knew he could tell I had cried. *Are you going to speak to the children?* I asked. *I'd like to be there when you do.*

My partner is speaking to them now, he said, brusquely clicking the end of his pen. *I just have a few questions for you, Frank.*

Through the bus windshield I saw his partner standing beside the driver, addressing the children. Down on the beach, a crew of people walked around the body, staring at the ground. I watched them long enough to see that they were moving in a spiral, looking for evidence. Another crew walked toward the beach with a long zippered bag. It looked too light, like a breeze could take it from them.

I shook my head. *I can't—I didn't see much.*

You saw the decedent, he said.

Something flooded my chest each time I heard the word. *I saw it,* I said.

Buckingham coughed, thick and wet. *Did you move or touch the body? Did you pull anything off it?*

No, I said.

What were you doing when the children found the body?

I closed my eyes. The newspaper, the men in the boat. Unzipping my jacket. *I was speaking to a student,* I said.

How much time elapsed between discovery of the decedent and when the children alerted you?

I didn't answer. How could I know?

Frank, Buckingham said, smiling tightly. *Did they all come at once?*

My eyes were still closed. The group of them, all looking down. Emma behind me. The group that left when I said to. The small, stone-faced cluster that remained. Jacob, bent at the waist, and his dry, scraping cough. *I have a student with asthma,* I said, looking up. *Do you know if he—*

Do you have a sense of which child made the initial discovery?

I looked past him, silent.

Buckingham's false smile disappeared. *Mr. Mason, I need to get a feeling for how long the children were unattended with the deceased, for evidence reasons.* He leaned down, his face not quite level with mine.

I watched his lips move, the wind wheezing around us. On the bus, his partner's chin turned toward her shoulder as she pressed a button and spoke into the radio there. The crew began moving up the beach, carrying, in tandem, the bag. It was no longer amorphous, no longer light. It bowed in the center and came up at either end in the shape of a smile.

We had just moved to this part of the beach. I searched his eyes. *It was only a moment,* I said, turning to watch the crew place the bag onto a gurney, *that they were alone with her.*

Buckingham recorded something in his notebook. *What a thing to have happen.*

I squinted, feeling queasy. *I never imagined that . . . I didn't know there could be so much damage,* I said.

That's the water, he said. *Not the jump.*

We were dwarfed by a rocky hill, beyond which stood

the bridge, swaying and red. *You must see a lot of these,* I said.

One is too many. He put his pen into his shirt pocket. *There's no greater waste.* He extended his hand for me to shake.

I'm so embarrassed, I said, stifling a smile of pure discomfort. Behind him, the ocean looked restless. I turned and watched the ambulance silently proceed down the narrow beach road. Buckingham dropped the hand I hadn't shaken. He waited a moment for me to continue speaking, and when I didn't, he left me alone.

I found Mrs. Stone leaning against the bus, the knees of her pants dirty from the wet sand. Her face was pinched, and her small billow of graying hair had flattened. It was nearly six o'clock.

Margaret, I said. *You've called everyone?*

She nodded.

How bad was Jacob's attack?

She didn't meet my eye. *He's asleep now. A few of the others, too.*

We climbed into the chilled bus, the yawning driver long into overtime. I sat beside Jacob, and without waking him took the inhaler from his limp hand. His breaths were ragged, the beds of his fingernails faintly blue. A few rows ahead, Mr. Noel held his son, Caleb, tightly against him. I could see him leaning down to whisper. I placed Jacob's inhaler in my backpack, daring to close my eyes.

But the image that came wasn't the body—it was Jacob, gasping for the air that escaped him. Jake, hunched over, and then lifting his head like a baby bird, mouth wide, trying to do on his own what I was supposed to help him do. The first time I saw him have an attack had been six months before. He had scrambled up to my desk and choked out, *Mr. Mason, I need it.* I blinked. *Like, soon,* he said. I remembered his mother approaching me on the first day of school, the package she had placed in my hand. Fumbling, I had retrieved his inhaler from my bottom desk drawer and watched as he gripped it for one, then two minutes, throwing his head back with each intake of air, his eyes meeting mine each time he lowered his chin. The din of the other children reverberated from what seemed a great distance and then fell away, as I felt my breathing sync with his.

I opened my eyes again, the bus rattling as we rode home. We drove over the Golden Gate, the city on the left, the sea to the right. The kids were quiet. They looked so small. They were so little it startled me sometimes.

When we arrived back at school, the parents were lined up against a portable classroom. I exited the bus with my hands in the air, shouting, *They're okay.* The sky darkened above us, as I began to explain what I could.

2

On the first day of the last week I knew you, we stood beside the mausoleum, watching people arrive. The limousines pulled in first, neon placards tucked in their windshields, headlights on at midday. Then came the dusty hatchbacks and squat minivans, their tires crunching the gravel. On the top edge of the nearby chapel, birds alighted between the splayed spikes meant to deter them. *Thanks for coming, Francis,* you said, breathing through your open mouth, your nose skinned from wiping. *You want to do something tomorrow?* You pushed tears away with the butt of your hand, eye makeup striping your wrist.

Sure, I said, loosening my tie. I was surprised that you asked—in the four days since the accident I hadn't left you.

When the call came, I was searching the channels for the next day's weather forecast before I left your apartment. You were making French toast for your dinner, opening and shutting the fridge. The phone rang. *I have egg on my hands,* you called. *Could you get that?* I answered and a man said his name, Officer something. He asked if you lived there. He called you *Miss Lucas,* above the buzz of his radio. I was, despite a flash of guilt, sorry I hadn't left sooner. From the way I said your name—*Nora, you should take this*—you knew to come quick. You took the phone with your dirty hands, confirmed that you were indeed you, and hung up.

He said he'd be here shortly, you said.

I started to speak—*What else did he*—but was interrupted by a knock at the door. He had called from outside, had been parked on the street. He stood in the entryway and took off his hat—you followed it with your eyes as he held it to his middle—and told you swiftly, like it was burning his mouth, that he was very, very sorry.

The first thing you said after he finished was *How did you know where I live?* You chewed on your lip. He explained the process a bit too gamely, like he was showing you a new toy. He told you they ran the plates on the totaled car—that was how they identified your parents in the absence of their identification. *Your mother's purse landed some yards away,* he said. *We haven't found your father's wallet, if he carried one. I'm assuming he did?* When you didn't answer, he went on to tell you that they had looked up your parents' records and found your birth certificate, and checked the directory for your name. You were listed.

It was actually pretty easy, he said.

Oh, you said, reaching behind you, feeling for something. He shut the door as he left; the TV was still making noise. I wasted a few seconds wondering if I should step toward you and when I didn't, you told me to: *Come here, please.* Since then we had spent every hour in your apartment or mine, the funeral director's sweaty office, our cars. And finally, the gritty parking lot above the graveyard.

In the vista beneath us were hundreds of gravestones, sprouting from the hills like teeth. We had just learned that no one is buried in San Francisco anymore—one must choose from the twenty cemeteries in the necropolis next door, where the residents have bumper stickers that read: *It's good to be alive in Colma.* You chose that cemetery because it was at the top of the list; the day of the service was the first time you saw it. The only trees stood at the outer edge of the lawn, and so the sun was everywhere, stone markers shooting glares like a laser show. The graves were coarse with crabgrass, the studded expanse enclosed in chain-link. On the mausoleum behind you was an old lady's rounded cameo photograph, embedded in the marble face of the stone drawer that contained her body. The type on her monument was harsh and certain. You were twenty-two, slouching in a discount black dress, about to absorb the sympathy of people you rarely saw or had never met. We roasted like tender plants, flushing beneath our black clothes, until your aunt came over to tell you it was time. She was a big, burdened woman, bent like she was dragging something. She put her arm around you and pulled you away, and you let her, because this was too big to fight: not the goldfish and hamster death we knew from childhood, but real death, searing and complete.

Inside the chapel, everyone shivered in the aggressive air-conditioning. I chose a seat a few rows behind and to the left of you, next to a string of business-casual strangers. You stared at your lap. *When young people are taken,* the man at the podium began, rustling his papers. The sound crackled through the slender microphone. He had merely been given dates and names, had never met you or your parents. Two caskets sat side by side in front of the altar, flowers spilling over their contoured lids. You had requested that they remain closed, and had declined a viewing. The director had leaned forward like you were six years old. *People want to say their good-byes to the faces they knew and loved.* You had pulled away from his mouthwash scent as you said, *Well I don't.*

The chapel had one wall of streaked glass that looked onto a small rock garden furnished with plastic ferns and fake frogs. An electric fountain emitted a weak stream, an extension cord growing from it like an orange tail. The pews were nearly full, people dabbing at their eyes with their sleeves, mothers transacting bribes to quiet their children. Your parents hadn't been religious, but the man at the podium spoke of the many rooms in His house. You blinked slowly. You could have been a passenger on a commuter train; you could have been waiting in a dentist's office. And then you jerked a little, your lips pulling in disgust, your hand batting at something. I couldn't see what.

Afterward, most people went to the lawn, others to their cars. Together, we approached the flimsy white tent at the graveside, the folding chairs sitting crookedly in the knotty grass. A bulldozer rested in the near distance. *It was a beautiful service,* I said, trying to think of what people say in movies.

But you were somewhere else. *I have to host a party after this,* you said. We qwalked, my hands in my pockets, yours clutching a purse from which you pulled tissues and gum. *And guess who cleans up afterward!*

You don't have to clean up, I said. *I'll do that.*

You pulled at your clothes, smoothing your dress, and asked me, *Do I look okay?*

Your face was puffed as if from too much sleep, though you had gotten none. The edges of your nostrils were abraded red hoops. You were pretty, but that day you looked like what you were: someone over whom sadness had triumphed.

Yes, I said. *You look very nice.*

Keep her talking, I thought. Just keep tossing questions. *What were you twitching about in there?*

There were ants on my leg. The corners of your mouth plummeted. *This place is a shithole.*

And then you saw the open grave. There was only one hole, cut deep for the two bodies that would share it, but you didn't understand. You had chosen this when you were making decisions by pointing at glossy pamphlets, half-awake, forgetting things the moment you said them. You glanced around like a spooked horse, trying to catch the eye of someone in charge. You wanted an explanation. Your aunt pulled you close to her, misunderstanding, and you pushed out of her embrace like a distracted toddler.

My mind clearing, I rushed forward and gripped your hand, hard, like a parent; I pulled you to me briskly enough that you dropped your purse. I whispered in your ear, *It's okay. Sometimes people are buried one on top of the other. This is fine.*

Everyone watched you. I knew they were waiting for the fireworks moment I dreaded, the moment you hit the ground wailing. I hated each of them, imagining them wanting privately, selfishly, to be the source of your comfort.

And standing there, holding your hand, I had a sour sensation of pride: I had won.

Okay, you said, pulling your hand away. You picked up your purse and took your place at the grave. *Okay,* you said again. And everyone exhaled, beneath the soft, enervating waft of pollen, as the proceedings commenced.

You left with your aunt as soon as it ended. Once everyone had gone, a casket began to descend. I didn't know which of your parents was inside. I waited until I felt the lowering mechanism stop vibrating, until I knew the first coffin was safe at the bottom of that hole, before I walked to my car. I had the irrational thought that you might worry about this, later. And I wanted, at least once, to be able to reassure you with some conviction.

When I arrived at your parents' house you were sitting on the steps alone. I jogged up the drive. *You beat me.*

My aunt had to get her lasagna in the oven, you said, motioning behind you to the house full of people. You pulled my arm so I would sit. Before I smelled your breath I knew: your gaze was bouncing around.

What, do you have a flask on you? I asked, but then I saw that behind you were two minibar bottles, their twist lids nearby like spent shells.

You showed me the place beneath the bushes where you had shoved the other three. *Catch up,* you said, pointing. *Watch out for the cop, though. He keeps driving past to see what all the cars are about.*

I picked up the bottles and downed one, then two. I asked, *Have you eaten today?* though I knew the answer.

We sat for a while in the October air. I imagined every one watching us through the window. *We have to go in,* I said. Soon, all the bottles were empty, the lids littering the stoop. I felt heavy, embarrassed. So when you leaned over and put your hand on my knee, I thought it was because you could tell I was sick. I had my lips poised to say, *I think we should drink some water.* But before I could speak you had pushed your palm up the length of my leg, fingertips pressing. The back of my throat made a noise, low and involuntary. You dug your nails in and waited.

I felt automation take over, my fingers straining to touch you back. But it was simple: I was afraid. I would have felt the same fear had your fingers landed there in high school, in college; I would have been afraid if you were sober. I would have been afraid if nobody was watching us through the window; or if nobody had died—if you had ten parents, twenty of them. I couldn't touch you. I couldn't do, at that moment, what you were asking me to do.

Don't, I murmured, stopping your hand with mine. You snatched your hand back, got up, and stumbled inside. You slammed the door as the cop came around the block again, peering like a predator. I swept the bottles to the dirt patch beneath the bushes and trudged up the steps, then through a small crowd milling in the foyer. I scanned the room and didn't find you there or in the dining room, the kitchen, the den. I walked up the steps and went into your old bedroom, the room where we had watched bad TV in high school and whispered our earnest, youthful convictions. The place where I had once cried after confessing some dumbfuck misdeed: I had, without any real motive, defamed a kid I had known for six grades, and though I forget what I was telling people—he was gay? A virgin? A gay virgin?—I know it was wholly invented. In that room one evening, after two pilfered lite beers, I had wept, *I'm not a bad person.* All I could do was hope it was true.

Of course you aren't, you had said, because you believed it.

The same posters, now comically dated, were tacked to the wall, and dried roses hung upside down from the ceiling fan's beaded pull-chain. Next to your bed was the novelty phone you had had forever, translucent plastic that lit up from within when a call came through. There was a sharp air-freshener smell. I hadn't been in there in years.

I suddenly knew where I would find you. I walked down the hallway, passing a picture of you as a baby: surrounded by plastic blocks, nestled in shag carpet, naked apart from a diaper. One of your hands was in the air, holding up three fingers. You were smiling, mostly toothless. I passed the open door of your father's office. His reading glasses sat upside down on a desk calendar beside a half-empty glass of water. The wastebasket was full. I opened the door at the end of the hall and found you on your parents' still-made bed, your dress twisted around your waist, wearing one of your shoes. You were unconscious, your mouth open, and I pulled the skirt of your dress down to cover you. In the bathroom I spit up my three bottles of hotel vodka, avoiding my eyes in the mirror as I washed my hands.

Downstairs, someone had put on the evening news. I joined the morose club on your parents' couches, eating turkey casserole and fielding stares. I knew what they wanted to know: who was I, to you?

3

I scanned my mind, opened my eyes. It was Saturday. I could hear Greta's metronome—it helped her insomnia—and my head throbbed to the familiar tempo. I awoke fully, my stale breath permeating the air, and the memory came: the body, the beach, the crying.

The sheets had tangled around Greta's waist in her sleep. Her breasts rolled toward her flanks and her squared stomach puffed around her navel like a cushion punctuated by a button. Sleep didn't calm Greta's face the way it does most, smoothing lines into angelic peace. Instead, she appeared elderly—feeble and uncertain.

She was four months along. Recently, I had been catching myself staring at her stomach. As she slept, I put my hand there and watched her face twitch; I pressed as though I were a doctor testing her appendix, feeling for something hard, defined. She awoke with a quick breath, her eyes wide. I reached over her to still the metronome, my hand lingering tenderly on her rib cage.

Good morning, she croaked, watching me until I forced a smile.

The previous evening returned in bursts. A gauntlet of parents, armed with questions. The sense that it wouldn't be over soon. It wasn't a situation I had thought to prepare for. It wasn't a situation I could have imagined. And even their simplest question couldn't, it seemed, be answered satisfactorily—*Where were you?*

This, more than anything, was what they wanted to know. They wanted me to tell them whom to blame. That is, they had an idea, and they wanted it confirmed. And they wanted to hear, *Don't worry, your kid barely knew what was going on.*

The children were tucked safely inside the classroom, waiting to go home, and still their parents had persisted. *Did Bridget see it? Did she in particular seem upset afterward?* They wanted to know what their child had said. They wanted to know if their child had been quiet or withdrawn on the way home. They wanted to know if their child had cried. *Did Mariana mention anything about my mother dying last year? Was Benjamin one of the ones that came and got you?*

I told them, *These kids are tough, and smart, and they'll get through this. They will need your help. They will want to talk about it with you. Together, we can create a network of support.* But their questions continued. They didn't ask their children; they asked me. They asked me questions as though I were holding out on them. They asked me questions so that I would see how concerned they were. How angry they were. They asked me questions because they genuinely wanted the answers, yes, but none of them asked what they truly wanted to know: How badly is this going to fuck *my* kid up?

My attempts at reassurance tacitly accused them of melodrama, my tone implying that all this clamor was an overreaction. But I was transparent, standing before them. My clothes were soaked; I didn't even have it together enough to carry an umbrella. The ink on my credential certificate wasn't dry. I was twenty-three years old—some of them were my parents' age—and I was being exposed as a fuck-up, a kid. I remember saying, *I'm sorry, but I really must use the restroom*, and being ignored.

In the end, though, they would have to accept my answers. They had no choice. They hadn't been there. So we continued this pained one-act until they realized that I had nothing else to say, then they tapered off, holding their kids' hands tight. Mrs. Stone stayed behind a moment, placing three fingers on my arm.

Mr. Mason, she said, *go home and get some rest.*

After everyone had gone, I walked back into the classroom and grasped the phone as though I were strangling it, shaking as I dialed my home number. Greta answered on the first ring—*You're still there?* she said—and I felt myself go inexplicably mute.

Frank? Her voice sharpened. *Hello?*

Greta, I said.

Yeah, I can hear you. Why are you still there?

I don't—I don't know, I said stupidly.

Did something happen? Are you okay?

What? I don't know.

Frank, can you just—

There was a suicide at the beach, I said. *The kids saw a girl jump from the bridge.*

She said nothing.

Hello? I said.

I'm here, she said. *Are you alright?*

Through the window I watched the cars pass, the fierce red glow of their brake lights irradiating the classroom. *I don't know,* I said again.

Her voice was stern as she said, *Come home.*

After we hung up I went outside and sat in my car for a while, thanking God for the weekend—a break to gauge the Sisyphean weight of what would come next. I realized I had never answered the parents' first and most primary question: *Where were you?*

And where had I been? Close enough to pretend I had my eye on them, far away enough that I could miss something like that. I pressed my head against the steering wheel and mistakenly hit the horn, a sharp blast echoing down the side street. I didn't want to think, didn't want to experience anything except quiet: a white room, a soft landing. But all I could hear were the questions still to come.

I drove in silence, examining everything like it held an answer. At a stoplight on Fourteenth Street a bum walked a leashed cat; on Fulton sat an orange tweed armchair, abandoned on the sidewalk. The houses rubbed shoulders like people in an elevator, fog obscuring the edges of things, erasing what couldn't be seen in direct light.

I turned onto my old street and stopped in front of the house where I had once lived. It was a San Francisco house in the style of most San Francisco houses—tall and narrow, pastel-colored, floors joined by a perilously steep staircase. Requisite bay windows on the first and second floors, one set stacked atop another; a pointed roof; sunken concrete leading into the garage. There was no car in the drive. The lights were off. The bush out front had grown wild. It was a habit of mine; when I felt nervous or unsettled or lost, this was an easy destination.

I let the engine idle and closed my eyes, exhausted. I could pull up the image—the most repellent, magnetic thing I had ever seen. And it was most definitely a *thing*, having ceased to be human. The basic form was there but had shifted, like a totaled car. The skin had split from the inside, like pavement after an earthquake. It was no longer the color of flesh but green-black as a crocodile, features swollen into a ballooned mask. The hair was mostly gone; what was left was discolored and bleached white apart from a few red-orange strands, splayed against the bug-addled sand. Wounds pocked the skin all over. The absent limbs hadn't been removed cleanly, the joints bore rip marks: some creature or rock or undertow had tugged until the arms and legs came free.

I left the car, headlights illuminating the walkway and porch. The next-door neighbor's lamp flickered on, a curtain moved. I knelt on the stoop, reaching toward the bush beside the porch, pulling the branches away. The minibar bottles glinted in the faint streetlamp glow. Their paper labels had corroded into pulp. I still had a key. I held it, my hand in my pocket.

I pressed my forehead and hands to the window on the front door and peered in. Mail lay strewn on the foyer floor. I fingered the key uncertainly. The lights in the fish

tank were on, visible in the living room beyond the entryway. I put a hand on the porch railing to steady myself.
The parents would want deeper answers, would think
of more questions over the weekend. The children, too,
would need reassurances. There would be no more room
for glossing, no more needlepoint phrases. I walked back
down the steps, got into my car, and headed out of the city,
toward home.

Greta was chewing a fingernail when I walked in. I glanced
at the clock, forgetting the time even as I looked away.

We spoke two hours ago, she said, her irritation a
fungus growing over the words. She saw my smeared, reddened face and relented. *Frank,* she said.

I know, I said. *I'm sorry.*

I walked to the kitchen and retrieved our lone bottle
of alcohol: spiced rum, kept above the refrigerator for the
holidays. I fished some flat ginger ale out of the fridge and
mixed the two in a coffee mug.

She followed me. *Will you tell me what happened?*

I shook my head.

Please, she said.

We were on the bridge, and we saw a woman jump,
I said. The refrigerator motor switched gears, the sound
gnawing. *She went right over, no one could stop her.*

Oh my God, she said.

Nobody could have stopped her.

How old was she?

I downed the drink and poured another.

Our age, I said.

. . .

Debt had aged us. We were in our early twenties and poor in a way that felt like being ground into a fine powder. We scouted out ATM machines that dispensed ten-dollar bills because we never had twenty in checking; we kept a ledger of what we owed Greta's Aunt Janine even as we borrowed more. Living in San Francisco would have been financially impossible, so after my graduation we had taken up residence in Vallejo, a dirty East Bay suburb on I-80: less a town than a series of half-liquidated strip malls. Greta found us a two-bedroom rental house that we couldn't afford but took anyway, and we set about destroying our credit. I thought that was what adults did: they bought bookshelves to fill, placed four chairs around a dining table though they never entertained. When we didn't make our loan payments for six months, we started parking our cars in a 7-Eleven lot to throw off the repo men. We never thought to sell one, to make a choice to live differently. If we couldn't afford a comfortable life, we wanted at least the semblance of one.

Though it was just the two of us, the space was never enough. Even with the extra bedroom, our possessions choked the house. To move about, one had to turn sideways or lift a leg over something. And our sloppiness made it feel smaller: tiny stains hovered above the stove—tomato sauce stirred too vigorously and never wiped—and striated dirt caked the place where the wall met the floor. Greta dug up prizes from thrift stores and antique markets. To me, age didn't improve status—it had been junk in '65 and would be junk a hundred years hence. But here was a bust of a girl, chin in hand; there was an orange piece of banded china. These items were showcased around our house as though pride of place overrode worthlessness.

The two bedrooms lay at opposite ends of the hall. Our bedroom, though the smaller of the two, received plenty of sun. The other bedroom had trees outside both windows and stayed dark and cool even in the summer. When the shades were up, light filtered across the wood floor. It was peaceful, serene. *This room is perfect,* Greta had said as we unpacked, *for the nursery—*

I remember the phone rang as she spoke, and before she finished her sentence I had run, relieved, to answer it.

And despite all of that—all the sharp words, the household annoyances, the moments when our mutual disgust sat up and made itself apparent like an intrusive houseguest—I loved her. Greta was my first girlfriend, my first sex. Being around her was like being in a warm bath. She made me laugh; she left me alone most of the time; she was smart, kind, and uncomplicated; she didn't begrudge anyone's happiness except her own. In the beginning, I often looked at her with a feeling I couldn't quite identify—a feeling like she needed my protection, like I should bear our burdens for her, like I should be the one to guide us. I thought at the time that this was kindness. I understand now that the name for what I've just described is condescension.

It was never that I didn't love her. It was that I loved her, from the beginning, incorrectly; the motives were wrong, rooted in politeness, comfortable companionship, inequality. It was that I loved her wrong and she let me. She erected no limits. She might bite back, but her innermost impulse was to forgive. Those who are weak, as Greta was weak—and I say this with no malice, only honesty—are like tests to people like me; I often wondered if she solicited my cruelty to know what sort of man I was. I suppose I showed her.

She told me once, not long after we were married, *I know this isn't what you wanted from your life.* She searched my eyes. *You can tell me. I want you to tell me, so I know we're always honest with each other.*

I told her what she already knew: that things had turned out so differently than I had planned. That we had never planned anything, really.

She turned to the wall beside our bed and sobbed. In the morning, she woke, dressed, and made pancakes and bacon. *Good morning,* she said at the table, smiling, her eyes like pink pillows.

From the moment we met, she had extended an unknowing invitation to hurt her. In a shorter time than I would like to admit, it became a challenge not to accept.

■ ■ ■

The metronome mercifully off, I cleared my throat. *I don't think I can go today,* I said.

Of course not, she said.

Despite her words, I could feel her disappointment, the sting of this new indignity—we got so few weekends together; we had planned to soak up the outdoors now that it had finally stopped clogging our gutters with leaves. I had even said the words—*I promise*—and now I was canceling. And why? To deal with a tragedy, yes. But one I had at least partially invented.

Why had I told her what I had told her? It had just come out; it had seemed, unaccountably, like the right thing to say.

Greta fidgeted, rubbed her belly. *I understand, Frank.*

I just feel a little worn out, I said.

As she nodded, stretching her calves, I saw the rest of the day unfold: she and I both quiet, moving about the house like ghosts. Finally, we would settle on the couch, collapsing into a state of paralytic stasis: television, takeout, movies left maddeningly on pause as she chatted on the phone with her mother. The thought of what was surely to come—that halting, dulling day—drove me from where I sat on the bed; I went into the bathroom and started the shower, fighting the headache as it slipped into my stomach to become nausea. I would keep my promise, and go hiking with her in Glen Ellen at the historic Jack London estate.

The drive there was an hour of stretched bucolic highway, the orderly vineyards tapering into paved woodland and then a cement parking lot. I parked the car at the base of the main trail. A wall of heat hit us as we opened our doors. The microclimates of northern California could astonish the uninitiated—the penetrating, foggy chill of the city, the bone-dry sear further inland, the wet green lick of the North Coast. Yesterday, I had crouched in the rain; here, it was parched and desperate. We approached the visitors' center and, beyond it, the thick expanse of woods.

We held on to each other despite the heat. I grazed her stomach with my fingertips. *Are you up for this?*

She squinted cheerfully into the sun. *It's barely a hike. It's a walk that curves.*

The flat straightaway of the trail opened up beneath a canopy of trees, the sun needling through the branches. Despite two aspirin, the jostling steps cemented the pain in my head.

Thomas, she said. *Thomas Mason. Thoughts?*

It's stuffy, I said. *Thomas wears tweed and sneaks Latin into conversation.*

An elderly couple passed us, the man wheezing slightly. He hunched over, his arms out like feelers, and took an indulgent gulp out of his water bottle as they clamored past us.

William, she said.

Mom would love it, I said. *William was her dad's name.*

Your parents aren't allowed around my baby, Greta said, and we both snickered.

William is nasal and phlegmy. I let go of her hand to rub my temples. Scores of black butterflies hovered above the trail, and we stepped carefully.

You know, when you touch a butterfly, it dies, she said.

I was just telling a kid that three days ago.

What'd he do?

What do you think he did, he touched it. Whatever I say, they have to test it.

Like, 'don't eat crayons,' she said.

There had been a rash of it a few months earlier. They all went for the brown ones—burnt sienna, raw umber—I suppose because they looked like chocolate.

Even the simplest stuff, they just don't know, I said. Then I reconsidered and shook my head. *But then they know all this other stuff. They hear shit and then just carry it around and spit it back out at the most random moments.*

Like 'butt sex,' she said.

Exactly.

At lunch, there was a small group that ate with me at the multipurpose table. A few weeks earlier, we had each been digging into our unsatisfying meals and covetously eyeing Marisol's hand-delivered McDonald's, when it happened: *Butt sex,* Adrian said. *Yeah, butt sex,* Angelica chimed in. And then they had all looked up at me, and that was the weirdest and worst part: they didn't know *what* it meant, but they knew what it *meant*—that it was naughty, that it would produce a reaction. *Don't say that,* I had said lamely. *Don't say 'butt sex' or any other kind of sex.*

Greta's voice lowered. *Do you think they're freaked out about yesterday?*

I don't know, I said. *I'm sorry, I don't mean to be— but can we please just not talk about it?*

A sweaty old hippie passed by, beaming, as his armpit bouquet wafted toward us. She waited for him to be out of earshot before she continued. *Did anybody call the police? Did they try to talk her down?*

I pictured how it would have happened. *Yeah,* I said, tentatively. *It seemed like she was set on the idea.*

So why'd she talk to the cops at all?

I don't know.

Why didn't she just—

Why do people do anything? I snapped. *Did I not just ask you to drop it?*

Immediately, her face—how can I say this?—it crumpled, as though instead of barking at her I had taken her head in my hands and compressed it like a ball of paper. There was a tightness to her breathing, and I could almost feel what was happening inside her body: that sensation like your chest cavity is filling with remorse and hurt. I had to look away.

And then, as ever, she tested the waters with her standard conciliation—one with a built-in response:

I love you, she said.

I pulled back, examining her face once more. Now, the harsh moment behind us, she looked softened, illuminated. I wondered if that was the outdoor lighting or the pregnancy. I remembered back to when she had been pregnant before and tried to remember if she had looked different those times; whatever it was, I hadn't seen her this way in a while—I hadn't had this sort of thought about her in a while. I looked at her and thought about how I so rarely looked at her. I had one of those out-of-body moments a marriage can provoke: this person is My Wife. Out of everybody in the world, she picked me. I had the impulse to thank her.

She searched my face. *I said I love you, Frank.*

I love you too, I said.

We approached the stone skeleton of London's home. It had begun to disintegrate with each earthquake and passing year and was now buttressed by steel scaffolding. A huge staircase flanked one side, built for visitors to ascend and view the ruin. We stepped up the staircase slowly, Greta in front of me. She placed one hand on her stomach and the other on the railing for balance. Greta carried herself, in those relatively early months of pregnancy, in the manner of a woman about to deliver. She often placed her hands soothingly on the small of her back and leaned as though balancing an enormous load. As yet, however, she hadn't really begun to show. Her pants fit tighter, but only she and I noticed that. To the rest of the world she was a well-fed young woman, maybe bulbous around the middle but in a way that appeared healthy, nourished, like she could swing a baseball bat or give a nice volleyball serve. In truth, though, she was just weak—carrying groceries in from the car meant an aching back; this walk would knot her calves into fists. As we reached the top of the steps, she was winded.

I always forget how enormous this is, she said. A mosquito investigated her face and she slapped it away. *How about Jack? Jack Mason. Jack is the guy who mans the grill. Jack is a good dancer.*

Weeds sprouted in what had been the study. Twin chimneys rose at opposite ends of the house like goalposts. We stood there, done already: we always did that—drove forever and then stayed fifteen minutes.

Sure, I said. I leaned into her, placed a hand on her hip, wanting to touch something soft. *Whatever you want,* I said.

Heading back, we came upon a little boy standing on the trail. Though he looked to be only six or seven, he was alone.

Where's your mommy and daddy? Greta asked him.

I heard a woman's voice in the distance: *Avery! Avery!*

Is your name Avery? I said.

Avery nodded.

He's here, I shouted back. *Over here!*

Greta knelt and put an arm around him, her face grim; she awaited the parents' arrival, almost posed, as if they would show up and take a photo. *It's okay,* she said to the boy. *They'll be here in a minute.*

The parents arrived and clutched Avery to their knees. They thanked us sheepishly, even as their eyes—you could see it—measured us, trying to decide how trustworthy we were.

Isn't that the worst panic there is? Greta said.

Oh, absolutely, the mother said, kissing Avery's head. *He's always running off. Do your kids do that too? Tell me it's a phase they outgrow!*

Greta smiled into the distance. *Nice meeting you,* she said. The couple walked away, each holding one of the boy's hands.

We walked a while, stopping at the decades-old water fountain. Greta planted her feet, bending her torso at a sharp angle to avoid getting her shoes wet. I looked at the trail ahead, but turned around when I heard a sudden cry. Greta's hands were clamped to her face as she stumbled backward.

What? What happened?

She was sputtering. *A spider! A spider came out of the tap!*

I snickered. Her eyes went cold.

Frank, she snarled. *It's not funny.*

I'm sorry, I said, not bothering to hide my smile.

She stormed toward the trail, leaving me behind, and in spite of every impulse to rejoin her, apologize, nip the argument in the bud, I did nothing to close up the gap. After a quarter mile I could no longer see her, and I let the heat wear down the tempo of my steps. Here and there, ridges were cut into the ground in improvised stairs, alleviating the natural incline. At the trail's fork I weighed my options, unsure if Greta had gone to the car or toward London's grave. We usually skipped the grave site—it was a lot more walking, uphill at that, to see very little: a rock the size and shape of a sleeping dog, a half-rotted fence, a plaque we didn't read.

The things I had to do to fix a fight with her—the explaining, the backpedaling, ten thousand close-range reassurances that all missed their mark—would have felled me on that day. So I delayed, walking toward the grave, the blond fields darkening into moist woods. The walk was far enough that my throat went dry, my quads burned, and when I reached the grave site I rested my arms on the fence. It occurred to me that Greta might have left. She could be halfway to Sonoma right now, heading toward the blackened landing strip of the interstate. The thought was laced with dizzy exhilaration, a hope that she would almost reach home, remember what had happened the day before, and realize the insult she had added to my injury.

The plaque said London had been cremated, that his widow had poured the ashes here before the rock was placed above them. I wondered how many small pieces of London had broken free, floating to the visitors' center, the parking lot, the extravagant restaurants that lined the bottom of the hill.

I noticed something at my feet. I had forgotten—a few yards from London's grave were two others: two children, a girl and a boy, were buried there. Another small fence surrounded their redwood markers. The plaque said they had been buried there long before London bought the property. They had died the year he was born. My headache began suddenly to intensify, a string section reaching crescendo, and I leaned over and vomited on the edge of the fence. I braced myself against it, wiping my mouth.

Greta found me not long after, sitting on the ground, my head in my arms.

I've been waiting at the car, she said tersely. *You're sick?*

A cluster of birds flew over the grove and began to shriek. I felt my throat catch. *Yes,* I said. A thin, icy tide of bile rose inside me and I shuddered. *Yes,* I said again.

She squinted at me, suspicious. *Why?*

Why what?

You drank too much last night. You always drink too much.

I barely had—

I stopped myself. We had had this argument a thousand times. If I came home with a forty, she winced. If I ordered a second drink in a bar, she eyed it like it was a live grenade. She accused me once of being an alcoholic—we had just left her cousin's wedding, and by some unfair and temporary metabolic quirk my three flutes of champagne had rendered me fully drunk, careening into pillars and resting my head on the table during the toasts. I hadn't overindulged; I had, thanks to an empty stomach, gotten unlucky. She shouted it at me in the parking lot—*You're a fucking alcoholic!*—and I turned on my heel, stunned and amused: *I must be the world's only alcoholic who drinks once a month,* I said.

Above the graves, the birds approached frenzy and then passed by, the sound vanishing as though a conductor had lowered his wand.

You know what, strike that—it's not how much you drink, Greta said. *It's why. You do it so you don't have to feel anything.*

Make up your mind, I said. *Do I drink too much or do I drink incorrectly?*

49

She ignored me. *You don't ever deal with anything. You just push it down.*

I looked away.

You ignore everything you don't want to see, she said.

I felt myself detach, felt the lightness, the quickening, that always prefaced a lie.

I think it was Nora, I said.

Silence.

Greta, I know it was.

She stared at me, expressionless. *That jumped, you mean.*

Yes, I said.

How? she said coldly. *Why did you say you think?*

I know it was. The police—I paused, waiting to see what I would say—*they identified the body.*

She turned away, and for a moment I thought she was disgusted—by the obviousness, the desperateness of the lie. But when she turned back, she was crying. She stepped toward me, extending her hand. She had asked me never to say that name in her presence, and now she was crying and holding out her hand.

She loved me so much that my grief was her own.

She drove us home. The sky had turned an angry shade of peach, and beneath the settling sun I felt weakened. We had gone all day without food.

You can't do that, you know? I said. *You should really carry a granola bar around at least.*

Greta was allergic to correction of any kind, fuming when I asked her to wash the dishes, snapping at me if I said the chicken needed salt. Suggestion, to her, was condemnation.

She had no problem, however, asking me to sweep up, unclog the toilet, never buy that brand of sliced turkey again. But that day she said nothing, and I knew I would get a pass: I had been through enough. I was untouchable.

You need to start thinking about this baby, you need to start taking care of this baby better, I said. *We can't take any chances, Greta.*

Her jaw set. *You're right.* Her voice was sharp and cool.

Though money-wise, not having a baby right now would probably be—

She slapped me, or tried to—she was driving and couldn't get a good purchase on my face. Her palm bounced against my open mouth, my tongue touching her finger long enough to detect the dim tang of salt. She wiped her hand on her lap as yellow highway stripes passed beneath the car, both of us stunned. Finally she spoke, imitating calm: *I know what you're trying to do.*

Instinctively, I touched my mouth where she had hit it. *What I'm doing is trying to get you to eat a granola bar.*

You think I'm stupid, but I'm not, she said.

Then the granola bar won't present a challenge.

It was always like this. I held it back as long as I could, and when it arrived it surprised both of us.

You think just because—

But I cut her off, punching the dash hard enough that a thin curl of skin lifted from my knuckle and blood began to bead. I watched her flinch, glaring at her profile like a dog about to spring, our hair fluttering in the breeze from the open windows. The sun was retreating. I looked away, feeling the wind begin its nightly easing of the heat.

Once home, she walked into the bedroom and shut the door. I saw the answering machine, blinking an angry red 6. I sprawled across the cat-scratched couch and put the television on mute. I tossed the remote above my head, catching it some and dropping it some. Blood had dried on my knuckle. I was starving. I walked over to the answering machine, pressed play, heard a woman's firm, clipped voice—my boss, the principal—and held the erase button down until the flashing ceased.

Outside, a half-dozen neighborhood kids played tetherball with their flimsy rig: the pole, anchored by a plastic base filled with sand, wobbled whenever someone got a hit in—too hard, and it fell against the pyramid-shaped topiary next door. Another kid rode by on a bike, taunting the rest. *How come you only got some shit to say when you're on your bike?* one of them called back.

I could hear Greta moving in the bedroom—opening dresser drawers, walking to the bathroom to wash her face. I felt a still calm overtake me, felt myself sinking into sleep and then dream. I was hunting for ladybugs in my grandmother's backyard at age nine, like I always did in the summer; the dream wasn't invention, just replayed memory. I placed hundreds of the insects into a mesh prison fashioned with scrap from the garage. Their insect feet crawled along, poking through the holes, and I held my hand against their flutter. As the sun left the sky, I pulled a final ladybug from a bowing blade of grass. I held it up to the mesh jail, but instead of putting it inside, placed it on my tongue and crushed it against my mouth's ridged roof. And then I stood in the grass and felt my head lifting, my legs lengthening, the smeared bug on my tongue. And in the way of dreams, where every shift makes sense without explanation, I knew I was growing up, becoming big in time lapse. Once my body had stretched itself fully, I was standing on yesterday's beach, looking down at a depression in the sand. The police had just gone. The bridge was swinging like a lazy hammock. In the parking lot was a tiny red car; it belonged to me. *Put your shoes on,* said a voice. I laughed, looking at the sky. The voice came from there. An airplane flew over in air-show loops. I waved to it. *Put your shoes on,* the voice said again, and my laugh halted sharply when I realized the voice was closer. The words were coming from beneath me—I looked down and the body was there, filling the depression. Ladybugs were crawling over it, lifting off and away. The face was hers, familiar and devastating; her red hair was speckled with wet, filthy sand. *Put your shoes on,* she said once more, as I looked up and saw that the red car was gone. I was stranded; Nora's body and I were stranded together. I knew there would be no escape.

I woke with a snap as the streetlights buzzed on, hearing the tetherballers start to leave and walk home. My pulse was in my ears. On the television a bounding dog covered stretches of grass in slow motion before a man entered the frame to hawk pet food.

There were no sounds from the bedroom. In the kitchen, the faucet dripped. The muted pet-food commercial continued, the text appearing in bold white letters at the bottom of the screen: *Don't waste your time with imitators,* it said.

I had forgotten all about eating that bug when I was nine. In my tiny twin bed that night, I had felt, bizarrely, as though I had stumbled upon the way things worked. My mother often cried to herself in the kitchen, my father often sat grimly on our apartment's balcony, smoking for hours—now I understood that adults felt pain because they carried burdens, and those burdens resulted from the choices they made. I had made a choice, too—to eat the ladybug. No one had seen. No one would ever know. Just as adults had secrets, I had one, too. My thoughts and actions—my choices—I realized, were my property alone. No one could take them from me.

4

The summer camp where I met you had been less a camp, really, than a holding pen—just a broken-down old rec center a few towns beyond the city. We might have been at school, save for the absence of desks. Three times a day, we moped our way outside to the tangled-chain swings, to goalposts without soccer balls. We swung from rusting parallel bars, our palms blooming with wet, cratered blisters. Inside, the mancala game was played with kidney beans, the marbles long since lost. We sang *Fish and chips and vinegar, vinegar, vinegar!* as we sat on stale tweed couches, the bottoms of our feet nowhere near the floor. When we got too loud, a counselor turned off the lights and put her finger to her lips. We were supposed to raise our hands in answer, to show that we understood. That year I wore thick glasses, and without them the world was underwater. I would take the glasses off and pretend to swim through a private ocean, cupping the air in broad, slow strokes until I ran into something, or a pale, face-shaped orb came into view and placed them back on, saying, in my mother's voice, *Keep your glasses on so you don't fall down.* At camp once, alone on the soccer field, I set my glasses down in the grass and swam away, leagues deep before I understood with a shock that I would have no way to find them again.

The night of your parents' funeral, I dreamed of that place. You and I were in the soccer field, both of us wearing glasses now—four feet tall, eight years old again. The neglected grass came to our waists. But we were also us at twenty-two, and I was frantic; I wasn't sure if you knew they were dead. If you didn't, I wasn't prepared to tell you. Next to the field was a swanky restaurant, its lighting tinted amber like those souvenir Gold Rush photos taken at the county fair. The waiter seated us at the only table left. There were two chairs, though the table was barely comfortable for one. Our knees smacked. *Don't bring us any meat,* you said to the waiter accusingly. *It's gone bad.* It was Christmas, suddenly, and so from everywhere came hackneyed carols sung in sped-up voices. *We're little again,* I said. *We have to do it all over, I guess.* We accepted this glumly, looking at our hands. A plate of meat came. *I'm sick,* I said. *Because we drank on the stoop after the funeral,* you said. I smacked my forehead. *Right!* You remembered. You did know. I wouldn't have to tell you.

I woke with a start on your parents' sofa, beneath a blanket I hadn't fallen asleep with. The cable box's clock read 12:00. I blinked at it, and it blinked back. I sat up, sticky with sweat, and cleared my throat loudly. It was pouring rain, the water falling in sheets. The streetlights had gone black.

Power's been in and out, you called from the kitchen. *Because of the storm.*

There was a pause.

You don't have to stay, you said. *The lawyer's coming, plus I've got stuff to do.*

The first part was true, about the lawyer. I don't think you knew why, but you disliked him: you deleted his messages until it hit you that nobody else was going to take care of it, that nobody else *could* take care of it. You didn't even know what "it" was—just that he was coming to tell you the surreal, formal things that you would now need to know.

But the second part was bullshit—you had nowhere to be, nothing you needed to do. The bookstore had told you to take as much time off as necessary. You called to tell them what had happened, and I could faintly hear the voice you spoke to. My God, what kind of accident? *A car accident,* you said. You used the same flat tone as the officer who had come to your door. By now, I knew the story in detail. On a rural highway, witnesses saw the car take a curve too fast and hit a patch of gravel. The fishtail marks meant your dad had tried to recover, but they had hit the guardrail. The momentum pushed the car up from behind. Here you paused, as whoever was on the line made a sympathetic noise. They didn't yet know how the story ended. In a moment, when you told them, I knew they would reframe the conversation in light of the final revelation, wondering if their reactions had been hitherto appropriate. You continued. It might have been okay—maybe a busted eardrum from the airbag, bruises from whatever projectiles escaped the glove box. Worst-case scenario a punctured spleen from the seat belt. But they were driving along the edge of a wooded ravine. It was steep. When they rolled, they went over.

I imagined the reply: *Oh my God, were they hurt badly?*

They are dead, you said.

I heard you say *they are* instead of *they're*, my skin tensing at the sound of your calm, android voice. You needed time off to make arrangements, you told them, though by then they had all been made. Of course, they understood completely. Whatever you needed. And then you just never went back. When they called, you erased their messages too. You cashed your last paycheck after they finally gave up and mailed it.

I came into the kitchen, finally. The way you looked at the paper, I knew you hadn't read a word. You still wore your black dress. Your pin-straight red hair was rumpled in the back, your eyes raccooned with makeup. Every breath snapped inside me like a cracked knuckle.

Hung over? I whispered.

No, actually, I feel okay. You looked up. *Relatively.*

I poured some orange juice. *Lucky you.* The house smelled like cigarettes and the sink was full of lipsticked butts. You didn't smoke, your parents hadn't: the guests had left them. *I feel chewed up and spit out,* I said.

You don't have to stay, you said again. *You've missed enough class.*

I told my student teaching supervisor I have the flu. It's fine.

You gave me a tight, false smile. *I know you're probably needed elsewhere.*

I set my glass down. I had a nasty remark ready without knowing why. So I held it there, like a sore on my tongue. You had every right to say it: I knew what would be waiting for me when I checked my messages.

I'm sorry, you said, smoothing the skirt of your dress. *I had no right to put you in that position.*

The light in the kitchen was clinical and sallow. You looked like a Halloween costume of yourself, like your face was on crooked. You looked like you had been up for hours. You probably had been. You probably woke up on your parents' bed, dazed and ill, suffocating beneath your grief; the funeral over, all that remained were the beginnings of your life without them. You tossed me that pitiful apology and I imagined you fretting upstairs, certain that your hand on my leg had split things at the seam, that I had gone disgusted into the night. I stepped forward to tell you not to worry.

No, I said. *No, don't be sorry. You were drunk, it was a rough day. To say the least. I mean, for God's sake . . .*

You glowered. *I meant I'm sorry for making you stay with me for four days.*

My fingers went numb. *Fuck,* I finally said.

I'm going to take a shower, you said, getting up. *I'll call you in a couple days.*

You disappeared up the stairs, and I heard your footsteps above me. I pulled on my shoes, gathered my keys and wallet, and made for the door. I turned the knob, listening to the water starting in the upstairs shower. And then the humming flow of electricity died once more, taking with it the soft layer of noise you never hear until it's gone. The room turned gray. I heard the water stop, the shower-curtain rings jingle. You were up there in the dark. I let go of the doorknob. Plastic cups were stacked on the coffee table, the stereo speakers, the lid of the fish tank. I gathered them, feeling the vague and pulling sense that I was expected somewhere else. But the dead clocks and the gray October sky made time a mystery, and I couldn't tell what part of my life I was missing.

You came back in pajamas, startling at the sight of me.

Thought I'd tackle these dishes, I said.

Francis, you said, looking around the clean living room. *You didn't have to—*

I'm not doing this for my health. I expect to be tipped.

You gave me a sleepy grin and walked into the kitchen to the refrigerator. *I can offer you rotting casserole, rotting lasagna, rotting cold cuts . . .* You groaned softly. *All of this is gonna go bad.*

A knock came and you went to greet the lawyer, letting him shake your limp hand before you both sat in the dark. I lingered in the living room, standing helplessly. You curled your feet under you on the couch, and we caught a glimpse of each other. I smiled. You smiled back and I understood: all I had needed to do—all you had wanted me to do—was stay.

I left the room to wash the dishes and give you some privacy. He talked for a while, and over the water from the tap, I heard your answers. *I can't,* you said.

I turned off the water and began pretending to dry.

Both. Either. Selling it or living here, you said.

So you have your own place, then? You and your boyfriend?

There was a pause.

I don't have a boyfriend, you said.

Another pause.

And renting it . . . just, the idea of somebody else living here . . . You sat up. *Aren't there costs people have to pay when they own a house, even if they don't have a mortgage? Special taxes, or something? You'll have to explain this to me like I'm six years old, because I don't know anything.* Your voice broke. *My dad does my taxes, I don't even—*

The lawyer cleared his throat. *Ms. Lucas,* he began, lowering his voice, *your parents have bequeathed you a significant amount of money.* If this produced a reaction in you, you said nothing to indicate it. A beat passed, his voice returning to normal volume. *You need to understand that ownership means there's no landlord to call when a pipe bursts, or the toilet overflows, or whatever else.*

Okay, you said.

He gave you his card. It was hard to hear what he said before leaving, but I could guess. *I'm sorry for your loss. Let me know if you need anything. Take care.*

I came out and we sat by the window, watching the lawyer's car wiggle tediously from a tight parking space, creeping to and fro in a sad, eight-point maneuver. Your face was lit by the weak sunlight as you said, *I don't know what to do.* We watched someone walk down the street, shouting over his shoulder at no one.

You don't have to decide today. Sleep on it. You've barely slept. My voice took on a pleading quality that surprised me. *Go take a nap. I'll get us some lunch.*

I can't live here, you said. *Sleep in my old bed, like they're just down the hall?* You motioned toward the things in the room. *Look at all this stuff.*

I knew you were wondering how to even begin. How much strength would you have to muster to empty their closets, pile their toiletries into garbage bags, cancel their magazine subscriptions? Your dad's golf clubs were propped against the wall in the foyer, mud from the course on the bag's metal stand. Your mom's cooking was still wrapped in foil in the rapidly warming fridge. Their fish swam placidly in the illuminated aquarium. Mail would come, the envelopes flitting through the slot in the door like dispensed candy. And it would all be up to you to deal with—only you who could see to these things.

Get me out of here, you said. You stood, grabbed my car keys, and held them out like an offering. We both looked at them, like they might answer for me.

Yeah, okay. You got it.

You ran upstairs to change into some of the ill-fitting old clothes from high school that remained in your dresser drawers. Any suggestion that you wanted me to leave was abandoned. You had no destination in mind. Neither did I.

But in the car you decided where we should go. At Fort Point, the structure beneath the bridge's webbed under-arch, there were tours you could take, and at the end they fired the old cannon. We both remembered the sound it made from our fourth-grade field trip there. I could still see the arc of the cannonball going into the water; I said so and you said you could too. Our class had run circles around the musty cots, spitting over the ledge into the bay. When the cannon went off we all jumped. After, our teacher walked us across the bridge—it was how field trips always ended in elementary school. You walk and walk through the German and Japanese tourists, irritated joggers and cyclists, and then by midspan everyone remembers how long the bridge really is and so you look out at the jutting city's plump hills and sunlit steel, the bobbing boats in the marina, the blinking drone of the Alcatraz lighthouse, the pubic foliage surrounding Coit Tower. And then, because you're cold no matter the season, and tired, and everyone else wants to, you walk back to the bus, defeated.

Seeing the fort again was one of those things we talked about doing but never did. But then there we were. The parking lot's edge was a jetty of sharp, stacked rocks, and beyond them men in wet suits drifted in shadow, prone on their neon boards. The water frothed beneath them. We looked for dorsal fins. You wondered about the pile of cannonballs accumulated on the ocean floor. *One day,* you said, *they'll shoot one off and it'll land at the top of the pyramid, it'll nose right out of the water.* Your voice was hoarse, your eyes drooped—you were worn down but excited. *Imagine all the whales they've beaned,* you said. I put the car in park as you shoved your purse under the passenger seat.

I'll get the admission, I said.

Francis, you said, *it's free.*

The power still wasn't on in that part of the city, and it felt as though we had been plunged back in time. The tour was going on as usual, except the dark corridors of the barracks were shut off to visitors. We met up with the crowd, following the guide through the gray chill as he

63

quizzed us on Civil War battlefields and sneezed into a stained handkerchief. It was evidently still a popular field-trip destination—names were tagged in correction fluid on the outer walls, an occasional knife intaglio set into the wooden door frames. *This is boring,* you whispered. One of the Golden Gate's pillars loomed nearby, like a massive foot that had just missed us. We looked at the sun and pretended to be warm. *Get to the cannon already,* you said to no one. The air smelled like rot and salt, and I dug my nose into my sweatshirt to see if that was how I would smell once we left.

When the tour was almost over, everyone gathered around the cannon, the guide clearly getting excited. Dressed in his Union garb, he began his practiced speech. We could see the belly of the bridge, could hear the sustained rumble of the cars. Everything was covered in white bird shit, the gulls circling near the bridge's underside. *Ten thousand homeless in this city and I have three bedrooms,* you said. I shoved my hands in my pockets. We were against the fort's ledge, and you threw over a crumpled tissue from your pocket. The wind held it at eye level for a moment and then it dropped. *I don't have enough stuff to fill the one.* People turned around to shush you with their eyes, but you had opened a door to something inside you. *I want to lie in a hammock. I want to do a paint-by-numbers.* You sniffed. *I'm gonna need some pancakes.* You kept going, listing things that wouldn't, in the end, make any of this easier.

We watched the tour guide wipe out the cannon's mouth. It was almost time. I tried to think of anything that wouldn't sound like an empty recitation: Go with your gut, You'll figure it out, Everything will be okay. You worried your lip with your teeth. *First you swab the bore,* the guide said. Behind us, the open ocean stretched out, as uninterrupted as prairie, the people around us taking pictures of all that horizon.

My dad took me here one time, you said.

I made sure you saw me listening with my whole face.

At night, you said. *It was something you could do here.* The cold had brought up the purple veins in your hands. *But we didn't go in.*

The guide said, *This is called 'wadding.'* He balled up a piece of paper and shoved it down the cannon's throat. You watched him with dead eyes. *I remember I wanted to go to Mel's Drive-In after. But I asked if we could and Dad said no.*

How old were you? I asked.

The guide held up the fuse, explaining how far away to stand.

Old enough that I shouldn't have whined about it. We rubbed our hands together, the sun behind a cloud. *But I did,* you said. *Whine about it, I mean. I whined the whole ride back, and he didn't answer me.* The guide took questions, pointed at people with their hands raised.

I keep having dreams about them, where my mom says something thoughtless. You swallowed, buying yourself a moment. *And then I wake up angry with her.*

I'm sorry, I said.

This whole thing. You shook your head, and your face softened. *It was this thing you could do. You walk around the fort with candles. My dad and I got to the parking lot and I cried and said I couldn't go in because it was too dark.* You started to say something else, but this guy next

65

to us said, *Oh, the candlelight tour? I've heard about that, how is it?*

You gave me a look.

Mind your fucking business, I told him.

Your hand went to your mouth, and, behind it, you finally smiled.

As we watched the guide push blackened objects into the cannon, explaining everything in his pinched voice, I thought about the last time I saw your parents. It was New Year's Day, ten months before. You had spent the night at their house, and I came to pick you up the next day. I drove beside the trees on Park Presidio, the jammed-together houses in Easter-egg colors, finally double-parking alongside your mom's car. Your dad came to the window and waved, then disappeared behind the curtain. He came back holding up a bottle of wine, pointing at it with his eyebrows raised. But I didn't want to get stuck there, explaining what I was up to nowadays, fielding questions about my idiot roommate, my little sister, the Giants' prospects this year. When I waved no, your dad batted his hand in my direction, like, *No problem—we'll catch you next time!* I saw him turn and speak, and your mom came to the window. She stuck her tongue out at me and laughed. I laughed too. You had a good mom and dad. When we graduated from high school, they sent me money in a tiny red envelope; when I came over for dinner they made things they knew I liked. One year, they gave me nudie playing cards for Christmas.

You met my parents only a handful of times, mostly at mediocre dinners celebrating my meager accomplishments: graduating junior high, growing one year older.

You were unfailingly polite to them, though I could tell that you regarded them with puzzlement, as though they were of a subtly different species—a boorish genus not yet evolved toward self-awareness. After a birthday lunch of mine one year, standing outside a suburban Red Robin (I don't recall how old I was turning, only that my deepening voice was unreliable during the proceedings), my mother spent ten minutes bitching at herself for lighting up around you, frantically waving away the smoke from her Camel instead of extinguishing it. My father said nothing—not just to you, but to any of us. Until, finally, someone mentioned his recent purchase of a puppy. Dad grunted. *We had a puppy when Frankie was little,* he said. *It got a nasty case of the trots and sprayed shit all over the walls, at a full run, and howled all night.* He spit into the bushes; one of his habits. *Chewed through our plastic kiddie pool, bit a hole in the hose, ate the jack-o'-lantern.* He gave me what was meant to be a playful slap on the back of the head. *And I thought my kids were a pain in the ass.* It was the sort of comment that, coupled with a slight indication of lightness, could almost pass for humor.

You gave him a nervous, school-picture smile, and I felt the sting of envy. Your family didn't do the playful-teasing thing. Nor did they do the not-very-playful-teasing thing. They certainly never got piss-drunk and teary over some old record turned to full volume, bouncing a knee to an ancient guitar solo. And they never slammed their kid against a wall, picture frames rattling and then splintering on the wood floor. You never had to smell, in those moments, for booze on your father's breath—you never had to find it absent and be shaken by that absence, and by what it meant:

no easy answer, no method of prediction. Your parents asked you questions and you were happy to respond. Your parents protected you from the inevitable truth: that they were regular, fallible people. Mine were openly flawed, unapologetically inconsistent. My sister and I gathered, on our own and early on, that no adjustments ought to be expected from their end. And because you saw them only in public, on their best behavior (such as it was), you never knew what it was really like at my house.

Your ignorance only fueled the crush I already had on you. I fostered it all through high school, fiddling with it incessantly like a wound inside the mouth. I admitted it to no one. After a while, my feelings for you and the truth about my parents seemed connected, inextricable. That you knew none of it was a kind of guarantee that of all the reasons you cared for me, none were based in pity. You remained untainted by the dismal truth about me. It was one more reason to love you, among the many.

. . .

When the guide finally stopped speaking and all questions had been answered, he gathered his swab and his foil, saluted us, and walked away. A beat passed and we looked at each other. *Hello?* you said. *I think we're forgetting something?* You checked your tour pamphlet, and we saw it for the first time: "See the cannon-*loading* demonstration." *Oh for fuck's sake,* you said. We stood there laughing, your long wisps of red hair whipping you in the face. I didn't say so, but I was relieved. I had been dreading the sound.

I said, *What do you want to do now?*

You blew your nose and said, *You know, I'm a little relieved?* Above us a gull flew forward but was beaten back by the wind. It hovered there, flapping and stationary.

Yeah?

You nodded. *I kind of hate loud things.*

We walked toward the car. I still felt a kind of desperation each time I thought of you, still stole glances at you when you looked away. Looking at you was easy. Standing there at the edge of the Fort Point parking lot—and I wish I could say it better, but I'll have to resort to this—you looked real, and alive, and I had a strange bout of tunnel vision suddenly, where my eyes almost watered at the sight of you.

Hey, I said. *Let's go to Mel's.*

When we pulled in, the neon sign was lit, the power on. You ordered pancakes and a chocolate milkshake. *Bid your teeth farewell,* I said. The 1950s jukeboxes at each booth blared music from the 1970s; children ate burgers out of paper Cadillacs. You grinned big as the waiter walked toward us, carrying your short stack. As he set it down—the moment after it touched the Formica table—the lights overhead died, the music distorting and then cutting out.

How about that, you said, lifting your fork.

We left Mel's food-sick, so full we unbuttoned our pants. Their fridges were again losing their cool—the staff turning people away at the door. The day was a wash for everybody. Before we started the short walk to my car, you paused and fished around in your purse for a mint. Outside a little market on Geary stood a man in a bloody apron, his face somber. He lifted packages wrapped in white paper from where he had stacked them, six-deep beneath a parking meter.

What? you said, turning to look. The butcher lifted the packages and tossed them into a dumpster. The echo reverberated like weak thunder as the wasted meat hit the dumpster's steel belly; first two, then three or four at a time, as the butcher hastened to finish the job.

I'm freezing, you said.

I pulled your coat tighter around you. You held my gaze, waiting for something, and exhaled. Your breath altered so slightly that I thought I had imagined it, until you inhaled again and your breath jumped along that same ragged catch, and the place we were headed became real to me: you were going to be mine, no matter who was waiting for me across town. I could push back pangs of guilt, or I could embrace this in a spasm of denial. But either way, it was going to happen. My hands were still gripping your button placket.

Let's go for a walk, you said.

By the time we reached Golden Gate Park it was raining again. Beneath one of the gray stone archways, a man slept on the ground. You grabbed my arm as we passed him in the small tunnel. *Francis,* you said, but I ignored you. Having passed the man, you continued to hold my arm. Just beyond the archway a tourist ran toward us. *How do you get to the bridge?* he said. He held a water-logged map out in front of him. You let go of my arm and gripped my hand as we stood there, getting drenched. *The bridge, the golden one.* His accent was gravel in his mouth. Behind him, a car full of nervous faces peered out at us. I looked down at our fingers, and then at the small orbs of water collecting on your eyelashes.

That way, you said to the man, pointing. It would have been easier to point with the hand I held, but you didn't let go.

We walked back and got into my little white car, soaking the seats. I shifted with two fingers, the other three still clamped to yours.

Are we holding hands? I said.

How could we have thought that they fire cannonballs aimed at the city?

Into the marina, no less, I said. *We're idiots.* I took the turnoff toward your house. *Are you okay?*

My feet are like blocks of ice, you said. I was hot, but I let go of your hand and turned the heater on full blast.

Can we do the just-feet one? you said.

I turned the heater on so it blew only on our feet. *Such an ingenious invention,* I said, feeling for your fingers again, and finding them.

. . .

Maybe you don't remember all of this, the way I do.

That day at camp, when I lost my glasses out there in the soccer field, I sank to my knees and began feeling for them in the grass. I saw, gliding toward me, a white glow with a red top and a glint. *These are yours,* you said, and the glint twinkled as the lenses refracted sunlight. You were wearing them. I took them from your face and put them back on mine. You became crisp: a white cotton dress, dirty sandals. Your red hair was in a bun like a ballerina's. Later, you came up to the pole and asked to play. *My side, my way, I get first hit,* I said: the tetherball mantra. You nodded, and then we were friends. Maybe you don't remember that. Maybe you remember us becoming friends in high school, the circle of acquaintances that slowly brought us into the same social orbit. Or maybe you would say we really became friends in college, long after those acquaintances disappeared—after our exiles to different towns, when we set aside our adolescent self-consciousness and finally showed ourselves to each other. Maybe you don't remember everything, but I keep those memories for the two of us, like valuables in a vault. If you need them, you can have them. And there are other things I keep—things I found out after it was too late to tell you. Like this: before a sound that loud would have incited panic, Fort Point used to fire blanks at the end of the demonstrations. They would put gunpowder in the cannon and set the fuse without any artillery: no cannonball, just sound. So maybe we did hear that colossal boom on our fourth-grade field trip. Maybe at least some of those memories were real. What I'm saying is that it's possible. What I'm saying is that there's a chance, Nora, that we didn't just invent it all.

5

Monday came.

I woke to the predawn sounds: the garbage truck whining around the block, neighbors starting their cars, drive-time traffic reports audible through their open windows. I fought an ache in that lymphatic region neither ear nor neck, ricocheting between agony and panic. Greta came into the bathroom, where I was shaving with her pink razor. *You want me to take the night off?* she said. *You look awful.*

No, I lied. I wanted the lazy momentum of a married evening—dinner, dessert, prime-time pap; canned laughter and bowls of ice cream. I wanted anything that felt normal, secure, mindless. I wanted someone to sit beside me. Still, I told her no. *Don't call in sick,* I said. *We can't afford it.*

She paused, then spit out what I knew she had been holding back: *You shouldn't have done that yesterday. It's not healthy.*

I know, I said. The previous morning, I had opened my eyes at 6:00 AM sharp—a habit from two years of alarm clock enslavement—walked to the bathroom, downed three of her ten-milligram sleeping pills, and slept for another eight hours. When they wore off, I took three more, and so on. I had been snowed under for a solid twenty-four hours, had exceeded the recommended dosage a half-dozen times over. Greta didn't bother to scold me. Each time she had noticed me taking more, she had made quiet clucking noises, and then finally, she had begun softly to cry.

Now, her tears renewed. *It's not safe, either,* she said.

She inspected my face, lifting a leg of her pajamas to scratch her knee. Greta worked late every weeknight, waiting tables at the one high-end place in Vallejo. With tips, she made more than I did. We sometimes crossed paths as I came home from school and she left for the restaurant, blithely waving to each other. Once home, I could piece together her day from the dishes in the sink, her stacks of movie cases, her bottle of nail polish on the scarred coffee table.

I'm sorry, I said. *I know.*

I wiped my jaw, pulled on clothes, and kissed Greta good-bye. She let go of my shoulders when the kiss ended, but I didn't move. She drew me to her again, both of us silent, until finally I pulled away and left.

I slid into the car through the passenger-side door— the only door that opened. I swallowed two Vicodin, left over from a long-ago wisdom-tooth extraction; I kept them stashed in the glove box. A moment later I shook out two aspirin.

I had been commuting for only eight months, but I had discovered what stop-start driving does to a body. The muscles in my right leg were permanently tight, sore from the feather touch necessary to hover above the gas, then the brake. I knew when to change lanes to avoid potholes. I had the phone numbers from the billboards memorized. I recognized cars on the road from their bumper stickers, the fading foam-paint football-team cheers scrawled on rear windshields. In twenty minutes I would inch over to cheat in the carpool lane, until the CHP trap where a motorcycle officer surveyed the passing cars like a cat. I would join the shining mob pulled toward San Francisco's magnet, paying the toll in nickels from the ashtray. I could cue the route in a mental reel.

But I-80's usual gridlock was weirdly absent that Monday morning, and I coasted, wracked by nerves, through towns I saw every day but had never visited. I flipped on the radio for an explanation, but every station was at commercial except one almost out of range, playing a gargling duet of static and "Eleanor Rigby." I knew there was no holiday, no easy out. Nothing was going to save me. I left it tuned to the barely audible Beatles. The words were muffled, but I knew them by heart.

I got to Hawthorne early but didn't go in. I had forty minutes before the kids arrived. I had taken the Vicodin on an empty stomach, and I gnawed on my nails, fearing further nausea.

Up the street was a truck just like the one I had driven in high school—a manual transmission that took me weeks to master. It rattled if you managed to push it up to seventy. Senior year it began screeching when I started the engine, the sound trailing off in quavering vibrato, like someone was strangling a violin. People around me would stop and stare. After a while, it made that sound whenever it liked; I didn't know what was wrong with it, but I kept driving it anyway. I took it to get smog-checked, and the guy heard that noise as I pulled into the garage. *That belt's gonna snap,* he said, cigarette flapping. *And then the engine'll shut down.* He glared at me. *You drive on the freeway, son?* He nodded emphatically, the cigarette going nuts. *You drive with people in your car?* I had stood there dumbly as he leaned down and growled, *Goddamn tires are near bald, too—Jesus, man. You're gonna be one of those sad little fuckers on the news, with the yearbook photo and your parents crying . . .* He waved a hand in the air and left to go print up my paperwork. The car passed inspection but I left terrified, walking everywhere for weeks. I wasn't certain if what he had said was true or if he wanted to scare me into costly repairs, but even so—I wasn't taking the chance.

Then, slowly, the immediacy of his words dissipated. Once again I took my friends to movies, drove three blocks to 7-Eleven, skipped class to haul seventy-five miles to the Santa Cruz boardwalk.

A few of the other teachers parked nearby, setting thermoses on their roofs as they gathered up books. I touched my jaw, found a spot I had missed shaving. I glanced at my watch. It was time.

My classroom wasn't far from the street, just through the side entrance and then a hike up the sloped hallway. I rattled the keys in my pocket. The kids in the early-bird program—corralled in the library with juice and word searches—were starting to waft toward their rooms. The place smelled like bleach and chicken fingers, with an undertone of ancient paper. *Morning,* I said to the janitor. My ears burned when he didn't look up.

I got to my classroom and inserted the key, pushing against the door with my shoulder. It didn't give. I tried the key again: nothing. Jesus Christ, I thought, breaking into a cold sweat. Not even a stern talk first? They changed the locks, locked my things inside? I felt someone coming up behind me. Every hair on my body stood on end.

I haven't had a chance to fix that lock yet, the janitor said. *Excuse me?*

He stepped forward, jiggling the key into position. *The lock went loose, you said.* He squinted, pointing at the door. *You said last week . . .*

While I stared at him, he turned the key and opened the door. I mumbled a thank-you and walked into the classroom; there were five minutes left. I had prepared nothing in particular to say. Then there were four minutes left. Usually by now there were a few kids waiting in the hall. Three minutes. I sat at my desk, which was littered with cassette tapes, splayed books, an apple core turned brown. Still three minutes. Think of something else, I thought. Remember that time you went to the Grand Canyon? I watched the second hand swing around, bringing me down to two minutes. I was eight when we went, worrying the whole trip about riding the mules. My mom kept saying, *It's like the pony ride at the fair.* But I nursed a heinous anxiety during the twelve-hour drive, thinking I would have to ride the mule straight down, perpendicular to the ground, attached to the cliff with some kind of spiked horseshoe. I smiled. I couldn't remember the actual mule ride. One minute left. All I remembered was what I had feared.

It was 9:01. Then 9:02. Still no one was milling around outside. 9:04. 9:06. I heard footsteps coming up the hall and froze: a grown-up's shoe.

Frank? The principal poked her head in, a jowl pressed against the door frame. *May I?*

My face went hot. *Yeah, no problem. Come on in. Of course.* I couldn't get the words out fast enough, emphatically enough. I had learned it from the kids: when they got ratted out for cursing, for hitting someone behind the monkey bars, they knew nonchalance suggested blamelessness. *How was your weekend?* I said lamely.

She squinted at me and I shriveled.

Frank, I'd love it if I could borrow you for a moment. She held out her hand.

Class starts in like . . . I checked the clock again. *It started eight minutes ago—*

It's okay, Frank, they're in the auditorium.

I shook my head. *Why?*

Let's go talk for a sec. She made the "come here," swing-arm motion; she may as well have bent at the waist and slapped her lap.

We walked silently up the hall. I knew she wouldn't speak to me until her door was closed. I took the chair in front of her desk, the room thick with potted ferns and posters of children's book covers: Max dancing in his wild rumpus, the selfish boy gazing up at the doomed Giving Tree. I saw her pick up a piece of paper and hold it in her lap, taking the chair next to mine, both of us turning to face each other. She leaned forward enough that I could see part of the reinforced, masking-tape-colored apparatus that held her gigantic breasts.

Frank, she said.

I thought, If she says my name one more goddamn time.

Did you get my message? I asked—the lie was automatic, unrehearsed.

She ignored it. *You should have called me immediately, from the beach. I tried your house ten times this weekend. I left message after message—*

I began to speak, but she stopped me with a lifted hand.

Let's come back to that. Her anger had congealed, spreading over her voice like a film. She gripped the paper; I tried to look through it but couldn't make out the backward lettering. *I spoke to Callie Stone's mom on Saturday morning, and Caleb Noel's father on Saturday night,* she said.

She waited for me to say it for her: they had told her everything. That I was staring into the bay as they took regular head counts and answered questions about pickleweed and barnacles. That I had let the children have free rein on a beach punctuated with pointy rocks. That I was reading a newspaper. Grenades of shame and terror detonated in my head.

You've had—she looked down at the sheet of paper—*six absences so far this year.*

She waited for me to speak. I didn't.

You've called a substitute in six times, Frank.

I get these chronic neck aches—

You've been asked repeatedly to attend district-wide teacher development days and thus far you have—she consulted the paper—*done so only once, at the beginning of the academic year.*

I looked at her with the same expression, I imagined, as someone being addressed in a language he doesn't speak.

This is the part where you tell me, she said, losing patience, *that you understand my concerns and will take steps to address them.*

I closed my eyes. When I opened them she was leaning toward me, her irritation nearly propelling her out of her chair. I could smell her baby-powder scent. I felt rage begin to replicate like cancer cells. It had always been my way: regardless of my own culpability, the anger of others made me angry.

The body was my wife's, I said.

She squinted again—that tight face of disdain and disbelief.

My first wife. It was her body they found.

Her eyes widened in perfect concert with her mouth and nostrils—every hole in her head dilated in shock.

God almighty, she said. *Oh Jesus, I'm just—*

The police identified her, I said. *They told me.*

One phone call—that's all she would need to find me out.

I'm so sorry, Frank. She grabbed my hand, enveloped it. *Why didn't you tell—*she stopped, correcting herself. I experienced a relief so strong I actually sighed: already, she was censoring her criticism.

God almighty, she said again. *Was she missing?*

I sat back in my chair, looking everywhere but at her—the junk on her desk, a terrarium filled with moss, the wood-beaded macramé hanging in her window. *Yes,* I said.

She had been missing for a while. I picked up a glass paper-weight from her desk and held it.

She watched the paperweight as she spoke. Her words were careful, precise. *We can offer you some time to get back on track . . . whatever time you need to do that.*

I leaned back, dazed. *You want me to take time off?*

We can't offer you paid leave, of course, because you've only been here—

Sure. I know. She watched me set down the paper-weight.

We'll get you a sub for a couple weeks. Would that help? I didn't answer.

God almighty, she said. *I just had no idea.*

I rubbed my palms on my knees like I was juicing oranges, my head swimming from the pills. *No,* I said.

No?

They need me, I said. *I want to see this through with the kids.*

She nodded, believing me.

We walked to the auditorium together. It also served as the gym and cafeteria: a basketball hoop hung opposite the small stage, and folded tables leaned against one wall. The children sat Indian-style along the three-point line, conducting their usual squabbles. The girls were braiding one another's hair, the boys raising their arms in threat-ened punches. Marcus, my problem kid, taunted another student, his head bobbing in practiced provocation. Jacob sat very still, and I watched his breathing for a moment before looking away. Edmund sat beside a couple of girls—a rarity among kids their age; mostly they divided

81

into gender-based teams to regard the opposite squad with disdain. Ed was tucking his knees into his shirt, showing Emma and Marisol his makeshift breasts. The three of them laughed wickedly. Sitting to the side was a petite brunette maybe a few years older than me, in hip eyeglasses and a snug pink T-shirt, her hair pulled into a tight ponytail.

Good MOR-ning, Mrs. Norman, the kids said to the principal in their robot voices.

Good morning, little ones, she said, pausing to bend and smile at them as she walked to the dais. She reached the foot-high stage and stood at the podium, thought better of it, and with great effort and imbalance, took a place on the floor. I stood against the wall, the light switch in my back.

You guys, she began, *something happened that I think we should talk about. Can anyone tell me about Friday?*

In a stuttering chorus came the simultaneous replies:

We went on a field trip.

We went to the aquarium.

We saw a shark at the aquarium.

We saw something on the beach.

We rode the bus.

The principal nodded. *Those are all correct answers, but can anyone tell me what happened that was scary and sad?*

Marcus piped up without raising his hand. *I ain't scared or sad about it, it wasn't even scary. I seen it, and me, Ben, Ed, and Jeff seen it, and we wasn't even scared.*

Amber raised her hand and gave the principal that hungry look: pick me, pick me. It took no imagination to see her giving that same look someday to some man. The principal said her name and Amber began her fidgety recitation. *We were at the beach looking for flora, and we saw something, and it was a dead person's body, and that means that their soul went to heaven.*

You only go to heaven if you're good, said Marcus.

Marcus, the principal said, pinning him with her stare. *Hands raised.* He went quiet, the kids tittering.

There's a very special someone here, the principal said, *who can help us talk about what we saw. Her name is Dr. Jennifer.*

The brunette stood up, eyes twinkling behind her cat-eye glasses, and took another spot on the floor. The principal stood, walking laboriously across the room until she reached me. As Dr. Jennifer reintroduced herself, the principal took my hand and held it for one, two seconds. *I'll stop by later,* she said.

You don't have to, I said. *I'm fine, really.*

She smiled, and mercifully dropped my hand. *I'll see you in a few hours,* she said, and then left, the equine clop of her shoes echoing behind her.

Hawthorne's in-house psychologist had been laid off the spring before—one in a series of desperate budget cuts—and I knew immediately that Dr. Jennifer had never worked with children this small. She appeared to believe it required a louder voice than usual, more deliberate enunciation. *Has anyone ever had a pet that died? Or a grandma or grandpa?*

Cautiously, a few kids raised their hands.

Rebekah spoke after being called on. *My mom died,* she said.

Dr. Jennifer looked stunned. There was a pause as she recovered. *What did it mean when she died?*

Rebekah shrugged.

Dr. Jennifer sat up straighter. *What does it mean, to 'die'?* She made the quotation marks with her fingers.

Marcus spoke up again. *It means you never come back.*

The kids turned to Dr. Jennifer for confirmation the way a game-show host consults the judges. *That's true,* she said. *It does mean that.*

And as she spoke, she looked up and saw my pink face, the tearful tributaries meeting at my chin. Before the kids could see, I ducked out and ran up the hall to the boys' bathroom. I untucked my shirt, drying my tears with the bottom as Buckingham's words returned. *The greatest waste.* The phrase repeated itself, changing shape, losing meaning. I fought back a rapid succession of childish urges: I wanted to suffocate in the warm embrace of my own arms, to stretch T-shirt over knees and duck into that fashioned cave. Let yourself think it, I thought. You're allowed to think it: she doesn't call you because she's dead. You'll never see her again. *It means you never come back.* And as though I had touched a live wire, I went weak as suddenly as I had on the beach. It didn't matter whether it was true or not; the very thought shut me down, blew me backward like a blow.

No one in my family had ever died, apart from the four grandparents who went before I was born. The closest I had come to death was cheating it: when that pickup truck's belt did snap, I wasn't on the freeway. I wasn't even on the road. I was in the driveway of my aunt's house, about to go to my cousin's Little League game. There was an abrupt jolt. The interior lights went off; the motor stilled. The car rolled back—the mechanic had been right, I had lost all control—and I yanked the emergency brake at my knee. It stopped rolling. I sat for a moment, sweating. That was it.

I understood then that nothing like that other scenario—speeding unanchored into oblivion, dying in the crush of a renegade metal machine—would ever happen to me. I felt certain in that moment that I would spend my whole life doing normal stuff, watering my lawn and yelling at my kids. I believed I would grow up and grow old and have money enough to pay my bills; I would vacation in Hawaiian shirts, push a stroller, bitch about property taxes. I would never have a hallowed, tragic name, would never be a sad story parents whispered about. My curse would not be adversity, but banality. I knew I might not get everything I wanted, everything I asked for. But things would move forward. I would get rid of that truck and buy another. And, in fact, a month later my dad fronted the down payment for the little white car, the one I still drove despite a busted cassette player and a smashed driver's side door.

Sitting in that deceased truck, I knew that life, for me, could always go on—that life, for me, *would* always go on. I was still years away from this moment in the boys' bathroom—sobbing, bereft, half-high on pills—still years away from this compelling evidence that I had miscalculated the future ease of my life. I was seventeen and already certain that my time on earth would never carry an ounce of tragedy. I was seventeen, and already disappointed.

I stared at my chest in the child-height mirror, crying into my sleeve. I felt myself succumbing to a genuine uncertainty: I had no idea how I would survive the day.

But I did. And I did it by doing one thing at a time—bending to wash my face, tucking in my shirt, counting to ten. Then I had the first clear-headed thought in recent memory: don't let today be different. I watched my hand open the door to the auditorium, where Dr. Jennifer was just finishing up. At the sight of me she stood and waved good-bye to the kids. They looked to me for direction, and I told them to please gather their things and line up. Dr. Jennifer gave me her card as she left, shaking my hand and avoiding my eyes.

I walked my class down the hall to our room. I brought up the rear and took deep, nourishing breaths. Just maintain, I thought. Do whatever you have to do to survive this. The kids stayed quiet, moving forward in in-stitutionalized cadence.

After they had settled in, to the degree that any group of second graders can, I told them to gather on the carpet for another two chapters of our group-reading book. They stared dumbly up at me. I knew they had assumed the day would be devoted to grief management; they had been certain I would take my turn dispensing wisdom, showering them with an intense interest in their feelings.

Carpet, please. I did say that out loud, right? I heard my voice quaking. They stood, chairs scraping, and began to gather. I had a sudden brainstorm, an answer to my most immediate problem. *Be right back,* I told them.

I left a classroom of small children alone to go out to the car, open the glove box, and fish two more painkillers from the bottle. Edmund—my pet, my favorite student, one of the boys who had serenely stood there with a corpse as I shouted at them to leave—watched me from the window. I waved. He waved back, frowning. The hand holding the pills went instinctively behind my back; I had a momentary fear that Ed understood what I was doing.

The principal returned that afternoon, opening the door and *then* knocking on it. She sat in my classroom for nearly two hours; when she left it was clear she wanted to stay longer but couldn't spare the time. In those two hours I felt the atmosphere compressing, as more and more time passed without any further acknowledgment of what had happened on the beach. I observed the slow degradation of her pleasant, comforting smile—first a beaming presence, and then a thin-lipped glower, and then a cold frown. The principal saw that I had no intention of addressing the subject again. She heard me slur my words. And though I worried in some corner of my consciousness that I was signing my own termination, I couldn't bring myself to give her what she wanted. My mouth, that afternoon, refused to form the words *Class, tell me what you saw, tell me how you feel.* I watched her reconsider her own faulty thinking, kicking herself: you don't ask, *Do you need time off?* You dictate. You insist. And then, cyclically, I erased all those thoughts—wasn't I just being paranoid? Wasn't I just overreacting, as I so often do?—only to watch them slowly return—I was, my excuses and grief notwithstanding, going to pay for this, and it was going to hurt.

But all of that was still an hour or two away. Walking back to the building, I took the pills with a bottle of stale water from the car's cup holder and came back to find the kids all off-task. I turned to the light switch next to the door and shut it off, capturing their attention. *Quiet, please,* I said. And, one by one, each child put a finger over his or her lips and another in the air, to let me know they understood.

6

Ask me what I most remember about high school and the answer is the back of your head—the freckled nape of your neck that was so soft it looked out of focus. Your last name was Lucas and mine Mason, so in high school you sat in front of me in every class. It was easy to cheat off of you; a lucky thing, since you did well in school and I never cared to. Sometimes I saw you writing long, spiraling lines of text, winding in circles around the page. I imagined they were poems, lists, entries in some kind of strange diary. Once, Mr. Zelner, a human steel-wool sponge, caught you writing one in tenth grade driver's ed and snatched it from your desk. You looked like he had yanked a hair from your head.

Don't write letters in my class, Zelner said, crushing the page into a compact ball. He sank an arthritic jump shot, the paper arcing into the trash.

I froze. A letter? I ran down the list of possible recipients, sweating.

It was in Zelner's class, sophomore year, that you told me your house was haunted. *I'm serious,* you said, because my expression warranted convincing. The front hall closet in your house reeked of roses. Not the faint, earthy tang of a garden, but the syrupy choke of drugstore-grade perfume. And it was contagious—a jacket hanging in there for an hour emerged as ripe as if a bottle had broken in the pocket.

Come look, you challenged me, *and tell me if you find anything rose-scented.*

So one Saturday I took the bus up Nineteenth Avenue, ready to prove you wrong. We were supposed to see a movie, but the afternoon got away from us as we pulled out unmarked boxes, baseball mitts, board games coated in dust. The smell was astonishing. It was the difference between air and fog; you could almost see it. We searched the corners, the baseboards. We ran our hands blindly over the high shelves, provoking a mouse-turd rain. In the end, we found nothing rose-scented besides the junk we had dislodged, and, once we were done, ourselves. I was freaked out. But it was my job to stop *you* from freaking out, so I spoke:

Isn't it possible something spilled into the cracks of the floor?

Would it smell for this long, and this strong?

If ghosts existed, would one live in a closet?

You don't believe in ghosts?

Of course not, I said.

You frowned. *You don't think people stick around waiting for their final wish to be fulfilled?*

We stood there, silent: you, embarrassed, and me, embarrassed for you. It was uncomfortable, seeing someone want so badly to believe. Finally, I began restacking the board games. *I think they decompose,* I said, *and that's pretty much the end of it.*

Though I had said this several years earlier, after your parents died I was scared that you remembered it. If there was no afterlife, your parents weren't just dead but permanently so, without hope of reunion, without the redemptive existence of a "better place." But if there *was* an afterlife, then it was possible there were ghosts. And if it was possible that there were ghosts, then it was possible your parents were among them, wandering, waiting for their last requests to be satisfied. A classic lose-lose.

After Mel's Drive-In and our walk in the park, we went back to your apartment. The lights had come back on, and in the streetlight glow I shut off the engine, still squeezing your fingers. If a move was to be made, it was now. I scanned my brain for something to say, but you beat me.

Have you even called her? you said.

Our fingers recoiled.

Since before the funeral, have you called her even once?

The car ticked, the engine settling. I swallowed. *You really know how to pick your moment.*

You slipped your hands under your knees. *Go home, Francis.*

You're angry with me?

No, you said, *but I assume she is.*

You may not believe me, but I'll say this anyway. In all the years I had liked you, I had never thought of you the way

91

I did other girls—bending them over things, whispering nasty coital rejoinders I would never utter in real life. I thought instead about us watching a movie on a couch. I would shut off the overhead light. I would choose a film we would need to be quiet to understand. I wanted to be quiet with you. Your head would rest on my shoulder, my hand on your knee.

The fear I had felt on your stoop was now diluted by recurrence: what had happened there was now of a piece, part of a pattern, and both times it had been *your* hand reaching out, touching me. You told me to go home, yes, but it was empty; the last thing we said that night was *See you soon.* I knew what you were doing. Once we had caved in and become something more than friends—in spite of my obligations elsewhere—you could pretend you had resisted.

That night, I did call Greta. I waited until I knew she was halfway through her shift, dispensing fried eggs for five-percent tips at the diner on Market Street. I stuttered through a willfully upbeat message, keeping it short and vague, and went to bed feeling like I had paid off a bill.

. . .

It was two years after we cleaned out that ghostly closet, a few months into our senior year, that you and I had the fight. It resulted in a long period of silence between us—in a grandiose show of my hatred I asked permission from each teacher to switch my seat. Most of them distractedly complied, letting me publicly drag my desks through the dingy orange classrooms, the hole behind you like the site of a pulled molar. I may as well have written it on my forehead: Fool in Love.

Only Mr. Wilkerson, our AP Economics teacher—a pony-tailed wearer of purple slacks, who showed us *Roger and Me* and got misty-eyed during the Beach Boys–scored montage—refused to redraft his seating chart so late in the year. *So you and your girlfriend had an argument,* he said.

She's not my girlfriend, I said.

He sipped his coffee. *You're almost an adult now; deal with it.*

And so each time he asked us all to pair up for an assignment, I watched a red bloom spread across your freckled neck. I came to dread Wilkerson's class. Once the anger dissipated (it took perhaps a week), being that near to you was torture.

I missed our small, stupid diversions. Driving through rain puddles to create stegosaurus fins of water above my truck; playing badminton in the lakeside park in Berkeley; eating supremely unhealthy food. We had been perpetually without destination, and often we just went places and watched strangers. There was a game we played. I would goad you into saying something mean about passersby— something that came naturally to me. You were so reluctant, so unwilling. Each time, finally you would give in and speak with only moderate unkindness, and then hide your face behind your hands, laughing. *I don't trust people who aren't mean,* I said to you once. *They're hiding something.*

And then, though I had been a normal kid with pals and laughs and weekend hijinks, I killed my whole social network with that stupid, belabored fight: when we drew up our opposing sides, everyone chose you. I didn't speak to you for seven months. I ate lunch alone like the kids I had once made fun of. All the while graduation loomed; a massive gate, we believed, to the unchained future— low-tier state schools, unexpected offspring, a sedentary attachment to the outlying suburbs. One could weep for all we didn't know.

That year, I wore a leather cord necklace that never left my body. When it fell off one day I failed to notice; I un- dressed for bed to find it gone. You came into Wilkerson's class the next morning with a fidgeting quality about your hands and I knew immediately that you were going to speak to me. My heart clenched in its small chamber, and then your gaze paused at my chest, my chin, my eyes. You set the necklace down on my desk. *I found this outside the science building.*

I refused to look at you—even as I did it, I hated doing it—and you waited, and then finally turned away, sitting down. *Thank you,* I said to your back, shoving the neck- lace into my pocket.

That night I retied it around my neck, thinking about how it was hidden, almost always, by my shirt. Thinking about how one would have to look very close to see it.

The next day you came to class with the invitations to your graduation party and wordlessly set one on my desk. I put it in my pocket and spent the rest of the day verifying periodically that it was real. After school, as you walked toward the bus I ambled a few yards behind, solidifying my courage. You sensed someone there, I guess, because you did that old trick: you followed a passing car with your eyes, all the way around. You saw me and stopped,

three sidewalk cracks between us. I tossed a tentative *Hey.*
You started to answer but sneezed, your *Hello* coming out
at ninety miles an hour.

Bless you, I said. And then we drove to Taco Bell in my
screeching truck, to eat bean and cheese burritos and begin
the short trek back to friendship. For seven months, that was
all it would have taken: a lost necklace, a sealed invitation—
you sneezed, God bless you, and I knew you again.

. . .

You decided you were going to keep the house. After I
dropped you off, I found a message on the machine: you
needed help moving in, quick, before you changed your
mind—*Meet me at my place at 10:00 AM sharp*, you said.
You had already phoned the lawyer, though it was nearly
midnight. The decision didn't surprise me; it would let
you avoid a lot of cumbersome paperwork. Most choices
you made right after the accident had one criterion: you
chose whichever option required no further choices.

The next morning, the streetlights shone in protest of
the persistent fog. The rain had washed the city clean. You
had said ten, but I was in my car, ready for the fifteen-
minute drive, by nine, having waited as long as I could—
that is, were I to say that *I couldn't wait to see you*, it
would be painfully literal. I came to a four-way stop a few
blocks from your apartment, waited my turn and pushed
forward. A kid in a rust-marred Honda rolled through the
stop sign, and the thought came as clearly as if someone
had spoken it: he's going to hit me. He did. The small
impact pushed my car sideways, and I felt the skidding

vibration of tire treads scraping asphalt. The door on my side crumpled, one side of my elbow hitting the armrest, the other bruising my ribs. I tried to get out to look as the kid rubbed a hand through his white-blond hair—so light his eyebrows were nearly invisible against his cherry skin. I pushed the driver-side door a few times, gave up when it wouldn't open, and exited from the passenger side. *Fuck,* the kid said, his voice thick with mucus. He sniffed some of it back, approaching me. I felt a twinge of pain progress the length of my neck. He didn't have insurance, he said, already had a point on his record, was on probation besides. *Don't do this, man,* he said.

Do what? I said, sneering. *Fucking idiot. Do what?*

Don't, man—I can make it up to you. He held out his hand as though I might shake it and then we could be friends. I stared at his palm. *My name's William,* he said, fishing in his jacket pockets. *It's all good.* He pulled out a foggy plastic bag of weed. I collected myself as he twitched with worry, standing there like a stupid animal, mouth half-open. A double helix of repulsion and mercy wound around me—I could have hugged him, I could have killed him. I said, *Watch where the fuck you're going.* There was nothing more to say. I got back in through the passenger side, and the adrenaline flood subsided, giving way to tremors in my hands. When I got to your street I just sat there. The previous twelve hours' irrepressible excitement, reborn every time I remembered our clasped hands, was flaking off, scraped raw by my jangled nerves and sore body. I got out and didn't bother to lock the car. My neck felt as though something inside had ripped. I knocked, but you didn't answer. Your car was there. I tried the door and found it open.

I yelled a hello toward your bedroom at the end of the narrow hallway. *You want me to start loading the car?* In the living room were three measly boxes piled in front of the built-ins. All you had was a small collection of movies you never watched, thrift-store clothes, a half-dozen used textbooks never traded in after college. *This should be easy,* I called.

You didn't answer.

I walked down the hall and knocked on your bedroom door, the ache in my neck sending shocks down my arm. *Nora,* I said. A few seconds passed. I rapped on the door with the fleshy side of my fist, hard enough to rattle it. *Nora, open the door.* I went short of breath, air clotting in my lungs. The intuition gripped me, hard: I didn't know what you were capable of. I pushed the door open, and after a searing moment my eyes adjusted to the glare of your desk lamp.

You were naked except for yellow cotton panties and a pair of headphones, which were screaming as you stepped into faded jeans. Where you bent, ripples formed in your skin. Your vertebrae were knobbed punctuations along your freckled back, your wet hair a red curtain against your pale arm. That was all I saw in the half instant before I moved back, taking the door with me. I listened in the hallway to the faint, bleating echo of your private music, barely audible through the lit crack at my feet. An involuntary smile came to my face—a pleasant ache stabbed me somewhere deep, followed by an aftershock of guilt.

You came out, clothes askew, startling at the sight of me in the hall. *You keep sneaking up on me,* you said. *Why are you rubbing your neck like that?*

I tried to think. *I just got here.*

You were jumpy. You smelled like a shower. In the kitchen you held up two beers. *It's nine forty-five in the morning,* I said. But we each emptied a bottle and you finally said what I knew you were going to say: *I don't really feel like moving today.*

I rolled my neck and felt tendons grating, a distinct pop as something already tender slipped farther out of place. *What then?*

Let's get out of the city, you said. *Let's get out of the state! You have to be anywhere today?*

I hesitated. *No.*

Outside, you went toward my car, but I scrambled to dissuade you. *I'm almost out of gas,* I lied.

I drank a beer, you said. *Can you drive my car?*

I nodded, and you tossed me your keys.

We skirted the north-facing lip of the city toward the Bay Bridge, looking for something new in places we had been a thousand times. We played songs over and over, mutter-singing the lyrics. You asked me some Who Would You Rather Do's: Bob Barker or Pat Sajak, Chuck Norris or Bruce Lee. As I hunted the Alameda streets for a good burrito, you slept. Waking up, you asked if we were still in California. *It's been an hour,* I said. On Buena Vista Avenue you saw a heap of junk with a sign saying FREE and wanted to investigate. In the pile was a citronella candle with four wicks, cylindrical and flesh-colored, the size of a small keg. I held it at crotch level until you swatted at me, laughing. A woman walked by. *That lady saw you,* you said, like we were in trouble.

Watching you right then, I fostered a self-satisfied burst of foolishness. I looked at your smile, coming easier than it had in days, and imagined that I knew what you were thinking, what you needed. But I didn't know shit. My parents, after all, were alive—divorced, watering cacti on their patios, arguing over who got to ignore my little sister on Thanksgiving. I didn't have the first idea what you felt.

In a Berkeley shop that sold animal bones you lifted a fossilized fish, wiggling it like it was swimming. I ran my finger over the rigid, pearled surface of a severed chicken foot. Tremendous antlers sat in vases like branches. In the corner a little boy was wailing, terrified, his mom laughing nervously. You leaned toward something but abruptly stood up and cursed. I looked over your shoulder at the hollow blue eggshell in your hand and the hole you had crunched through the top of it. We set down the pieces and walked briskly outside, something pulling at the edge of your mood. I knew what you were thinking—that you were always so goddamn clumsy—because I had heard you complain about it a hundred times.

We ate lunch at a place in Oakland that had peanut butter and jelly pizza on the menu, but even though you dared me I was too strapped to throw money away on chances.

Where now? you asked.

The world is our oyster.

Vegas! you said.

I'll put it this way: the world is our oyster within a hundred miles.

You spoke with a mouth full of bread. *Tahoe! Reno!*

Christ. If scabies was a place, it would be Reno.

New York City, you said.

I stole one of your bread sticks. *You're not very good with numbers.*

I've always wanted to live there, you said. *Like every Bay Area kid.*

It was true. We all fought the suspicion that San Francisco was a sort of training-wheels city. Life in northern California was embarrassingly easy—yes, the rents necessitated lifelong roommates, but there were also working wages and reasonable parking, Mediterranean weather, proximity to an array of natural wonders, access to exceptional weed. The prevailing wisdom held that the breakneck glory of that fabled East Coast city was one of the few draws worthy of giving all this up.

In the end we landed about twenty miles away, at your alma mater, a wooded, bright campus beneath a drooping halo of eucalyptus, their little pods plinking around us like dangerous brown hail. We parked at the bottom of a steep hill, a thin walkway worming up the incline to a cluster of dorms. It was a pretty, improbable place, located just off the rank, decrepit avenue that plowed through east Oakland's cement ruins. I had visited your dorm, but only rarely and usually after dark, summoned to comfort you when some guy did what all guys do. I remember us eating a lot of packaged cookies in there. A creek ran through campus and now we walked over the footbridges that strapped chunks of earth together, relaxed in the shade of all those trees.

I want to show you something, you said, taking me on a short hike rife with poison oak. We stepped carefully, our canvas shoes growing damp. You put your hand through the triangle of my elbow and I hardened my bicep: the only thing to do when a girl touches your arm.

I'm allergic to poison oak, I said.

You pulled your gloves off and gave them to me—pink with a velvet ribbon around the cuff, about two-thirds the necessary size. And then we reached a concrete drainage pipe, roughly eight feet in diameter, emptying into the creek. Beside it was a large flat rock. *See, just down that little slope,* you said. *I used to come here to read.*

The slope was more like a three-foot cliff. *How do you get down there?*

You have to run down and hop.

I didn't think, just moved, covering the distance with more grace than I had hoped. I took a breath and turned. *I've got you,* I said, holding out my hand. You took it.

From that planar rock we watched the afternoon die, the orange light shifting to gray. I asked you an idle question, forgetting myself.

Do you still believe in ghosts? I said—cursing silently as soon as the words left my mouth.

You retied a shoelace. *Yes,* you said.

I want to say it now, because I was too afraid to say it then: *I'm sorry I asked you that.*

I drove us through the quiet residential streets. We were holding hands again, and we were happy. Do you remember how that felt? It fed itself, existing not because everything in our lives was perfect, but because nothing was and we were *still,* in that moment, content. Right then, we could both say something monumental: we didn't want to be anywhere else.

. . .

I never told you how I felt in high school—not because of Greta, but because I was a coward. If you knew, you never said. And then we went to college in towns separated by an hour's drive, and things changed. Though we spoke less and less, the conversations morphed, intensified: now, the quotidian minutiae fell away, and we talked only of tremendous things—careers and death and Achieving our Visions. I didn't know what classes you took or who your friends were. I didn't know what you did for fun or what music you liked. It didn't matter. We were vaults for one another. I heard from you every five months or so—I don't think I could have withstood more frequent interaction. Every time we spoke I felt like I had been laid bare, fully seen.

Our connection became more acute than in high school, something deeper and more abiding than friendship; I don't know that there's a word for it other than *peace*. You gave me a kind of peace, and I think I gave it back. When you heard my voice on the line, you sighed with relief. I would show up at your job, and just like in the movies—those scenes in which the unresolved love walks in unannounced, there to settle some old score—you would flash your wry smile and say, *Well hello, stranger.* Because we reserved a certain place for each other, a privileged place. And I tried to believe that was the same as you being in love with me.

Because I was in love with you. I didn't figure this out until our junior prom. That night, you and I and our now forgotten friends paid forty bucks each to split a limo. You wore a cream dress, the color just darker than your skin. At the dance, we didn't dance. We sat at a table and I made fun of people. (Zelner, for one: the old bastion of the *Red Asphalt* educational doctrine was chaperoning, in nylon track pants, a sport coat, and a heinous plaid tie.) It was a joint prom with five other schools, and I hoped the strangers mistook me for your date. I couldn't stop looking at you. *Are you having fun?* My voice was drowned by the cranked-up bass. *You want to go outside?*

I had this idea that we would stand on the balcony overlooking the Berkeley marina—its chain restaurants, corporate-convention hotels, and glittering black water—and you would kiss me. I thought you might be overcome by the view, the moment, enough to see me differently. I remember actually having the thought, This is when it's going to happen.

Just let me hit the bathroom, you said.

I stood against the railing, loosening my bow tie. A blonde in orange casually leaned next to me, the bust of her dress sagging.

Are you from Armijo High? she said.

No.

Vallejo?

No.

She shoved her hand at me. *So what's your name?*

Francis, I said, shaking it.

Do you go to Oakland Tech?

Lowell. In the city. I motioned behind us. *I'm actually waiting for—*

My name's Greta, she said. *I go to Skyline.*

I shook her hand again as you came out and found me. You told her your name and held out your hand too. Greta motioned for her friends to come over. Awkward conversations sprouted. I kept waiting for them to wander away. They never did. The tables got dismantled and the

DJ threatened last dance, and we all moseyed toward the sea of limos. Greta asked for my phone number, pulling a pen from her purse, and I wrote on her hand, thinking, She brought a pen to the prom.

I was sixteen, so rabidly in need of sexual stimuli I scoured my school-issued copy of *The Scarlet Letter* for blue bits, engineered homemade stick-figure porno. You talked about your crush on Greg Linderhoefer incessantly, before apologizing for talking about it incessantly. There was a live girl two towns over who seemed lonely, and dim, and giving. I cut my losses and took what I knew I could get. I could do both: pine over you, and flail over her.

Our friends met Greta at caravanning jaunts to the mall during which none of us bought a thing. Greta never spoke first, just answered questions: Yes, she liked the Clash. Sure, the Mongolian barbeque place was fine by her. They all pretended to like her, which worked out fine. They were all pretending to like me too.

Greta, like you, was only an occasional witness to the embarrassments that trailed my parents like a stench—their casual swearing, my mother's confessions (*Honey, I was twenty-six before I had my first orgasm . . .*). Greta reacted, like you did, with polite puzzlement. If she sensed that things were worse than what she saw, she never brought it up, and I never told her otherwise.

Until a day early in our senior year, when I came home from school one afternoon to find my parents waiting. They had some mundane grouse: I had promised to drive my sister somewhere and, having forgotten, never showed. My father yelled, a caricature of an angry man— he was beet-faced, out of breath. I hardly needed to be there; this was for his benefit, not mine.

You told me you were going to take her, I said. *Don't you remember?*

As I spoke the lie, an involuntary smirk came to my face. I saw him register my expression. He looked at my mom as if to say, *The balls on this kid!* The three of us hung there, suspended. I felt the ice break, like we had stepped out of our scripted roles. He knew I was lying; I knew he knew it. The whole thing was absurd and suddenly lighthearted. We were still smiling, a triangular exchange of deflated tensions, when my father began to undo his belt. He grinned, so I grinned—it was a joke, he was miming like I had gone and done it and so he was gonna stripe my ass good; a pantomime from another era. He liked to get tough, push me around. He liked to tell me that I made him sick, and why. But he had never whipped me. I knew not to take the gesture seriously. He lightly flung the belt outward, using the buckle as a handle, so that on the recoil it licked me on the upper thigh—he had expended no effort, and still it nipped at my skin through my jeans. *Hey!* I said, laughing through the sting.

I was about to speak. That's what I recall most vividly—I was about to apologize, concede. I was opening my mouth to form the words *You're right, I'm sorry for forgetting*, when I was interrupted: a salty, throbbing pain, thick and cutting, across the side of my neck and shoulder blade. I never got the words out. The hit came hard, and it was enough to pop a white burst at the outer edges of my vision, my teeth biting down on my tongue, my mouth filling with the taste of blood.

You little piss-ant liar, he said.

When my vision came back, I saw my mother's hand on the dining room table. I didn't dare look up. I put my hand to my neck, then my face: it had happened fast enough that I was still smiling.

Without pausing I walked into the bathroom—the only room with a lock. A coral-colored welt had already taken root, suppressed enough by adrenaline that it didn't yet hurt. It would linger for days, doggedly visible and impossible to explain.

I found my keys and walked to a pay phone. I had six digits of your number dialed before I reconsidered. I couldn't tell you this.

I called the studio where Greta had piano lessons; I knew her exhausting, application-padding honor student's schedule as well as my own. A man answered and I could hear someone playing in the background: uncertain, faltering notes among more confident ones, and then the mistakes being repeated, corrected. I asked for her and the playing ceased.

She answered. *Greta,* I said, loathing the desperation in my voice. Fucking disgusting, asking for help like this. *God,* I said. *Fuck, I'm sorry, this is—*

I heard rustling on the other end. *I'm packing up,* she said briskly. *I'll meet you at MacArthur BART in an hour,* she said. Her voice was clipped and efficient. *Get out of there,* she said. She had known, without my saying, if not the specifics then the tenor of what had happened.

At the BART station she cried. *I wish I could keep you safe,* she said.

It was the sort of remark that usually made me ill with embarrassment, stupidly angry, or derisive toward its weak-hearted source. But I wanted, in that moment, to take from her anything I could. She was the only person who knew this, who knew me. I was so grateful to Greta it frightened me.

And once she was the keeper of that information, it took so little time for things to change. When I looked at her I saw my shame. She thought of me as a victim, and gauged my actions accordingly: he's not unkind, only injured. She told her parents. The next time I came for dinner, her father cornered me in the den. *This is abuse,* he said. *What your father did. What your father does.*

I smiled, shaking my head. *Mr. Carver,* I said.

Your father is a bad man, he said, his hands on my shoulders. His breath smelled like butterscotch.

No, I said, looking away. *He's just an idiot.*

That night at the BART station, before Greta and I parted, she kissed me good night. I had to go home. I was seventeen—where else was there? She reached up to caress the mark on my neck but stopped herself, pulling her hand back.

It's okay, I said. *You can touch it.*

Her cool, gentle fingers grazed the reddening welt. It was when they pulled away that it really began to hurt.

■ ■ ■

After we left your college we drove back to your apartment, and, distracted by your hand in mine, I forgot to avoid my car: it was still right where I had parked it that morning. You gasped. *Oh shit—somebody sideswiped you!*

I parked your car in a stranger's driveway, my ears burning, and you ran to mine, touching the gash in the paint.

Maybe your neighbors saw something, I said—realizing a beat too late how unconcerned I sounded.

You peered at me. *You're not upset?* You bent back down, touched the massive dent again. Your voice flattened. *This isn't a swipe, somebody hit you for real. Somebody T-boned you.*

I rubbed my neck without thinking and you watched my hand as I did it. *It's no big deal, just a fender bender,* I said, stepping toward you.

What happened to your neck? You stood against the crater in the door. Your voice broke. *Somebody hit you? You were in a car accident and you didn't tell me?*

Yeah, but I'm fine, Nora. Nobody got hurt.

Your tears came anyway. A spiteful burst of speech came to my lips, and I rolled my eyes: *Oh God, I can't—*

I had started to say, *I can't do this anymore.* I could no longer handle having to anticipate, moment to moment, what would make you cry. I wanted you to stop crying. I wanted you to get over it, to banish your parents' ghosts. I wanted to get where we were going, for a move to be made, without the specter of your heartache sucking the air out of the room.

I put my arms on the car, on either side of your body, pinning you without touching you. I got close enough to smell your car's sun-cooked vinyl scent on your clothes.

What is this, I said, inches from your face, my voice gentler than I expected. *Tell me what we're doing.*

You paused. *We're deciding what we'll regret more.*

What? I said.

These things only end badly, you said. *You know that. Everyone knows that.*

I stood there in disbelief. It was like you had suddenly become someone else.

Fuck that, I said. *You know what?* Seconds died like weak snowflakes, disintegrating as they hit the ground. *Fuck you.* I walked around the car, opened my passenger door, and finagled my way over the gearshift. Your torso eclipsed the window as you pleaded through the glass. But I ignored you, taking off toward my apartment, gunning through stop signs and blasting the radio. The cassette player had cannibalized a tape that remained there, dormant. I found a Christian rock channel, some honey-voiced young thing basking in holy light.

As I walked into the apartment, sounds came from my roommate's door that didn't compute right away—a mélange of male earnestness, rickety carpentry, a girl's barks of pleasure phrased as questions: *Unh? Unh? Unh? Unh?* A wave of revulsion rolled the length of me, and I shut my bedroom door, hearing them just as clearly.

I looked around the place: toppled fast-food cups, fragrant socks, a stack of loose CDs next to cracked CD cases. Down the hall my roommate approached liftoff, groans stretching out and growing frenzied, and in that queasy moment it felt unfair to be born male. I would always be a messy, grunting animal. My face, if left alone, would grow coarse with hair; I would have to wage a lifelong war not to smell like an armpit. I missed you terribly right then. I had acclimated to you like a new time zone. You knew a lot about strange things, like old typewriters and Eastern philosophy. You tipped well and sometimes did a goofy little prospector's jig when you were happy. You were effortlessly lovely. Your hair smelled like tropical fruit.

You were so sad, and so strong. You were good at being a person; you were a good person.

I got up, lifted my rolling desk chair, and readied myself to hurl it at the wall of bookshelves, 1, 2, 3 *NOW*—

I stood there with the chair in my slightly raised arms, muscles locked. It suddenly seemed like a stupid thing to do. Am I really this angry? I thought. It made no sense to be this angry. You were right. You were deciding if being together was worth ruining our friendship, and I already knew that it was. The only thing you had phrased incorrectly was the "we."

Stop thinking so hard, I said quietly. And then I threw the chair.

The shelves—planks of unfinished wood on cinder blocks—dissolved. The books, the CDs and their cases, the swimsuit issues, playing cards, and loose change—all of it avalanched. The house went silent, my roommate and his girlfriend apparently suspended. *Shit,* I said: it was a mess, *my* mess, with no one to attend to it but me. The stillness held until a framed Bob Marley poster, seconds late, hit the floor and splintered. The girlfriend's frantic yelps resumed.

Suddenly, I *was* that mad, and heartbroken too. Angry and sad was a recipe for violence in men of conviction—but I knew whatever painful rage I felt would manifest itself in wallowing self-criticism, binge drinking, phone calls soliciting your sympathy with a telemarketer's shamelessness. I fished a clean pair of boxers from my laundry. I would drive up to my mom's house, block her car in the driveway, let her feed me low-fat pudding and vodka-Sprite cocktails. She owed me—she said it every time I saw her. When my mother was, by virtue of a highball or two, willing to speak seriously about my father, she apologized for him breathlessly, emptily, as though begging pardon for stepping on my toe. There was always a new permutation. *He seemed so different when we were younger. You kids adored him when you were babies. We thought if we were better than our parents then we were good enough.* I think she believed it was a matter of locating the correct phrasing.

Being a parent, she said once, *isn't like you think.* She closed her eyes for a moment, ruminating. *You, as a person? You're gone. Your past is over. You watch your old self die.*

Her eyes were like a startled cat's. She clutched her bathrobe to her chest. I looked away.

I shoved the boxers into my pocket, hating that I had nowhere else to go. I had no real friends other than you. Greta would be primed for an all-night delirium of bitter rage, unanswerable questions, tearful recrimination. So I would regress alongside my mother, watch her terrible TV programs, wake up hungover with her twenty-pound cat on my chest.

I stepped into the hall and saw the front doorknob rattling. I could hear keys. I walked to the door and opened it. You looked up, sheepish.

I couldn't get it open, you said.

It sticks. You have to pull the door toward you.

We were interrupted by my roommate's noises; they were still at it. You peered down the hall. *You're not having an orgy, are you?*

Just taking a break, I said.

And then you pushed me against my bedroom door in the style of a locker-room bully. You put your lips to my neck, your hands on my chest. And then you worked my ear with your tongue, your breathing pornographic. But when I enveloped your shoulders with my arms, surging with relief, you slowed to hug me like I was a lost child.

I brought a toothbrush, you said into my neck.

For once, I didn't let myself think. As events unfolded, I would evaluate them on their individual merits. Thus far, the list was short. You had brought a toothbrush: plus.

I didn't bring pajamas.

Plus.

You looked into my eyes, except then I realized you were looking near them. *I want to take your glasses off,* you said.

Don't, I said. *I can't see.*

But you did anyway. *Do you take them off to have sex?* you asked.

I tried not to look startled. *Yes,* I said.

This is how you look, you said, your fingers touching my hairline. *Without your glasses you look like the purest you.*

Okay, I said.

You look weird, you said, smiling.

In my bedroom you saw the mess, and your smile faded. I kicked some of the spilled junk off my mattress. *Rough night?* you said.

Not anymore, I said.

I shut off the light and we lay down in our clothes. We were still: my nose in the red web of your hair, my arms around you—one you used as a pillow, the other I curled around your rib cage. The hand of that curled arm was the one you held all night, chastely, between your breasts. I slept, long and black and dreamless. When my alarm went off I waited for you to panic. Instead, you turned onto your back, grinning. I propped myself up on one elbow.

We didn't kiss on the mouth, you said. *I slept in your bed and we haven't kissed.*

No?

No.

We're all out of order, I said. *Do you want to kiss me now?*

You made a face. *I need to brush my teeth first.*

We walked to the bathroom in our rumpled clothes and brushed our teeth side by side, regarding each other in the mirror with pleasant suspicion. We went back into my room, and sat facing each other on my bed. You leaned toward me, eyes shut, and pressed your closed, dry lips to mine. Neither of us breathed. And then our minty mouths opened, and it was happening.

Before it all ended, in those few days we had after your parents died, our history was recast. Every trivial thing suddenly meant, meant, meant. We wanted to know all the stuff we hadn't learned in the first decade and a half. We wanted to line it all up and check for patterns, look in hindsight for prophetic synchronicity: Did we ever have pets that had the same name? Had we ever lived close by each other without knowing it? We needed to rehash it. I didn't touch you; we were happy to get there in due time. We barely left my room for eighteen hours, knocked out by the one-two punch of cinematic romance and easy, familiar company. If we left to pee we rushed back, eager to return to our private undertow.

I did something silly, you said. *When you went home the other night? I called the psychic hotline.*

The Jamaican lady?

The other one.

What'd you say?

The stuff you'd expect. Can they see me, do they miss me.

What'd she say?

She said yes, you said. *Everything I asked her, she said yes to.*

You were on your back in my white T-shirt and a pair of panties. The blanket was pulled down, your bottom half uncovered. In a first stab toward sex I leaned down, my lips brushing the hard knob of your hipbone.

I asked if they were proud of me, you said. *She said yes to that, too.*

They should be, I said, lying down again. *They are.*

You told me things I hadn't known: in Spanish II, the boy next to you showed you his penis during class. *Where the hell was I?* I said, retroactively protective. You said he gave you such a mournful look as he did it that you couldn't tell on him. You told me Ms. Jefferson had a retarded son, grown, who lived with her; that she could never get to class on time because he refused to put on his shoes. You came for a makeup test once and she told you this, sobbing. You told me all the small things I hadn't known about your college years: where you ate burritos, all the times you did mushrooms, the worst grade you ever got (a C-). You told me you had dated boys from your dorm. *Boys,* you said—you didn't name any. And you told me, too, that those swirling letters you had composed in class were addressed to boys. Some were to me. They stayed in your backpack until you threw them away. I confessed something myself: when Mr. Wilkerson asked us to pass our papers forward and you put your hand over your shoulder expectantly, I would hold the paper for two, three, four seconds, before passing it up, spiteful enough to make you wait. You said, *That was during our big fight?* Your head was on my shoulder. *What was it about again?*

I wondered if you could tell from my heartbeat that I was about to lie.

I don't remember, I said.

Twilight had made the room one encompassing shadow. I could hardly see.

This is cheating, what we're doing.

We haven't had sex, I said, bristling.

Promise to break up with her. Don't say you'll do it and then not do it.

In all the years I had lived in San Francisco—the nut jobs yelling, the noisy patrons at the Indian place downstairs, the thumping nightclub around the corner, the sirens, parades, marches, street fights—in all those years I had never experienced a more silent moment in that city.

I nuzzled your hair. *I will.*

I could say anything right now and you'd do it, you said.

Test it out, I breathed, my hand on your back.

You sat up, kneeling over your purse. You put something into my hand and I looked at my palm: a small bronze key.

Move into the house with me, you said.

. . .

Because you didn't remember, I'll tell you now. Our big fight during senior year was this: you said something true, and I said something mean.

I called you one night, upset. Greta and I had fought. She wanted me to spend Christmas Eve with her family

115

the following month, but I had no interest in the extended company of her Christian Scientist parents, who eschewed aspirin, kept pet parakeets, and regarded me as a charity case with a psychotic father.

She's going to break up with me, I said. *I know it.* I was genuinely sad, and pissed off that I even cared.

She's not going to break up with you, you said.

You don't think so?

You lowered the boom. *You think she's got guys waiting in the wings?*

Seconds slipped between us. I let my voice freeze over. *You're a bitch,* I said.

Okay, you said, ultracasual. I began to yell, calling you that again, calling you worse. You kept your tone quiet and lethal. It was only after I hung up and played it all back in my head that the waver in your voice was real to me—that I could hear me, hurting you.

You made it a policy never to say anything unkind, even when it was deserved. It's only these years later that I understand why you broke your code of decency. I met a girl, and you suddenly had something nasty to say. I missed the sign. And I moved those desks around, spending months pretending I was still angry, having increasingly boring sex with a girlfriend I had never asked for. The timing murders me. Say you hadn't gone to the bathroom at the prom. Say you had given me one of those spiraling letters in Zelner's class.

Say I had been brave, rushing you to that balcony. Say I had just said to you what I wanted to say: *Please let me kiss you.*

I kept thinking, when you were finally in my bed: all that time wasted.

7

As I drove to school on Tuesday morning, I devised a plan for survival: Be elsewhere, quietly retreat into your own head. I thought about feigning a sore throat, pretending my voice was gone—no one asks questions of those who can't answer. I thought about tasks that would take the kids all day and accomplish nothing. Here, sort these lima, pinto, and kidney beans; here, write down all the animals you can think of. I would create a baseline of normalcy and wouldn't attempt to better it. I downed more pills, which now seemed a given, in traffic; not enough to put me out, but plenty to achieve the spaced-out order of the day.

I parked outside Hawthorne, walked carefully up the hall, and found the door open. I stepped into the classroom, expecting to see the janitor.

Mr. Mason, the principal said gently. She was one of several adults in the room: six or seven parents stood along the walls or crouched beside their children. Mr. Noel was sitting at my desk, holding Caleb's backpack.

Mr. Mason, the principal said again.

You shouldn't lean against the whiteboard, I told Mariana's mother, swallowing. *It'll rub off on your clothes.*

She stepped forward an inch, frowning. The clock's second hand was deafening. The children were silent, curious about why the grown-ups were present. Some of the parents stared in my direction. I followed their gaze to my hands, which were thrust downward, clenched into fists.

Our task that morning was to learn to sing in a round, and I said a prayer of thanks that I had scheduled something easy. The parents were concerned. This I understood. I knew their children must have been saying alarming things. It made sense to me that the parents had come; they were offering their support, making my job easier—there were so many children and just one teacher. We would need to work together.

The principal pulled me aside and confirmed this. *Frank,* she said gently, *nothing to worry about, just—the kids had a rough weekend, as I'm sure the parents told you last night . . . I know I got several calls—*

No, I said, suspicious. *No one called me.*

She nodded. *Well, they just want to ease the kids back into the classroom, so they're all going to stay as long as they can today, and maybe tomorrow . . .*

I must have been frowning, because she started speaking faster. *But I really doubt they'll be here past then—*she put her hands up defensively—*and they'll stay out of the way, obviously.*

There was a pause, and I imagined her retracing her steps. She was realizing this was a breach of etiquette; it was dawning on her that she should have discussed it with me. She tried another approach, her face softening. *And how are you doing, in all of this?* She placed her hand on my shoulder. I looked down at it.

Okay, I think we should probably get started now, I said, turning away. I heard myself speak in a higher pitch than normal, like something was pressing on my throat, choking off my air. *Mr. Noel, maybe you can give me a hand moving these tables?* The class needed to divide into two groups—one to begin the song, another to come in seconds later. Mr. Noel stood slowly, his eyes bugged, and lumbered toward me. I saw the principal walk over to the parents, nodding and shaking hands and being gentle with them like they were children who had fallen down. I was aware of the eyes watching me as, with a pealing squeak against the floor tiles, Mr. Noel and I dragged the tables to the perimeter of the room. I could hear fragments of the principal's quiet speech to the nodding parents. *The important thing to remember . . . difficult time, certainly.*

Frank, Mr. Noel said, *I just want to mention that I've done some work in schools.*

I strained to hear the principal. . . . *Just up the hall if it seems like . . . my eyes and ears, here.*

Pardon? I said to Mr. Noel.

Some of us guys from the fire department go to schools and talk about what it's like. You know, to the kids.

. . . Don't hesitate to alert me to . . . benefit of the doubt . . .

Oh, I said to Mr. Noel. *That's great.*

So, Mr. Noel said, *if you need me to take over at any point, just holler.*

I frowned at him, struggling to stand up straight.

Caleb had wet the bed, Mr. Noel told me later. Rebekah had awoken crying and asked for her dead mother in the night, her father said. Their parents were afraid and helpless. And yet I couldn't help it when my compassion and trust—they were here to observe their children! They were doing the right thing!—gave way to resentment. What were they *really* doing here? What did they want from me? Every internal impulse lurched toward defensiveness and paranoia: I was in deep fucking shit.

Simon is having a recurring nightmare, his mother told me that afternoon. *He loses his arms and legs and can't move.*

I see, I replied.

Well?

I shook my head.

Is that significant? she hissed, looking at me with the expectant eyes of someone lodging a complaint.

When the recess bell rang at midmorning, I was half out of my seat to start lining them up when I looked out the window: it was raining. *Oh,* I said aloud. *Sorry guys, it looks like we're staying in for recess. They're probably just about to—*

The announcement interrupted me: we were rained in. The kids made their collective noises of disapproval.

Hey, listen, it's way too wet, I said.

But Mr. Mason! they chimed. I had heard these kinds of complaints so many times—anything said in this tone barely registered anymore. *Mr. Mason, that's not fair! We have umbrellas!*

Listen, Mrs. Stone said, standing authoritatively. *It's too wet out there. If the rain is gone in the afternoon, you can have recess outside then.*

The kids were silent. She sat down, triumphant.

When we were rained in, we played games. Barnyard, in which they were blindfolded and let loose in the classroom to moo and cluck and figure out who else was mooing and clucking and then gather by animal. I had to stop assigning anyone Horse, because none of them could neigh convincingly. Or we played Who Is Hiding; the kids all closed their eyes and sat in a circle on the grimy floor, while I led one kid to the back supply closet. It took them forever, figuring out who wasn't among them.

We had played Heads Up 7-Up once before, and they had a giddy kind of attachment to it. Seven kids stand. Everyone else puts their heads down and one thumb up. The seven wander the class, each touching one of the extended thumbs. If your thumb is touched you put it down; I would watch thumbs get sucked into fists like sea anemones disturbed by a passing fish. The kids whose thumbs are touched have to guess who picked them. If they guess right, they get to be one of the next group of seven.

I can still remember from my own childhood how it felt when my thumb was touched—the aching joy of being chosen. Some kids pressed their thumb against yours in a kind of mirror image; others tenderly swiped their palm against it. I can remember entire alliances formed and fumbled because of who did and did not choose whom in

Heads Up 7-Up. We played it in fifth grade, and so were old enough to know we should try to throw people off: we chose the people we hated, so they would never guess it was us who had touched them. But second graders don't know yet about strategy. They just pick their friends. So in my class, the presiding outcome of Heads Up 7-Up was that everyone always guessed right.

The rain was coming hard and fast, and it didn't take long for one of them to abandon his disappointment over the lost recess and shout out the suggestion. And then I was picking the seven kids, a sense of anticipation in the air, and the seven were excitedly making their way to the front chalkboard. *Eyes closed,* I said from my desk. I did a quick peek-check and called out the most egregious cheaters; they closed their eyes and the game commenced.

I watched them perform their exaggerated tiptoe around the classroom. Marisol picked her best friend, Monica, Henry picked the kid he sat right next to. I had a pair of first cousins in the class, a boy and a girl; Cody picked Brianna inside of ten seconds. They opened their eyes, immediately knew who had picked them, and it was time for round two.

The game was futile, but they loved it anyway.

. . .

Greta was scheduled for a sonogram that night. She had made the appointment for the evening, having taken the night off, and it was disconcerting to drive to a hospital in the dark. It was something I had only ever done in an emergency: slicing off part of my thumb chopping garlic, breaking my collarbone falling from a bike.

Is this a checkup ultrasound, or a particular kind of ultrasound, or what? I asked.

She shrugged. *What do you mean?*

Are they checking for something? A defect?

She rolled down the window, spitting out her gum. *The baby is doing great,* she said. *I can feel it.*

Good, I said, looking for parking. *That's good.*

Inside, the doctor confirmed her intuition. *Everything is looking a-okay,* he said. Greta's expression bore a whiff of petulance, as if she had won a bet.

I bought her an ice cream sandwich at the gas station, and when we got home, we lay down on the bed to listen to an old CD on the stereo. She rested her head on my shoulder, and I combed her hair with my fingers.

Are you doing okay? she asked me.

Of course, I said, my eyes clenched.

I know this is new to you.

It's new to you, too.

No, Frank—I mean that you've never lost anyone before.

She tensed, waiting for my response.

I'm fine, Gret.

We can talk about it if you want.

I sighed.

I know she meant a lot to you.

Stop, I said. *Please.*

She lifted her head from my chest and turned away. When I heard her breathing go ragged for long, difficult moments, and then slow finally into the rhythm of slumber, I knew that she had cried herself to sleep.

■ ■ ■

Both times Greta miscarried, the calls came directly to the classroom. The first time was shortly before Christmas, near the end of a student teaching assignment at a school in Oakland. I'd taught alongside an irritable woman named Miss Martinez. I don't remember her first name, since I was instructed not to use it. I had nearly completed the seventy-plus classroom hours necessary to graduate, and though I disliked teaching in others' classrooms, I told myself I would enjoy it once I had my own—the way prospective parents recoil from a tantrumming brat and tell themselves, *Ours will be different.* That morning, Miss Martinez answered the phone and scuttled over to chide me.

You can't receive calls here. It sounds like a woman, she said, scandalized.

I took the phone and heard a flurry of activity—intercom pages, shuffled papers, people shouting. *Mr. Mason?* the nurse asked. She coughed, apologized for having to be the one to tell me this.

I hung up the phone and retrieved my backpack from the closet.

Did you inform her of my policy? Miss Martinez said.

I walked to my car without a word.

When she complained to my professor—a bike-riding hippie with a T-shirt that read KILL YOUR TELEVISION—he nodded sympathetically and promised that next semester, my coteacher and I would *share the same vibe.* A few days later, Greta packed away the contents of the nursery.

Everything had been yellow, her one nod to the unknown. A yellow wall hanging with a quilted sun; a yellow set of curtains. Yellow clothes, yellow blankets. A yellow liner for the bassinet. By then all of the pregnancy books had been read, the suitcase packed though it wasn't yet necessary. Greta had collected an array of pants with elastic waistbands, had made lists, charts, budgets. We hadn't decided on names. She had been eleven weeks along.

I made the mistake of looking in one of the books to see what a fetus looked like at that stage. *Your baby may soon be able to open and close his fists,* the caption said.

The second call came to Hawthorne, about two months after school started, on a morning in November when I had given my students a photocopy of ten clocks and asked them to write the time below each. I came around to measure their progress.

Simon, how's it going? He had filled in only twelve o'clock, the simplest one.

What I don't like, he began, his voice edged with irritation, *is when the little hand is between the numbers.*

Okay, I said, *you have to see which number the small hand is—*

Am I just supposed to guess? he asked, exasperated.

The phone rang, and I patted Simon's shoulder, setting my pen down on his desk before walking away.

Mr. Mason, a woman said. I understood immediately—from the familiar sounds behind her, the discomfort in her voice, the fact that the classroom phone almost never rang.

You're from the hospital, I said.

Yes, she began.

I cut her off. *Has something happened to my wife?*

I watched Simon squirrel my pen away, slipping it into the plastic tub under his desk.

Your wife will be fine, the nurse said.

Give IT! one of the kids said, somewhere behind me. *I said give it!*

The baby's dead, I said.

The children closest to me looked up.

Your wife has miscarried, sir, yes. She'd like you to come pick her up. She paused only a moment before she asked, *Sir, did you hear me?*

Yes, I said flatly. *I heard you.*

The principal covered my class. I drove down the street beneath the elm trees that lined each side, their branches meeting above in a canopy. The world looked different—when I left school in the afternoon, the streets were always crowded with children walking home. But with class still in session the school looked abandoned, the swings moving in the breeze. I had the uneasy feeling of playing hooky, like when I stayed home sick as a kid and got carted around on my mom's errands, suddenly privy to the workaday world. I turned on the radio absentmindedly, whistling to an upbeat tempo, tapping the rhythm on the steering wheel. I caught myself and shut the radio off, sitting at a red light, disgusted by my still-pursed lips.

At the hospital I signed my name on a form and followed the blue line painted on the floor. The first time, Greta had already heard the doctor's briefing when I arrived. But now we sat in the exam room together as he explained what her body had just undergone. He described the idiopathic event that had killed our eight-week-old baby, shaking his head with practiced regret. Then he told us, *This isn't your fault.* It seemed, to me at least, an odd thing to say. But Greta nodded, holding my hand. I was alarmed by her inexhaustible flow of tears.

The doctor told us we would need to wait six weeks before another attempt.

In the car, Greta said, *Six weeks isn't so long.*

Greta, I said, *I can't do this again.* I surprised myself, but immediately I went from fear of her reaction to pure elation: the words had finally been spoken aloud.

I felt her peering at me. *You can't do what again?*

This.

She deflated in her seat. *This is the only thing I've ever asked you for.*

I stated what I viewed as simple fact.

You never asked me anything, I said.

Why are you with me? she said, her voice calm. Her question wasn't rhetorical; she wanted to know. *I don't understand anything you do.* She shook her head, puzzled. *I don't understand how a man who is terrified of people becomes a bully. How a man who hates children makes a career of teaching them.*

I leaned back in the driver's seat. *You don't have to understand me,* I said. *Because I could be anybody, as long as I gave you what you wanted.*

Fuck you, she said, wincing. It hurt her, matching my unkindness this way.

Tell me one thing, I said, *off the top of your head, that makes me different from anyone else.* I laughed; it was suddenly funny.

The stoplight held at red, threatening to change. I glanced at her. The wounded look on her face disappeared, replaced by a quickness in her eyes I didn't recognize. *You know,* she said, *I just figured it out.* She grinned through her tears. *There's no fucking mystery here. You're transparent.*

Enlighten me, I snapped.

She leaned in as though spilling a secret. *You choose the path of least resistance and then you find it boring. You choose the high road and you fall off it. You'll keep on doing things you hate so you can keep on feeling robbed, walking around bewildered, wondering how you got cheated out of everything you wanted. So you want to know the thing I like about you, Frank?*

She narrowed her eyes.

You're predictable, she said.

For the six weeks that followed, we were silent. I recall it now and half shudder. It was an endurance contest; it was the nadir of our time together. When I think about those weeks, I remember the house being unbearably stuffy. I remember feeling like there wasn't enough air. I remember that time being like a brief, reversible death.

Each night, we retired to our separate spaces—me in the living room, her in what she persisted in calling "the baby's room"—before, in an act of mutual masochism, sleeping in the same bed. We were careful not to touch. We ate separate meals, watched separate television, pretended we were fine in the supermarket's checkout line: the cashier would make jovial chatter and we would laugh in unison, chirping to each other and to him, turning the performance on and off at will.

And all the while, I watched the calendar, knowing what was to come.

A few days after the six weeks ended, I arrived home from school and found Greta standing in our bedroom, changing the sheets. We had only tentatively begun talking aloud again—post-fight, her inaugural words had been *Do you need any socks washed?*—and the way she said hello felt like a formality, as though she were meeting me for the first time.

Hey, I said, setting down my backpack. I took off my shirt, my pants, leaned down to peel off my wet socks. It was January, and raining so hard that driveways became lakes. I started the shower, feeling my full-body chill begin to ebb away.

A moment passed before she came naked into the bathroom. *Can I get in?*

I nodded, startled. As she bent to get a fresh towel I looked at her brown hair, wondering why she had begun dyeing it—her blondeness had been the one thing about her looks that people complimented.

She stole glances at me, reaching for the shampoo. I rolled my neck until it cracked, the harsh sound echoing.

How was your day?

The same, I said. I washed my face beneath the spout.

Do you want to go out to dinner?

We can't.

I borrowed some money from my dad, she said. *I'll drive so you can drink.*

I smiled bitterly. So I can drink. She was trying to liquor me up.

I haven't changed my mind, Gret.

There was a pause. She hadn't expected candor.

I know, she said.

I don't want to try anymore.

I know, she said again. She put her hands on my hips and her wet head on my chest, resting her ear against my sternum. I knew it like I knew anything—she was plotting the course by which she would get me to acquiesce.

And then I blurted out the words on my tongue: *You look pretty,* I said, awash in something like—I don't know, what? Empathy, maybe. It occurred to me that as awful as the previous weeks had been for me, they had likely been worse for her. I had only been insulted, taken to task. But she had been bereaved and let down and told, in so many words, that she was selfish. She had been manipulated into thinking she was manipulative. A spasm of guilt weakened my knees.

I'm sorry about how it's been, I said. *I'm sorry we fought.*

Her fingers were warm, like a dangerous, engulfing fever. I turned down the hot water and when I looked up again she was so close to my face, glancing at each of my eyes in turn, searching them. Her palm molded itself to the plane above my nipple. She was hunched, sighing. I squinted. It wasn't dye. Her hair had darkened over time. She had aged. Her hand moved down and grabbed me, too hard, and I winced. She didn't notice. She placed my hand on her breast. I held it there, unmoving.

She checked my expression, and when I didn't object—when I stared at her vacantly, breathing through my mouth—she turned and faced the tile wall. We hit our familiar marks, took our places like seasoned actors: I set one hand on her back as she bent forward, the movement automatic. I met no resistance. We made no noise. The water reddened my eyes and flattened our hair.

Weeks later, she would give me the news. The yellow accoutrements were pulled from their boxes, and she began to tally the days. I told myself the course had been laid years before, that I had made my bed. I tried to repackage my apathy as selflessness: hadn't I given her what she wanted? I would let her live this pain ad infinitum. I would sit with her in the doctor's exam room as she asked how long we would have to wait before failing another time, and again.

I braced myself with one hand on her hip, then I put both hands in her hair—her hair that had grown darker with age, with time, with everything that had come to her. I pulled, hard. Greta's head jerked back as I groaned and sputtered, calling out in bitter rapture, feeling something inside me wither and pass away.

. . .

That Tuesday night, the favorable sonogram behind us, Greta went into an upswing, cleaning the house with a fervor she pretended had been there all along. *This is how you're supposed to do it,* she said. Her actions took on a frantic, repentant quality, as though any show of capability would stave off what had come to feel inevitable.

As she cleaned I slipped into the garage through the hallway door, telling her I would tidy the boxes of Christmas decorations, old school papers, other unnecessary shit we kept out of obligation. But then I snuck out through the retractable garage door and walked down the driveway to retrieve a bottle of whiskey from my trunk. I drank, among the Christmas lights and mildewed boxes, until my belches were accompanied by wet trails. I spun my wrist, cracking it: click, click, click, the tendons vibrating like harp strings. I continued drinking until I couldn't stand.

I woke up on the cement a few hours later, walked back into the house, brushed my teeth, and was happy to find Greta silent, perhaps even sleeping, when I came to bed. I slept deep and heavy, like something was pressing on top of me. But at the sound of some nocturnal animal rustling outside I stirred, my hand going to my head. I turned toward Greta. Her eyes were open. *It's okay,* she said. *You had a nightmare.*

I did?

It's okay, she said again, brushing her hand across my temple. *What are you so scared of?*

I ran my dry tongue over the ridged ceiling of my mouth. *I'm not scared,* I said.

You're terrified, Greta said. In the dark it was hard to see. Her expression shifted with the shadows.

I didn't have a nightmare, I said. *Why did you say that?*

I can tell, she said.

There was a knock at the bedroom door.

Come in, Greta said.

A massive stroller, its seats lined up in a row, rolled forward and into the room, and around us swelled an awful, searing light; the paint on the walls began to blister. I looked down into the stroller. Four faces stared placidly back.

Oh good, Greta said.

When I woke a moment later, Greta was standing in front of the mirror.

It's okay, she said flatly. *You were having a nightmare.*

. . .

Wednesday morning, I skipped the shower and instead rose from bed, walked to the bathroom, ran the tap, and dunked my head in the sink like I was blanching a vegetable. I was so hungover my lips trembled; my tongue was still numb from the alcohol. My neck was destroyed—that familiar injury from the car accident, reawakened now and again by a hasty turn or an incorrect angle to my pillow, had this morning limited my mobility to a sickening degree: I wasn't sure I'd be able to look over my shoulder when changing lanes. I stepped back into the hall, dripping, and Greta was waiting.

I guess you got a lot of cleaning done, she said, holding up the empty whiskey bottle.

I opened my mouth, and closed it. She tapped the glass with a fingernail.

I need you to not crumble right now, Frank. I need you to do whatever it is you do when you're in need of solace—Jesus, she said, interrupting herself, *do something, anything, to keep it together. Do you want to talk to someone? Do you need medication?*

I pointed at the bottle, smirking. *I thought I was.*
What?
Finding solace.

She blinked. *I understand that you're in pain,* she said. *And you have a right to be in pain.*

I closed my eyes, my head against the wall. The water in my hair ran into my ears. I thought about the pills in the glove box. *Thanks for your permission,* I said quietly.

She shifted her weight, narrowing her eyes. *I think you ought to be glad, Frank, that I'm being as kind to you as I am.*

On the last word, she dropped the bottle to the floor. I think she had hoped it would smash, but it broke tidily into two pieces—*clunk*—and then the bottle's squat neck rolled toward the heater vent. She stormed into the kitchen, and I bent to retrieve the broken glass, then dressed in the first clothes I found, walked briskly outside, and popped the last of the Vicodin as I made my way to work.

I waited for her arrival, but the principal never showed. As the moments ticked past and she remained absent, I felt ever lighter, slowly filling with relief, bathed in chilly sweat.

Oh my God, I thought: it's going to get better.

Had I figured all of this wrong? Of course I had. I had been so eager, like always, to jump to the worst conclusion. There were a few parents still present, and once again I felt I understood their presence for what it was: not about me. They were here for their kids. They weren't spies. They were just attentive, engaged parents—Christ, was it any wonder I had trouble recognizing *that*?

Good morning, Mr. Mason, Mrs. Stone said.

Good morning, I said back.

They were there because they wanted to give their children one extra boost of support; they wanted to ease them back into life's inevitable trajectory, the parent-ectomy— *you go here during the day, and I go there*—before quietly backing out of the room, confident that their kids had readjusted. I just need to keep repeating this, I remember thinking. Just keep on believing this.

When Jacob's mom approached me midmorning, despite her nervous expression I greeted her with a reassured smile.

I want to tell you that Jake has loved being in your class, she said.

Through the thick muffle of the pills and the tremu-
lous hangover, I felt my face brighten even further. *Oh,* I
said. *I love having him. He's a great kid.*

She nodded.

Well, I said, when she didn't move, *thanks for telling me.*

She twisted the rings on her fingers. *You're welcome,*
she said.

I guessed that the parents had made their peace with
me, my methods, my state of mind—none of them approached me with further questions. Whatever doubts
they had about my ability had evidently been quelled by
their time in the classroom, by the news of my loss.

And then the cold sweat changed into something
disorienting—something viral, pestilent; a plague overtak-
ing every inch of my body.

My loss, I thought. All of it came back—they still
doubted me, hated me. They *are* here to watch you, you
naive, fucking *pathetic* piece of shit: none of them told you
they're sorry for your loss. My bereavement had gone un-
acknowledged. *Think this through,* I whispered to myself.
Look at the possibilities. Don't refuse to see what you
don't want to see.

Either they didn't believe it was the truth, or they
didn't care.

At lunch, some of the kids came to sit near me at the back
table, Simon and Marcus among them. The parents went
elsewhere; they took their kids off campus to a drive-
through or else left to grab coffee at one of the chains nearby.
When they returned, they always seemed reinvigorated, as
though returning from intermission to see the next act.

I heated a tuna sandwich in the toaster oven, and the classroom took on a fetid, familiar smell. I stared at the bread, the encrusted cheese. I was starving, but the process of eating felt imposed, laborious: why did I have to eat, even if I didn't want to?

Mr. Mason, your lunch looks nasty, Marcus said.

It stinks, too, Simon said, food falling from his mouth.

You eat the same thing every day, Marisol said. *You always bring tuna.*

It's my wife's favorite, I said.

What does your wife look like? Marcus said.

I thought for a moment. *She looks kind of like me,* I said. *We look a bit like brother and sister.*

Lunch is almost over, Simon said. *You better eat that, Mr. Mason.*

I shook my head, like a toddler. *I don't even want it.*

My vision was blurred, and faint white trails followed every moving thing. It was as though I had removed my glasses—the world was underwater again, everything distorted. The bell rang, and the kids moved to dispose of their trash. I looked at Marcus, who remained behind, until he stared down at his food, smiling in discomfort. *What?* he said, in an unconvincing attempt at defiance: in his voice was anxiety, clear as a bell. My gaze was unwavering.

I don't want to be here any more than you do, I whispered to him.

He lifted his chin, the remnant of his smile disintegrating.

Take your seats, take your seats, I sang out, corralling every ounce of my strength to say the words, to do this small thing, to exist. The food smells started to lift and exit through the open windows. *I'm counting to five and anyone still standing is last to go to afternoon recess . . .*

I mounted my stool before the wall of windows, legs bowed like a cowboy. *Time to play Description, gang,* I said. *Who's ready with an object?*

Amber's hand shot up. *Apple,* she said: a perennial, predictable favorite.

Okay, apple. Who's ready with a description word?

Amber's hand went skyward.

Let's let someone else have a turn, I said. *Who's ready?*

Me! Jeff said. *Apple is round!*

No it ain't! yelled Mariana.

Jeff looked at me helplessly. *It's almost round?*

I had my mouth open to speak when someone else did: *Hands raised, I think is the rule,* Mr. Noel said. The kids all turned to stare at him, dumbfounded. Before I could staunch it, I felt my face smear with snide shock. The words spilled from my mouth before my drowning brain could catch up:

Do you mind? I said.

The three or four seconds that followed had a high-pitched whine about them, barely audible, like a teakettle seconds from a full-on wail. I could feel each instant teetering on some kind of awkward fulcrum, deciding which way to go: all-out confrontation, as is always imagined in those sorts of moments in the corner of the brain that governs fight or flight—or what actually happened, which was absolutely nothing. Mr. Noel pretended I hadn't spoken; I turned back to the kids and smiled insincerely, and a few somebodies called out—without raising hands—*Red! Green!* and *Shiny!*

The kids went out to recess after we had gotten through six nouns—I was so exhausted that the final one, *pillow*, drove me to distraction—and I said I had to visit the copier and then carry out another small errand: *I'm just going to run up the hall to the photocopier to make a few . . .* I paused, delaying the stupid, inevitable final word: *copies*, I finally said. I had to get out of there. I'd gotten away with one sharp remark; if I stayed, I knew I'd make another.

I didn't even bother to walk in the direction of the copier once I left class. Instead, I headed, sure and purposeful, to the door that led to the roof, and once up there I grabbed my folded lawn chair where it leaned against the edge. But I lost my balance and fell to the tar; I stayed there, sitting cross-legged. I clapped a hand over each ear, my palms sliding to my mouth, and then my closed eyes, like I was hiding from a horror film. *Fuck me,* I said, and the words felt so good: pure, and deliciously wrong. Out on the soccer field two kids were playing catch with a kickball. I opened my eyes and looked at my watch. Another two hours. A plane droned overhead, and I watched the game of catch. *Jesus,* I said, engrossed. Sometimes, I didn't understand the way children played—like it was hate that drove them, not fun; as though they were exorcising demons. I watched them pass the ball in zipping line drives, these joyless, horizontal throws—I watched, suspended, as they chucked the ball at each other like it was something they abhorred; like it was a burden they wanted to be rid of, like they wanted their compatriot to have to take it up in their stead.

. . .

After the final bell rang, most of the parents escorted their children outside to begin the car or bus or cab rides home. I planned on staying late to correct the children's reading responses from the week before. Rebekah needed to stay, too—we had just begun double-digit addition, carrying numbers, and she was one of the many who was struggling. Her father often let her linger after school, until she could finish her reading or confidently spell CALIFORNIA.

I'd be happy to walk her through the math again today, I told her father that afternoon.

I should get her home, he said.

It's no trouble, I said. *I'm always glad to help her.*

He grimaced. *I'll come back at four thirty.*

Great, I said, trying to ignore his reluctance. *We'll have her caught up in no time.*

We went over it and over it, and then Rebekah returned to her chair; though I knew she still didn't understand, I let her. And then, sure enough, at quarter to four she finally caved in and walked back over, frowning. *Mr. Mason, I don't get it,* she said. Her paper was translucent, worn thin by erasure.

Here's how it works, I said, beginning again, repeating verbatim what I had already said. *The number is two digits long. There's only one spot for a number, so the other number gets carried.*

Okay, she said, not comprehending.

Rebekah, I started to say, *I think we should—*

The classroom phone rang, startling me. I set her paper down, watching the receiver tremble in its cradle.

Shit, I said aloud. I told her, my mouth dry, *Just a sec, okay?* before hesitantly answering the phone. *I can finish helping you in just a second.*

I spoke into the receiver. *Is this about my wife?*

A male voice cleared its throat. *This is Officer Buckingham.*

We took turns exhaling.

Mr. Mason, have you got a minute? I tried you at home, but—

I'm with a student.

This won't take long.

Rebekah watched me. I mouthed again, *Just a sec.* She ignored me, holding her paper up.

I'm wondering if you've been able to remember more about the time line that day, Buckingham said.

Is that my dad? Rebekah said.

Sorry, I said to Buckingham, shaking my head at Rebekah. *The time line? What does that mean exactly?*

I was just going over what happened, he said. I heard him sip something, heard the mug being set back down on his desk. I heard the faint air of irritation in his voice. *Just filling in the blanks in my report, really. I was wondering how long you'd been at the beach beforehand.*

Mr. Mason, Rebekah said, *is my dad coming soon?*

Bek, can you sit at your table for just a minute? I said, holding my hand over the receiver. *I'll be right there.* Into the phone, I said, *I think we were probably there twenty minutes before she jumped, maybe thirty, but I—*

Buckingham was silent. I felt my spine snap taut as a tripwire.

All I could manage was a whisper. *I—I didn't—*

He scoffed. *You saw someone jump off the bridge?*
No, I said, scrambling. *I didn't.*
You didn't bother to tell me this?
No, I didn't mean to say—

He cut me off again. *Christ,* he said. *Start over. Tell me whatever it is you're not—*

I think I interrupted you, I said, interrupting him. *What did you—you needed to know something. What did you need again?* I hastened to cover my tracks, erase what I had said with new words; I talked so fast I doubted he could understand me.

He said nothing for several moments. I knew he was sorting through our interactions, evaluating my motives. Gauging my veracity.

Start over, he said again.

I took a deep breath. Rebekah fidgeted in her seat. Outside, a motorcycle bellowed down the narrow street.

I know I should have said this sooner, I said carefully. *But the woman on the beach . . .*

Rebekah looked up. I turned my back on her.

. . . The body on the beach . . .

Yes? He sounded spring-loaded. I pictured him leaning forward in his chair. This time, I didn't feel the quickening, the lightness of a lie being borne out of my body—as I spoke what came next, it seemed pure, definitive, clear as water. Real and whole and impregnable.

. . . The woman on the beach was my wife.

Your wife, he said.

My first wife. I got confused when I said I saw her jump. I was just confused.

And why's that?

Because I had nightmares about it all weekend, I said. *I kept dreaming that I saw her jump. My ex-wife.*

There was a harsh little beat of silence. *Why didn't you tell me this at the scene?*

I wasn't certain then, I said.

And what's made you certain now?

I sorted through things. Evaluated my motives. Gauged my veracity.

I was in shock, I said slowly. *You saw me at the beach. I didn't understand why I was so upset, and then over the last few days I've . . .*

I turned around. Rebekah was standing at the window, watching the cars pass.

. . . I've had a chance to process.

Have you tried to call this woman—what's her name?

Nora Lucas, I said. *No, I haven't called her.*

Well, look, I can't just—

I stopped by her house, I said. *She wasn't there. She hadn't been there in a while. Look, isn't there any evidence you can, that you can divulge?*

I don't know what's going on here, Mr. Mason, he said. *But I think it goes without saying that I can't share anything with you about this case. Not until identity of the deceased can be established.*

I tensed. *But you know the identity, I'm telling you who . . .*

As my voice rose, Rebekah turned to watch me.

This is my wife, I said, weighting the final syllable.

So you said.

My chest tightened.

I need you to come down to the station, Mr. Mason.

You said you're with a student—can someone else take over for you?

I sputtered. *You're just going to ignore what I told you?*

There was a long pause, and when he spoke again his tone had shifted. In place of his anger was something new; he held it back enough that it took a finely tuned ear to discern its presence, but it was there: pity.

Frank, listen, I'll be honest with you . . .

I don't understand, I said. I felt a helpless, hiccupping laugh rise in my throat. *It's the truth. She jumped from the bridge.* I stared out the window, trying to collect my thoughts. *I didn't see her jump, I didn't mean to say . . . you could probably tell from the autopsy that—*

When he spoke again it was deliberate, slow. *Why do you think this woman is*—here he paused, I assumed to look at his notes—*Nora Lucas? The deceased wasn't in a state in which—*

I grabbed a piece of chalk from the chalkboard's rim. *Not with any accuracy.*

He sounded perturbed. *Right.*

She was unhappy. I waded through my reasoning. *She told me, 'This is where people come to die.' I saw the body, and it was her.* Her house was abandoned. The strands of red hair. My fingers ground the chalk into an ashy dust.

His voice was quiet, compressed. *Mr. Mason, I think you've—*

I haven't, I said.

Outside, a car rolled past, blasting its radio.

I'd like it if you would come to the station right away, he said.

I replaced the receiver without another word. Walking over to her, I sat in the miniature chair beside Rebekah. We looked at each other for what seemed like a long time. *Here's how it works,* I said again. *There's only a place for one number. Only one number can go there. So the other one gets carried.*

She looked at the paper, and then back at me. *Why?* she said.

At half after four Rebekah left with her father. I went to a bar about ten blocks from Hawthorne, where a group of pathetic men in Hawaiian shirts enjoyed a complicated trivia event. College kids played Connect Four in the corner. Slowly, I swiveled my head: the place was eighty percent girls, with their rainbow-colored cocktails and shared orders of six measly chicken wings. The chalkboard above the bar advertised two dozen shooters designed to mimic baked goods: the Pineapple Upside Down Cake, the Bananas Foster, the Jelly Donut. *Boston Cream Pie,* I read aloud.

The bartender swung a rag beside him like he was twirling his pistol. *That's what you want? That's our specialty.*

I shook my head and ordered a shot of Jameson. *And a beer,* I added.

The bartender frowned. *Heretic,* he said.

I downed the shot, then pointed to the tiny glass. He refilled it.

You look, the bartender said, *like someone in a movie playing a sad guy in a bar.*

I looked up at him.

Straight out of central casting, he said.

When I didn't return it, his smile faded.

Do you have a phone? I asked.

He set it down beside me. *Local, right?*

Do you have a phone book? I took a prodigious swig and looked down: the beer and the second shot were gone.

He set the directory next to the phone, motioning to my empty glass. *Another?*

Yeah, I said, skimming the pages—pet grooming, pest control, preschool. I stopped flipping, running my finger down the columns of numbers.

The bartender looked down at the page. *Oh, Lord,* he said, pouring my refill. *It just gets better and better.*

At seven o'clock, still vaguely drunk, I pulled up to the house across town, parking in the empty driveway—my thoughts abstract, tamped down, tolerable. I heard Greta's voice saying, *Do something, anything, to keep it together*; heard the sound of the whiskey bottle's stubby neck rolling across the wood floor. Everything felt distant and manageable. It was the best I'd felt in days: I had done something. I was drunk enough to believe I was being proactive.

Outside the house, I saw a woman standing next to her long, wide car. An old lady's car. She wore a fitted corporate pantsuit in eggplant, with a cheap paisley scarf knotted at her loose-skinned neck. Her gray hair was spiked and immobile. We shook hands, hers covered in ornate gemstone rings. I had made the appointment from the bar; it was easier than I had anticipated.

We spoke on the phone, I said. *Thanks for coming on such short notice.*

Francis, she said. *I'm Beverly.* When our hands let go she leaned in and hugged me, her touch as formal as an airport frisk.

I'll need to ask you a few more things now, she said, though we had discussed everything over the phone already. *How old were you when you married?*

Twenty-two, I said. *I told you that, I think?*

And you lived here together?

I'm sorry—why do you need to ask me again in person?

She was undeterred. *To receive the energy. When did you divorce?*

I felt my buzz wearing off, my hackles begin to raise. *I'm a little skeptical about things like this.*

Perhaps we should just get started, she said. *I'll need an object of hers.*

We walked up the steps. I took out my keys, hesitating, before I stepped forward.

And then we were inside.

The house no longer smelled of life being lived there. There was instead the distinct tang of neglect—dust, musty moisture leeching into softer surfaces, cracks in the floor alive with bacteria—like no windows or doors had been opened, no rooms disturbed. And there was something else, something sweet and deceased. The place was bleak, though still furnished. Emptiness hung in the air like a caustic vapor. I was suddenly so ready to be out of that place I impulsively took a step backward. I had a key, yes. But I wasn't welcome.

Do you have the object? she asked.

Hang on, I said.

I went up to the bedroom—the dated posters, the ancient dried roses. The same air-freshener smell. The space felt empty. I slid the louvered closet door on its rails. Apart from a white dress hanging against the back wall, its hem stained faintly with grass, the closet was empty. The sight of the dress made me wince. A clock showing the incorrect time ticked loudly from above the desk. I could hear footsteps outside the door.

I stepped into the hall to find Beverly waiting. *I felt her asking me to come up,* she said. I offered the dress to her as though I were surrendering.

She paused. *Oh, yes. There's definitely something.* I leaned against the wall, not sure what to do with myself. Beverly entered the master bedroom and moments later I heard her speaking to someone. *Yes, she's definitely here. Oh, I know. What are you getting? Oh dear.* I stepped forward, and saw that she was on a cell phone. Apparently her partner could get premonitions off-site. Beverly walked with her eyes closed, pausing near the bed. *Oh, I feel a great sadness here.* There was a distant chipmunk voice at the other end of her call, the words indistinguishable. *A great regret,* Beverly said. The phone voice buzzed in response. Beverly glanced down the hall and looked at me imploringly. *Francis,* she said, *I'll need you to help her pass into the light.* She motioned with her finger.

We sat together on the edge of the made bed. She took my hand. Her skin was dry and cool. The dress lay beside her. *Francis,* she began, *I need you to push all of your energy toward this spirit. Use your mind to tell her that you have only kind words to say.*

I closed my eyes and thought, I have only kind words for you.

Francis, I need you to help me fill the room with psychic light. She squeezed my hand tighter. *Can you help me do that?*

I pressed my eyes until no light penetrated. *Yes,* I said. I imagined the bedroom hosting its own sunrise. Orange, then yellow, then white.

Good, Beverly said. *Now I need you to tell her not to be afraid.*

Don't be afraid, I said aloud.

You don't have to speak aloud if you don't want to.

I want to, I said.

Tell her something wonderful awaits her, she said. *Tell her to walk toward the light. I can feel her turning back, she's afraid—*

Pass into the light, Nora, I said.

Tell her again.

Pass into the light, I said, opening my eyes.

I saw a menopausal woman with gym-teacher hair and a bad suit staring at me earnestly, and I thought, She really believes. It was comforting, and it was sad. I closed my eyes again and sighed, deep and rattling, like I was taking my last breath.

I walked her downstairs, both of us jangling our car keys. We paused in the foyer as I wrote her a check. *Walk you out?* I said.

That won't be necessary, she said, turning toward the door. She passed the entryway closet—still full, I assumed, of board games and junk—without a word. As her car pulled away, I opened the closet door and stepped back. The smell of roses was ripe and suffocating. She had walked right past it.

I realized the check I had written her would bounce.

I sat on the couch where I had slept the night of the funeral, sneezing from the dust and staring at the bookshelves, whole sections devoted to baseball statistics, half a dozen guides on quilting. There were pictures in frames on the shelves, arranged among VHS tapes, tchotchkes, dead plants, and lion-head bookends. I wandered upstairs, opening a dresser drawer in the master bedroom: a neat stack of men's dress shirts, folded and crisp. None of their things had been moved.

Across the hall, I picked up the novelty phone in the bedroom and heard the dial tone. The bill had been paid at least somewhat recently. How long did they give you before they cut off service? I dialed the old apartment phone number automatically, without thinking, and a female voice answered.

Is Nora there?

Who?

I need to speak to Nora Lucas.

There was a confused pause. *There's no one named—*

Fuck it, I said, setting down the receiver.

I knew I would stay there overnight; that that was the only option. Buckingham knew where I lived—if he didn't, he could easily find out. *I tried you at home,* he had said. It all felt like too much. I heard Buckingham's voice again: *So you said.* Despite the booze—God, I wished I had more pills—the gravity of it all, the sheer, abject snowballing fucking *enormity* of what was happening here was more apparent than I wanted it to be, than I thought it would be after a king's share of quality Irish whiskey and several watery domestic beers. Why the fuck had I said that aloud? *Before she jumped,* I heard my voice saying to him—it replayed again and again, like someone slapping me. *Before she jumped. Before she jumped.*

And then, from the landing at the top of the steps, I saw the aquarium. The water was still and clouded, the fish floating. The sides of the tank were coated in scum. The smell, the one I had smelled when we entered the house, seemed to intensify as I connected it with its source. The place suddenly felt more still, more ghostly, more saturated with death than it had after the funeral, or on the day we emptied the rosy closet. It felt like a repository for sadness. It felt like a tomb.

8

*Y*ou *want me to live with you?*
   I want this, without the commute, you said. *I like you a lot.*
   Oh, I said.

Your face flattened. *You're not sure you want to be with me.*

I had done nothing *but* that for days, putting everything else on a shaky hiatus, abandoning the daily responsibilities I had only reluctantly signed on for—lame record store job, crummy public university, ambivalent relationship. I had spent a week contemplating the fallout I was accruing, leaving phone messages intended to buy time before I was fired, failed, dumped. I had done it with no ulterior motive—and once I *did* see something with you on the horizon, I had been hopeful but not expectant, happy to receive whatever the future held.

How can you say that? I said. *Isn't it obvious?*

I have an idea, you said. *We'll look for signs. We'll get out of this bed and go forth into the world and look for signs to decide.* You stood to get dressed, pulling my T-shirt off over your head and revealing your naked back. *Though with these things,* you said, *you usually ignore the bad ones, because you already know what you want to happen anyway.*

You turned around, still topless. The freckles that covered your face and arms spilled, too, across your chest and shoulders. My hands and feet were suddenly warm. *We can pretend we're a couple,* I said. *Like a dry run.*

You lifted your bra from the floor and stood slowly, reaching behind you to hook it, a striptease in rewind.

It's a little late for that, you said.

Once downstairs, you walked wordlessly to the passenger side of your car, so I got into the driver's seat. My knees pressed against the steering column, your seat pushed as far forward as it would go. *What are you, three feet tall?* I said, turning the ignition.

I get nervous if I feel too far away from the pedals. It's one of my things.

Where to? I shifted into reverse. *Where do couples go?*

You would know, you said.

I put the car back in neutral. *Why are you picking fights with me?*

What fight?

I leaned back in the seat, flipping the sun visor down. *Rule number one. We'll always say what we mean.*

That's a good rule, you said slowly. *But I was. I did.*

I backed down the driveway and the tire hit something, sending a revolting crunch through the car. I stopped, got out, and inspected. *It's just a plastic bottle*, I said, my jaw still tight.

I thought, There's no hope for me if I fuck this up. I had waited years. Our feelings were finally aligned and I was snapping at you like a snotty teenager. I closed my eyes, the car idling. I wanted to be with you. But I didn't want to have to ask you to repeat yourself because I had stopped listening. I didn't want to say to you at night, *Do you feel like it?* I didn't want to argue; I didn't want to talk it out. And I never wanted to have to simulate interest—I never wanted there to be a day when I had to start acting. I didn't want to be with you the way I had been with her.

A plastic bottle, you said. *Not a cat. Our first sign!*

I leaned against the headrest and smiled. *I like you a lot, too.* I pulled back into the driveway. *Hang on,* I said, suddenly certain. I left the driver's side door open and galloped upstairs.

She answered on the first ring, her voice frantic. *Frank, is that you?*

Yeah, I said.

Where the fuck—

I don't love you, I told Greta. *Okay? So I guess we can talk later about the money I owe you, exchanging our stuff, all that kind of . . .*

I trailed off. There was no response.

Greta, I don't want to be with you.

I looked at the bed where you and I had taken up residence, at the mess I still hadn't cleaned—irrefutable evidence that this was actually happening. I was exhilarated, more proud of myself than I could remember being.

Where the fuck have you been, she said, finishing her sentence.

Somewhere else, I said. Through the window, in defiance of the October chill, shone a warm, blue day. *That's it, that's all I wanted to say. So long.* I hung up, catching my reflection in the mirror above my dresser. It was the purest smile I had ever seen. I didn't recognize it. I picked up my keys and went outside.

The car sensor was beeping and you were leaning over from the passenger seat, still in your seat belt, trying to close the driver's side door. *You left the door open!* you said, laughing. *I can't reach it!*

I don't need any signs, I said.

What?

I'm officially a single man.

Your smile dwindled. *What does that mean?*

It means exactly what it sounds like. I called her.

I shut the beeping door.

You were in there for ten seconds, you said.

I got to the point, I said.

Jesus, you said, turning to face the dashboard. *I had no idea you'd do it like that.* And then, suddenly, you were my friend again. *How does it feel to be single?*

I smiled. *Pretty fucking good.*

Well, too bad. You put your hand on my leg—the original gesture, the move that had started it all. *Because you're not anymore.*

I backed out of the driveway and we turned onto the street. I took us out of town, both of us aglow with anticipation. We had made a recent career of reversal, and the potential for surprise seemed infinite.

Oh shit, you said, on the freeway to Berkeley. *It's Halloween.*

Shit, I said back, though I didn't care that much. *Is that a good sign?* I pulled off onto University, then turned onto Fourth.

It's not a sign, you said, *it's just the date.*

We drove past the smoothed stucco buildings housing tony restaurants, four different makeup stores, a so-called ocean-view diner from which no ocean was visible. We ate in a New York–themed bagel place—I ordered an Ellis Island, you got an Empire State. *I have almost no money,* I said, *so you're gonna have to cover this.*

I'm calling that our first bad sign, you said, handing the girl a twenty.

In the bagel place we saw a ballerina, a Richard Nixon, a slutty French maid, and a six-year-old dressed in blue sweats with Styrofoam balls tied on with fishing line.

What are you? you asked him, putting a mint in your mouth.

The solar system, he said.

I love that, you said.

We walked up the street to a bakery and shared a blue-frosted cupcake. It turned your lips a pale blue. *You look like you need an oxygen tank,* I said. At the toy store, you found a little red toy car from the '60s about the size of my thumb and played with it on the floor. When you weren't looking I took it to the counter, paid for it, and hid it in my pocket.

We listened to Al Green and drove above Berkeley and then Oakland, parking on patches of moss to walk in the bitter forest air. On the trail, as we passed them, we took turns greeting people.

Happy Halloween, we said, beaming.

Happy Halloween, they said back uncertainly.

If they passed on your side, you spoke to them. If they passed on my side, I did. And then we passed a couple on my side and I didn't say anything.

That was your turn, you said.

I took your hand. *I hit my people threshold.*

You popped another mint. *Want one?*

What is the deal with the mints, already?

I have breath paranoia, you said.

We stopped at a clearing full of miniature train tracks. It was surreal; we had left the thick forest trail and were suddenly surrounded by a miniature railroad system, built alongside and above the trail, with little tracks to walk around and under, right there in the middle of the woods.

I loved trains when I was a boy.

I want to kiss you, you said, leaning in.

A couple walked past and startled you. *Happy Halloween!* you said, your face reddened. Everyone laughed, the situation clear. I liked that the world thought you were mine. An interior voice answered, She is.

We left, and I sped around the curves above the reservoir. You gripped the armrest, going white in the face. *Can you slow down?* you finally said. *I'm having some trouble being a passenger right now.*

I said it was no problem. *Another one of your things?*

You didn't answer. I slowed down, but then eventually forgot and started speeding again. Going around one turn that curved above a cliff side, you whimpered that I needed to slow down again. I smiled. *Hey, if we go, we go together,* I said. We passed a huge empty lot covered over with gravel. I looked at your hand on the armrest, your other hand now gripping the upholstery next to your leg. On impulse I pulled into the lot, sped up to thirty-five, downshifted, and yanked the emergency brake. The car spun a weak donut, rocks tinkling against the windshield in a silver hail. We stopped. Your hair was loosed from behind your ears, hanging over your face.

I grinned. *You can stop grabbing that armrest, scaredy-cat.*

When you pulled your hair from your face, you were tearing up. With an ice-pick's stab of horror I remembered it as you said it. *My parents died in a car accident,* you said softly. *Like a week ago.*

My head screeched. *Fuck,* I said, too loud.

I know, you said.

No, I just completely didn't—

I know, Francis.

Afterward, I stayed quiet, scared of what else I might ruin.

We ran out of Oakland ideas, so I just drove around the hills. You said, *A left, a left, a right, and then a left. We'll see where that takes us.* It got us lost. *The houses up here are so weird,* you said. And they were—overgrown and incongruous, ill-fitted to their lots. New ones sprouted up coated in polyethylene sheets, as though the building had been diapered. Nobody had a view anymore, apart from a clear sight into their neighbor's dining room.

The old ones burned down, I said. *Everything up here burned.*

Do you remember the fire?

We were in fourth grade, I said automatically. *I was going to an A's game with my cousin. The smoke made the sky turn black. The sun looked like an orange hole.*

I don't remember it, you said. *I never remember anything.*

We took a left, two rights, two lefts, and a right. We were quiet. Like magic, the freeway entrance back to San Francisco appeared.

Get on it, you said.

We went back to the city and parked off Valencia, wandering into a shop with a life-sized Superman and towering midcentury lamps. You read the old anatomical drawings on the wall, your mouth open in concentration. We walked up the street to a wood-paneled shop full of pirate supplies, poking our fingers into their barrel of lard.

I want to go somewhere outside, you said.

It's starting to rain. Do you mind it?

You didn't. I drove us across town, as slowly and carefully as possible, to the botanical gardens. As we got up to the entrance, the mist intensified into a drizzle. The gardens were enormous, sprawled out among flat grass planes. We walked over a wooden footbridge.

There was this architect, I began, *whose name I can't think of, and he designed these cathedrals. He started this cathedral that he never finished, and they're still working on it a hundred and something years later.*

You nodded.

And he made them first upside down, I said, *with weighted ropes, hung to let gravity determine the straight angles, you know, because it's just hanging there in a per-fectly straight line, and I don't know why I can't think of his name . . .*

You patiently listened to me ramble, and then spoke. *Where was the cathedral?*

Cathedrals, plural. Spain, I think.

You cursed. *I'd write this down, but I don't have a pen.*

Just remember it. Cathedrals in Spain, cathedrals in Spain.

Cathedrals in Spain, you said.

We passed a couple our age, near a huge bird-of-para-dise. The guy was dressed as a girl, the girl dressed as a guy. *Happy Halloween,* they said.

You cracked your wrist with a sickening pop.

That's disgusting, I said.

You looked stricken. *I can't help it. I do it so much it's just bone on bone now.*

We stopped and read the little markers describing the species. We turned a corner and found a dingy four-door sedan parked in one of the groves. *This is of the species Acura,* I said. You laughed and I said, *I can't believe you laughed at that.* We stepped into a tremendous weeping willow, its hanging vines forming a nearly uninter-rupted curtain. We looked at the nexus of branches over our heads. *Let's live here,* you said. Our canvas shoes squelched with rainwater. *We need to put on new socks or we're gonna get the jungle rot,* I said. When we came to a small, tucked-away grove, I said, *This is what I wanted to show you.* The bamboo rose so high in the air it was hard to see beyond the ringed yellow spokes. The rain filtered down through so many sharp, pointed leaves. There was a stagnant pond in the grove, alive with larvae. The dim gray light that came through the canopy bounced on the pond like pitched pebbles. You had your back to me, standing at the edge. I was very close behind you. The water was a color green I had never seen before. *That's a color green I've never seen before,* I said.

I know, you said. *Me either.*

Do you know how the bamboo can grow so tall?

You didn't.

Because its roots are so deep in the ground, I said.

The teeth of my jacket's zipper grazed the back of your collar. I felt us reset; however far we had come—sleeping next to each other, holding hands, your naked breasts gracing my lowly bedroom—every time the next step presented itself, it carried with it an undertaste of alarm. As we gained momentum, we were acquiring weight, not shedding it. I was growing more nervous, not less. The seconds plummeted past, the pond crawling over itself, tingling with activity. I could feel you waiting. The smell of that place was sharp and clean.

Ready? you said, turning to leave.

Yeah, I said, defeated.

We got to the entrance across the street from the car.

I wanted to kiss you in there, I said.

We have all the time in the world, you said.

We drove past an advertisement, hanging from a lamppost, for the Conservatory of Flowers. We wanted to go somewhere to warm up and it turned out to be just the place: inside that glass building was a fleshy, palpable heat, like being in a mouth. We passed a child in a stroller, laughing as an overzealous koi splashed water up out of the pond. I blinked and then the fish was on the floor, everyone exclaiming. *It jumped right out,* you said. An unaffected guard stepped forward and scooped it up, tossing it back into the pool. Everyone applauded. It took a moment for him to laugh at what he had just done.

There was a man-eating plant. *I thought it would have teeth,* you said. I don't know what made me do it, but before I had considered it, my finger was in the thing's mouth. The guard never stopped me. You gasped, but then we just watched my finger. *This is the worst man-eating plant I've ever seen,* you said. You inspected the plaque. *Oh,* you said, disappointed. *It just slowly dissolves your flesh with chemicals.*

I'll be sure to wash my hands, I said.

We were on our way out when we saw the bulletin boards. On one were pictures from 1906, and on the other were pictures from 1989. In the pictures, people had pitched tents on the park lawns, catastrophe looming in the distance—belches of smoke, sunken foundations, wire girding splayed like bent fork tines. And in the foreground sat those impromptu shelters; a campground at the foot of apocalypse.

Outside was a sundial that told the incorrect time. When we passed it I said, *Oh, it's early yet.*

You looked at your watch and shook your head no.

We had just parked the car outside your parents' house. We were on Eighth Avenue, walking toward Clement Street, when it happened.

My hair's all wet, you said. *I must look ridiculous.*

Yeah, I kind of can't look at you like this.

Oh, ha ha, you said, rolling your eyes.

No, I'm serious, I said, because I was. Your hair had plastered to your head like a skullcap. *You know the phrase you used earlier, bone on bone?*

Your face soured.

It's like that, I said. *It's having the same effect.*

Wow, you said. You stopped, absently mussing your hair. *I've never heard someone work so hard at being mean.*

I saw the injury in your expression and I couldn't move, couldn't talk.

Let me make sure I understand. You're saying that the sight of me, right now, is as grating to you as if two bones were rubbing together. You didn't wait for an answer: you hurried ahead of me into an aquarium store. You wanted to get away from me, you didn't care where. The worst part was, I had wanted to show you those fish tanks—dozens of them, alive with odd aqueous beings. It was why I had taken you down there.

I know now where that remark came from. We were too happy. I had to rough things up a little, break you down a little. I had to show you not to expect too much from me.

We ate in silence at a barbeque place on Clement, our fried chicken saturated with hot sauce. The waiter was rude, disinterested. Whenever you asked him for something he wandered away wordlessly to retrieve it. You were fuming. When the check came I didn't let you pay it, though it was just about the last forty dollars I had in the world.

I thought you didn't have any money, you said.

I pretended not to hear.

I think I'm out of things to talk about with you, you said.

I don't mind, I said, pretending as though your anger amused me. You sulked while I sat there acting pleased and impenetrable, vowing never to speak again.

Once home, after that silent dinner and a jaunt around the bookstore (*What are you reading?* I asked; *Someone you've never heard of,* you snapped), we settled onto your parents' couch in silence. And then came the most improbable moment. I put on a movie and dimmed the lights. I made us each a cup of chamomile tea. You curled your legs beneath you and leaned against the arm of the sofa. Your softening came in degrees. You let me lean against you, and vertical became diagonal. I rested my head on your hip. I paused the movie to get us a blanket, and when I came back I put my head on your chest instead, tucking your icy feet between my legs to warm them. You placed a hand on my forehead and stroked my hair, pulling the blanket up over us. We pretended to watch the movie as I put my hand under your shirt, against your back, the lace there like Braille. You put a hand up my long sleeve, holding my forearm. You would lean down, your neck at an awkward angle, and kiss my forehead, like a mother. *Can you get the blanket off my face?* I said. I didn't want to move my hands from your body. A moment later, again—*Can you get the blanket off my face?* We laughed. *I have a new idea,* you said. *Get behind me.* I did. The movie ended, and we stared at the revolving DVD menu. *This feels good,* I said.

We should have been like this the whole time. We were warm and dry, and outside it was quiet. Through the bay window we could see the people across the street knitting in their living room. Your back was suctioned to my chest, concave to convex, as though we had stumbled upon some stroke of anatomical destiny.

We fit, I said, without asking for confirmation. I was just declaring it.

I never apologized for what I said on the street. I ought to be glad that, by then, we had stopped looking for signs.

9

Before my mother lost interest in God—the result not of any great crisis of faith, but rather an increasing distaste for Sunday morning obligations—she put me to bed with Bible stories. She knew only the greatest hits: Bethlehem, the populous ark, David's victory. But one night, around my sixth birthday, she pulled out the big guns, and I was transfixed.

Who made the crown of thorns? I asked. *Why did they hate him so much?* The story made no sense: everybody I knew liked Jesus.

She forced out a raspy smoker's cough. *They didn't like the things he said. So they nailed him to a cross and he died.*

They used a hammer?

I don't know, she said.

They put nails in his body?

Yes, his hands and feet. And everyone was sad, because Jesus was—

How big were the nails?

Every night after that, I requested it. *Tell me about how they poked the holes in him.* Every night, she obliged— I wonder now if she mistook my interest for a budding piety. The story grew to encompass the days after, half explaining the mysterious link to the plastic eggs I found hidden, annually, in the mailbox and dog's bowl.

One night, she concluded with a question.

Do you know why it's good that Jesus did this?

I told her I didn't.

Because even though we're bad, he already got in trouble so we don't have to. God won't punish us for doing wrong.

I felt an instantaneous, shattering fear: I didn't put my toys in the right color-coded bin; I once hit another kid with the play iron in the domestic area at preschool—and God was restraining himself only because Jesus had those holes poked in him?

I don't like that, I told her.

No, it's a good thing, because when we die we get to be with baby Jesus and God in heaven. Her eyes were imploring. *Do you know what forever means?*

A long, long time, I said automatically.

She fiddled with her ashtray. *It's all of the time. It doesn't ever end.*

I closed my eyes and saw white: white, white, white, and then I installed edges to the white, and then I removed them—no ends, no edges. It just kept going. *I can see it,* I said. After she turned out the light, I kept imagining: installing hurdles in that great expanse of white and then plucking them out, reaching its parameters and then seeing there could be none. It felt like too much. I panicked, pulling my hands into fists and rapping my knuckles against my skull. I already felt too dwarfed by the universe to survive.

I cried the next time Mom asked if I wanted a story, because I didn't know how to say I wanted a story but not that one. She backed out of the room—*Okay, Frankie, okay.*

My father grudgingly took his turn. His stories were all about unsuspecting men—usually named Manute Bol or Clyde Drexler—out on a jaunt and encountering things on the street, every twist prefaced by "when suddenly . . ." The unfairness pained me: I didn't like that those going about their business could suddenly be called upon. *But Hakeem Olajuwon was just walking down the street, Dad.* I remember my father's face as I reached a breathless state of anxiety: pure puzzlement. Usually the challenge they encountered was only another ball player, and then they played one-on-one until the hero triumphed with the requisite three-pointer. *Goddammit, Frankie,* my father said, shaking his head. *Jill,* he called to my mother, *I give up.*

Then they installed a tiny TV/VCR in my bedroom, and I took comfort in *Peter Pan* and *Pinocchio,* singing along before bed. Even now, decades later, I can remember those movies from beginning to end. My eyes would grow heavy in the faint glow, and I'd wake up to whine if they turned it off too soon—I couldn't fall sleep without it. I dreamed in graphic cartoon outline. Around the house I used a plastic golf club as Jiminy Cricket's cane, singing, until my parents forbade it, about the benefits of whistling when my conscience threatened to fail me.

■ ■ ■

I slept in the master bedroom—her parents' bedroom. Or rather, I reclined on one side of the bed, staring all night out the window at lights going on and off in the homes along the street, and then at the slow crawl of the pink dawn. I witnessed the automatic snuffing of the streetlights, and listened to my breathing. I watched shadows pass across the ceiling and in my comedown discomfort—I was out of booze money—I considered never leaving that spot, that room. Who would know where I was? No one would find me; there was no one alive who would know to look for me there. And yet in my stupor I tensed with every passing car.

Thursday morning I got to Hawthorne later than usual, a few seconds before the bell would ring. Let them wait, I remember thinking, startled by the severity of the thought. The kids, the parents, Buckingham—surely he was in there, ready to discreetly guide me out of earshot before explaining to me that I was—what? A person of interest? A criminal? *A piss-ant liar?*

Let them all wait. I didn't cower, didn't flinch. I walked right up to the classroom, soles sliding against the buffed floor tiles. I saw the kids and some parents congregated outside the classroom, blocking the hallway in a swarm.

Morning, I said, nodding curtly like they were coworkers.

Hi, FRANK, Marcus said. It was a game they played when they were feeling pushy, nasty—they called me by my first name, testing my reaction. *You're late, FRANK.*

Hi, Marcus, I said, fiddling with my keys and chewing on my fingertip, my messenger bag hanging from my shoulder.

As they went inside and scattered to their desks, the parents followed. Their number had decreased. Mr. Noel had come again, and Mrs. Stone. Jacob's mother had returned. I was surprised to see Simon's mother absent—twice she had bent my ear for twenty minutes about Simon's nightmares, his every question since the field trip. I had imagined she would be the one who stuck around longest.

As I sat, Jacob's mother approached my desk. *Mr. Mason,* she said.

My mind dissolved into panic; instinctively, I stalled. *Just one second,* I said, beginning to take attendance.

I need to speak with you, she said.

I'll just be a second, I said again.

That was when I noticed Simon was absent. I glanced around the room to make sure, craning my neck to see behind various children. I looked back down at the list. A full four seconds passed with Jacob's mother standing beside me before I realized Jacob was missing, too.

Jake's not here today? I said, finally looking up at her.

I watched her hesitate, out of patience but not ready to say whatever difficult thing she was about to say. I swallowed, stood, and strode purposefully away from her. *Mr. Noel,* I said, walking toward him. *Any word on Simon and his mom? Did you see them outside?*

He shifted his weight and looked at Mrs. Stone, who spoke. *Simon won't be in,* she said. *I think it's better if you speak to his mother.*

I nodded. *Fair enough.*

I set the children up with their Xeroxed math problems, delaying, looking busy. Jacob's mother still stood quietly beside my desk. I looked out the window. Where was Buckingham? I was certain he would come for me.

Mr. Mason, my pencil broke! said Jamil.

Yeah, okay, I said.

And then clarity dropped on me like a cartoon anvil: come on, you think they're going to come *arrest* you? For what? Accessory to a suicide you imagined—an accessory from three hundred feet away, no less? Get a fucking grip, I thought. And the missing kids—they were probably just sick, absent for the reasons immuno-compromised small children are often absent. The flu, a cold, an ugly cough. Jacob might have had another asthma attack.

I was ready to put all of it out of my head—was actually walking toward the parents to say a formal good morning—when another possibility came to me. I stopped, turned on my heel, and walked to the telephone, mounted to the wall next to the chalkboard. After one ring the nasal-voiced Ms. Levitt—the only other second-grade teacher at Hawthorne—answered. I could hear the raucous conversation behind her.

Sharon, it's Frank.

Oh, she said.

In her voice I read the entire situation: she hadn't expected to receive the call so soon.

I laughed a short, miserable little laugh, hung up, and dialed the principal's office. Now I looked openly at the parents clustered in the corner, the rings trilling in my ear. I saved my nastiest expression for Jacob's mother, still hovering at my desk.

The principal answered.

You transferred my student, I said. *You put him in another class?*

Silence.

You didn't think I deserved to know?

Finally, she spoke. *It's my job to respect the parents' wishes.*

I suppose Jacob . . . I said, my voice cracking. I recovered, straightened my posture. *Transferred out too, I'm assuming.*

I looked again at Jacob's mother. Her expression was one I recognized—Greta used it whenever forced to tell me how short I fell of her expectations.

We can talk about this later, the principal said. She sounded tired, and suddenly it made sense: she was picking her battles, aware of how futile this interaction was. Because soon I would be gone. She was keeping me only as long as she had to.

I was going to be fired.

Right, I said, hanging up. The kids were watching. They seemed miles away. I looked one of them in the face and tensed with alarm: full seconds passed before I could remember her name.

I became aware of pain in the palm of my hand, and when I looked down four half-moons were branded into my palm—I had squeezed my fist so hard my overgrown fingernails had cut four red smiles. I was fully sober, buzzing with the agony of total awareness.

To Jacob's mother, I said, *Tell Jake Mr. Mason says he's sorry.*

She tried to speak, but I was already turning away. *Listen up,* I said to the kids. *Mr. Noel has something to talk about with all of you.*

I glanced at Caleb's father, his mouth open slightly.

He's going to tell you what it's like to be a firefighter, I said, motioning for him to take my seat: the stool before the wall of windows, the place from which I had delivered my energetic talks on compound words and A. A. Milne, where I had led the students in funny tongue twisters and quoted Fred Rogers.

Mr. Noel took the stool. As he spoke—*I was one of the first responders to the Oakland Hills back in '91*—I fumbled through my desk, resigned and exhausted. I nearly gasped when I came across five over-the-counter nighttime painkillers, like tiny morsels of salvation, rolling loose in my top drawer. Three times I pretended to cough, clapping a hand over my mouth, and turned to the wall to swallow the pills dry. I closed my eyes, feeling my surroundings soften and fade, suffusing with surplus light like an overexposed photograph.

. . .

For a little while, in the beginning of my career, I was sure that teaching was the only job I could ever do. That buoyant certainty had existed for me only once previously. It has been my particular curse to watch the only two meaningful things in my life fail utterly. In both cases, there were many indications of the coming defeat; I either ignored them or, more probably, was not smart enough to recognize them for what they were.

But now that time has passed, I can see the first moments when my belief began to falter—it survived intact for a blissful couple of months at Hawthorne, and then one November afternoon it cracked. I had stayed late to get ahead on grading. Through the wall of windows facing the street, I noticed Emma waiting for her mother.

I watched a dingy black car pull up to the curb; Emma tossed her bag into the backseat and then sat beside it. Through the open window, I heard her mother's voice jump to a sharp clip. *I told you not to slam the goddamn door.* She twisted her body like a wrung towel, popped Emma on the mouth with her knuckles, and drove away.

Breathing like a marathoner, I set my red pen down and retreated to the roof, to the lawn chair. One second I had been a confident man, a virtuous teacher; the next, I was certain I was of no consequence. Looking out at the gray water, I thought of that distance I had once found so endearing—the sense that I was watching them become people, that I was witnessing their first encounters with the world. I felt that distance reconfigure into something dark and baleful. They weren't enigmatic little wonders. They were miniature adults. They were just as weighed down by their own shitty impediments, their same painful burdens, as their grown counterparts. I was watching them become people, yes—I was watching them become people they someday would not want to be.

My conviction began to sag with a weight it could not bear. I vowed to continue despite my uncertainty, despite my fear that whatever I gave them—these children I taught, these children I would someday father—would be too little. In spite of me, they would coast forward on rails someone else had built, or rails I would build unknowingly, mistakes I would pass on to them without even knowing I had done so.

And that was how I came to be sitting on a beach, reading the paper, neglecting a classroom of children who trusted me. That was how I came to fail them. It was the story of my life: I performed by rote, dutifully persisting long after I'd ceased to believe in the endeavor—thinking that sacrifice made me noble, thinking it made me good.

. . .

After recess the children filed back in. I watched Jeffrey trip another kid and laugh hysterically when he stumbled. *Hey, Jeff,* I called. He looked up and I shook my head sluggishly. *Come on, guy, you know better,* I said. I scanned the room: they all fidgeted, chattering at one another.

Mr. Mason, one of them said. I looked down, and Benjamin stared up at me.

Yeah? I said.

I didn't do it, but the other boys did, he said.

Did what?

He stared up at me, dumb.

What? I snapped. *Did what?*

I leaned down and held his shoulders. My hands felt huge, swollen. *Tell me,* I said.

His nose was encrusted, his eyes glassy. His frame felt shrunken and bizarre to me, like I was holding a doll. I didn't touch them very often, and when I did, I was surprised by their size—the alarming lack of mass, the ease with which they could be overtaken.

I didn't do anything, he said.

I looked down and saw his hands—filthier than I can describe, dirt caked beneath the fingernails. I felt myself recoil, pulling away from him, walking backward toward my desk. Seconds later, Mrs. Stone jumped in to divert their attention. I pretended to be engrossed in a stack of papers. *Who wants to play bingo?* she said.

Get through today, I said under my breath. *You'll be gone by tomorrow.* The call was coming; I knew it. *Get through today,* I said again, picking up my attendance book to take post-recess roll.

B-24, Mrs. Stone called. *Who has their bingo card ready?*

I ticked down the list: *present, present.* Two kids, apart from those transferred out, were missing. Emma, the sickly girl with the quick-handed mother, and Edmund, my happy-go-lucky pet. I walked to the door to scan the hallway. We'd been back in class for ten minutes. I had seen them that morning. They had just been there.

Did anyone see Ed or Emma outside? I asked the kids. A few looked over.

I-14, Mrs. Stone said, as though I were invisible.

Hello? I raised my voice. *Did anybody see Edmund or Emma?*

The children listening shook their heads. Without thinking, I clenched my fist again, and before I caught myself I had opened the cuts on my palms, a wincing pain radiating up my hand. *Shit,* I muttered, beneath the din. I glanced around looking for a tissue to wipe away the small amount of blood, and when I couldn't find one, I walked across the hall to the boys' bathroom.

The irony is that I had a first-aid kit right there in my bottom desk drawer. I guess I forgot that, though I opened it at least three times a week—they were always hurting themselves, hurting each other. Band-Aids were cure-alls. They coveted them, begged for them even when they weren't necessary. I could have just opened the drawer, pulled out a bandage, slapped it on, and forgotten about it. This is how it works, in the wake of avoidable events: the moments prior beg for obsessive reevaluation. But this particular variable, upon reflection, feels too small, too stupid to be the catalyst for what followed.

The boys' bathroom smelled like piss and cleaning solvents. I pushed backward through the door with my elbows raised, like a surgeon avoiding contamination. I held a paper towel to my palm, stepping over a puddle in front of the sink. And then I held still, suddenly alert. I felt something in there: furtiveness, as though the air had quieted upon my approach. One stall was open, the other shut, and I sensed that I was intruding. A kid must be sick, I thought. He's waiting for me to leave. I grabbed a few more industrial brown paper towels from the dispenser, started toward the door, and heard a small human sound, like a sniff, a cough, some minute disturbance of the air that indicated a presence. It wasn't the right kind of sound; that's the best way I can describe it. Look in the stall, I thought. The thought came from somewhere far removed from intellect. I knocked on the door and heard a whisper, but couldn't make out thé words. *You need to come out of there,* I said. *This is a teacher. I need you to come out right now.* No answer. *I'm coming in, kiddo.* I pulled a coin from my pocket, pushed it into the lock's slit, turned it horizontally, and pushed the door.

Edmund had been pressed against the stall door, facing the toilet, so when I pushed it open he stumbled forward. He regained his balance, looking up and behind him, into my eyes. *Ed,* I said. That was all I said, just *Ed,* a small notation to myself: as in, that's Edmund. There's Edmund. Then I saw his panic; a look I knew well—I'm in trouble, it said. I'm caught. I peered past him into the stall. *Emma,* I said, still just arranging the information in my head: There's Ed, this is Emma. They aren't absent, just in the bathroom. Just here, in this stall of the boys' bathroom, alone together.

Ed, I said again.

She was sitting cross-legged, Indian style, at his feet, her eyes wide. He was short enough that Emma hadn't had to kneel. *You guys,* I whispered. *The bell already rang.* They didn't move. *The bell rang,* I choked out, bending down to help Edmund lift his pants, a distant scream radiating through my head. *Come on,* I said to both of them. We crossed the hall, went back into the classroom, and they took their seats. If the other kids had noticed I was gone, they didn't show it. Their parents had—they were talking heatedly among themselves when I walked in, and I watched them quiet at my approach. At my desk, I made two small amendments to the attendance form: Edmund and Emma, present.

It was mimicry, I knew that. And I knew what that meant: to mimic, one must have an example. Which of them, or if both of them, had had such a guide, I didn't know. I still don't know. I can tell you that what I felt wasn't sympathy, wasn't compassion. What I felt was nameless, taking up space but entirely abstract, without feature. The purest kind of nothingness. I can tell you that, given what it replaced, it was a relief.

As the children painted Mexican flags—it was Cinco de Mayo—the nothingness inside me sharpened, took shape. I finished my coffee and rocked on the back legs of the desk chair. On my watch, I kept thinking. All of this, on my watch. Mrs. Stone leaned over their desks, walking around, putting her hand over their small fingers to keep their paintbrushes inside the lines. I thought I could feel Ed and Emma looking at me, though I didn't look up. I thought I could feel them gauging how long it would be before the consequences came down, how long before they were taken aside. Maybe they stole glances at each other. Maybe they went on, oblivious. Maybe they plotted their next visit to the bathroom, the area behind the equipment shed, the far reaches of the soccer field. God knows where else. Maybe they thought they had gotten off easy, that they had beaten me: I had impotently let them slide. They knew what they were doing was something I shouldn't see. Whatever else they didn't know, they knew that.

I projected motives onto their act—lust, evil, predatory malice, weakness of character. It was idiotic. They were children. What they had done existed outside of thought, outside of contemplation. They were interpreting someone else's script. They were just babies. They understood nothing.

I knew all that. But when I looked up, finally, my vision trailing slightly behind from the medicine, all the kids were hovering over their paintings except for Edmund. He looked right at me, as though I were a show he wasn't enjoying. He looked at me like he knew exactly what he had done. I dropped my coffee cup into the shallow trash can and it splashed back at me, drops staining my pants.

They were just babies. They understood nothing. But he stared like his pupils could drill holes. I stared back, letting my eyes go dead. He looked away, cowed, and something inside me split. All this time, right under my nose there had been this one fucked-up little kid, hurting someone weaker than him. One evil child, poisoning the rest. And I was favoring him all the while. God knows what else the kids did when I wasn't looking. God knows what they did to those who were weaker—who else had been tormented, abused. God knows what they were doing on the beach before I knew what was down there. God knows what else I hadn't been told. Savage little bastard, I thought. You sick little shit.

I stood up, barking, *We're having silent reading early, take out your books.* They stared with wide eyes, trying to tell what was wrong. The parents, too, looked up sharply, and I quieted myself, saying, *Just a quick change of plans,* my voice reassuring. I scrambled around the room, snatching the still-wet watercolor palettes and shoving them into an empty box.

Mr. Mason? Mrs. Stone said.

I've got it, I said. I could smell myself—I hadn't showered in days, and the stench emanated from the collar of my shirt. *Come on, come on, put it in the box. Brushes, please.* I darted around the desks, ignoring their questioning eyes. I felt that blanketing whiteness in my head, a blizzard behind my eyes, a feeling like cold and distance combined—white tundra stretching out inside of me. It had no edges. It had no ends.

I found myself at Edmund's chair. I said to him, as the rest of them pulled out their silent-reading books, *I need your help putting the paints in the supply room.* He stood silently and began walking as though toward a gallows. I followed him.

In the cluttered supply room at the rear of the classroom, I unfolded two chairs. We sat opposite each other in the tiny space, his chair flush against the wall. I tried to speak a few times but kept stopping myself, looking for footing, the right way in. I gave up, leaning back.

Why did you do that, Ed? My voice was thick. I saw him hear the tears in my voice, saw his surprise, his worry. *Tell me why you did that to her.*

He looked toward the supply room door. It passed in less than a second, but it was a rare moment in which I understood without any doubt exactly what someone was thinking. He was thinking, *I'm not safe.* He was afraid of the way I spoke, afraid of what I was letting him see. He was looking for an escape hatch. He was thinking about how fast he would have to run, if it came to it.

Tell me why you did that, I said again.

He shrugged. It was exactly what I expected him to do, to shrug and sit there waiting for his punishment. There would be no moment of remorse, in which he professed to know what he should do different next time. How could there be? A shrug was the only response he could give, because it was no response at all. But it shook me, hard.

He does this, he does this to her—and he fucking *shrugs* at me?

It was the shout in the canyon, and the avalanche roared over both our heads—all of it came down: the previous days, the previous years, the goddamn unending sea of nausea that pooled inside me, the bones in my wrist ground to powder, my bloody palm, the hours I hadn't slept, the hours I hadn't wanted to breathe. Her mother's hand, popping against Emma's mouth. *I don't feel like playing soccer today.* The sight of that thing, that repulsive thing lying on the beach. The culmination of everything ugly I had ever known. All of it synthesized, began as a tingle in my shoulder and ran down my arm and I stood, like a hulking god above him, and with the butt of my hand I pushed his forehead so that his head bounced off the supply room wall. It rattled the shelf where I had stored reams of construction paper, a single blue sheet dislodging and floating merrily to the floor, and tears came to his downcast, avoiding eyes, as he began to whisper softly to himself, ignoring me, as though the little song or prayer or whatever he was whispering would save him. And at that moment I was glad. I was glad that his hair would cover the bruise; I was glad that I had hurt him in a way that wouldn't show. Edmund's impromptu lullaby caught in his teary throat, and the paper smell lingered like a dry, searing heat.

The children read for two hours, because I never told them to do anything else. After an hour, Mr. Noel came to my desk.

Are you sure this is what they're supposed to be doing? he said. *It seems like this is an awful lot of reading for a bunch of eight-year-olds.*

Just a little while longer, I told him.

Eventually, Mrs. Stone pulled out a notepad and began to write. That's how it is in any school district—everything requires documentation; no one gets fired until there's ample evidence against them clogging someone's file cabinet. That's why the parents came. Two of them had seen me fuck around on that field trip, seen me read that fucking newspaper. They had told the principal they were unsatisfied, they were concerned. They had given me a short grace period, maybe, once they were told that my wife was the corpse on the sand, but when they emerged from the fog of their sympathy, if they had ever believed I was bereaved, they remembered that I had been reading that newspaper long before catching sight of the body. That I had checked out months ago. That I was just a stupid kid. All ambivalence was gone—I was certain now. The parents were here to make sure I didn't do anything worse.

The children fidgeted and yawned. With about forty minutes left Mrs. Stone and Mr. Noel rose in synchronized indignation, pulled their children up by the arms, and walked silently out of the classroom. In my peripheral vision, I saw Mr. Noel glaring at me. I didn't meet his gaze. I expected the principal to arrive at any moment, but she didn't. I gather now that she busy securing the future of my charges—a final hour of my foolishness was tolerable, if it meant that tomorrow the kids would be in capable hands.

The phone rang. I picked it up, weakly saying hello.

Oh good, Greta said. *You're alive.*

I'm sorry.

Where were you?

I was—

It doesn't matter, she said. *Wherever you were, I'm sure there was a phone.*

I couldn't go home last night, I said quietly.

Last night, she said, *or any night from now on?*
I don't—
Maybe I should be the one to decide.

I put my head in my free hand. *Oh God, Greta, everything is like, beyond fucked up.* I looked up at the class. *Fucked up to the point where it's not even recognizable.*

Without knowing exactly what I meant, she called it like a pro: *You made it that way,* she said. *You took a difficult situation and made it worse.*

I didn't mean to.

It's your specialty, she said.

Greta, I need you right now.

She was silent for a moment. *I'm here for you, Frank. I am sitting around, just like always, filling my days with being very, very here for you.*

Please don't think that I don't care about you.

I don't think that. What I think is that you don't care about anything.

Edmund hid at his desk, his face in his arms. It began to rain, the drops clattering against the windowpanes, and the secretary's voice came over the PA, announcing that final recess was to be held indoors.

I love you, Greta. I mean that.

Someday, you'll have to tell me what that means. We'll have to compare notes, she said, before hanging up.

Most of the kids eventually passed out—they were so small, still so close to the age of obligatory afternoon naps. Edmund's face stayed in his arms and I thought, after a while, that maybe he had fallen asleep too. But when he lifted his pink face it was slick with tears. At some point

Marcus raised his hand. I shook my head with my dead-eye stare and he slowly pulled it back down to his side. If they woke up they read some more, or pretended to, cranky and worried until the bell rang at 2:49. They stood, bewildered, to leave. Edmund was among them. There was no moment of reconnection between us, no final word in which he approached me—no moment when I begged him not to tell. I didn't apologize. I didn't see to his wounds, if there were any. There was just silence. He stood up, put his lunch bag in his backpack, and went outside like everybody else. They were gone. I exhaled the deep breath I had held for hours. I was sore from sitting still all afternoon.

I stood, walked over to the classroom door, and locked it. In the supply nook, I grabbed the biggest box I could find, emptying its contents—cracked plastic rulers, straightened paper clips, a ream of graph paper. I brought it to the desk and began placing my things inside. I put it all away: the flashcards I had made to teach them addition, the pamphlet I had gotten from the Egyptian Museum. Red pens, rubber stamps, scratch-and-sniff reward stickers, sing-along cassette tapes. Whole stacks of curriculum papers. Whatever graded work I still had went into their plastic cubbies, sorted as deftly as a casino dealer's cards. I left the crooked posters up, left the chart showing the points they had earned for Cooperation, Extra Effort, Kindness. I sorted through the prizes these points could win them—glittery folders, cheap spinning tops, dollar-store junk bought with my own money. I placed one prize on each desk—I knew which one each kid would want most and tried to accommodate them. I erased the chalkboards, the whiteboards. On the one chalkboard facing the door, so it would be the first thing someone saw, I wrote my two-word farewell. *I'm sorry*, it said—more to the janitor than to anyone else, since it was his job to wash the boards at night.

My things packed, I closed the supply room door, then opened it again: Ed had put the fallen piece of paper back in its place. Up to that moment, I had done a pretty good job of avoiding thoughts of the following day—the custodian being called to open the door, the principal waiting for my arrival, to tell me the news, until she happened to open a desk drawer to find it empty. She would ask the custodian to take the posters from the walls. She would hire someone else, after the kids had spent who knows how many days with anonymous subs—retired ladies supplementing their social security, kids just out of college. The children would do more dittos than they had ever done in their lives. They would spend hours on word searches. They would watch the animated films that had inhabited my childhood dreams.

I fished around the bottom of the box until I found the striped pebble Ed had given me. I looked at it one last time, before setting it at his place. I put my key ring on the chalkboard ledge. I walked to the door, pressed the lock button from the inside, and pulled it shut behind me.

Between the outer door and the street, just beyond a hole in the playground fence, was a massive mud puddle left over from a recent storm. I heard Benjamin's voice again—*I didn't do it but the other boys did*—and remembered the filth on his hands: a small blue chair, bearing the construction-paper numbers I put on each of the ones in my classroom, was half-submerged in the gray water.

I said aloud, *Make it to the car.* I would make it there, sit down, close and lock the door, the weight of my body sinking in, bonding to the fabric. I would envelop myself in that small space, tightening the seat belt around my frame for safety.

By then, I had grown used to the sense that however far down I fell, there would always be another gradient to plummet. But now I thought, This is permanent. What you did today is permanent. *What you did today*—I couldn't bring myself to name it. I closed my eyes and tried to picture eternity, like I had when I was small. But what adulthood does to your imagination—limiting it, narrowing it, clogging it with too many associations for any pure thought to exist . . . I envisioned that large expanse of white and tried to see its infinite expanse, but all I felt was the opposite. Forever wasn't a wide-open span. Forever was something that fell on top of you. It wasn't a breadth of possibility. It was the reverse; it was suffocation. And that biblical, childhood terror reemerged: the fear of something so big that the mere task of comprehending it could crush me.

Make it to the car. I would depress the pedals and make that space move, so that it would take me to the warmth of my own house. I would walk past the greeting at the door and move swiftly inside, say that I was taken ill, lie down on the coverlet, and sleep, and sleep, and sleep.

Or I would stay in that car, bypass the house entirely. I would get on one road and just drive—until the road ended, until I found something else.

I sat and turned the ignition. The engine hummed and the car spurted forward, and I found the familiar streets, each one emerging from the ever-present fog as though it were coming out of hiding.

I went back to the abandoned house, the psychic's footprints still visible in the mud out front. The light coming through the bedroom window had turned a bleak gray, but I stayed a while without flipping on the switch, staring at the novelty phone, thumbing through the desk. It was full of stacked papers and nubby pencils, rubber bands, half-scrubbed erasers, bent thumbtacks, gum wrappers. It felt intimate, looking at those objects. All those odds and ends that belong to us say something: a person could know me if he looked in my kitchen drawer and saw three different-sized lightbulbs—because I never went to the hardware store prepared, I bought whatever seemed right and then found, once home, that I had misjudged. Junk has a language. Every piece-of-shit mistake I made, I hung on to the evidence. *Not with any accuracy* I had said to Buckingham: the other story of my life—miscalculated leaps, aims taken and overshot. The distance, always, between what I said and what I meant. What I wanted and what I got. What I hoped and what turned out to be real.

10

The DVD player finally shut itself off. We held still, reluctant to move. After being in the wet and cold, it had taken forever to get warm. *Are you ready for bed?* I asked, hopeful. I felt like it was time. I wanted it to be time.

You sat up and reached for your shoes. *Let's go out.*

We were out all day, I said.

It's Halloween. Let's go watch the Vincent Price movie.

The Castro will be packed.

We should find a party, then.

I didn't want to drink those shitty party margaritas, always ninety percent crushed ice. I didn't want to stand around watching you talk to people who weren't me. I didn't want to share you. But you were happy, feeling good despite my various bunglings. I had done enough to sabotage your night.

I know a party, I said.

By the time we arrived, it was clear that the event had veered from its intended trajectory: it was supposed to be grown-up and tasteful, but had slipped into your average college kid's chandelier-swinger. There were decorations, and not just silly drugstore decorations but really deliberate, arranged decorations: green Spanish moss over the fireplace mantle, white pumpkins nestled on the end tables, spice-scented candles strategically placed. My roommate Sam's girlfriend, Renee—she of the erotic auditory assault you had overheard—was our age, but it was as if someone's mom had thrown a party. She had spent a grip on top-shelf liquor, but only one bottle of each. The graveyard of empties held court on a card table. For a while we stood awkwardly by the door, and then gave in and headed for the booze.

The only thing left is gin, you said, holding up a teal bottle.

This isn't really a gin crowd, I said, people-watching. *How long are we staying?*

You want a martini? you said. *They've got vermouth.*

That's ridiculous, I said. *Make me one.*

Someone had put in a karaoke tape but no one was singing, just grinding to beats missing their raps, lifting drinks to a decade-old sample. Everyone was in costume but us. An embarrassment of bottled beer sat in ice buckets, cans of it sweating in paper cases. I swiped one and it was gone in moments, before you had even finished with the cocktail shaker. I opened another, and it vanished too. Parties were always like magic acts for me: making alcohol disappear, pulling drunken confessions from thin air. I was two beers in, draining the martini you had made, and already I felt sick. *What's the rhyme again?* I asked. *Beer before . . . no, whiskey before beer . . .*

This is awful, you said. *This is an awful party.*

I looked at your drink: empty. When had that happened?

Twenty minutes passed, the music getting louder. The revelers around us looked like they were melting, their costume makeup separating on their faces in greasy streaks.

You never said if you want to live with me, you said. *Was that a yes or a no?*

Oh, I said, *I guess I just—*

Never mind. I want to finish this and go. Another drink had materialized in your hand. *I'm going to have sex with you tonight.*

I took the drink from you. *What are you, drugged?*

I'm tired, you said, tearing up. *I'm just tired of how I do things.*

In the corner, somebody put on vintage Snoop and started dancing all ungainly. Some kid in a police uniform walked past and pointed at my two martini glasses. *Double-fistin',* he said.

What do you mean? I said to you. *How do you do things?*

I don't. I just wait around hoping things will change.

You looked small. *Oh God, Nora, nobody—*I gestured around the room—*none of us knows what we're doing.*

You do, you said. *You're going to be a teacher.*

Probably not a very good one, I said.

Do you want to live with me, yes or no, you said, your shoulders sagging.

Fireworks! somebody shouted. *The roof! Everybody on the roof!*

And before I could answer, you had turned to follow.

Up there, some guy had cigarettes and you asked him for one. He lit it for you, looking at your breasts. You picked up an almost-full beer from the roof's railing, taking deep swallows. Someone lit a bottle rocket and chucked it a few yards. It went off disappointingly, so more were lit, their bearers running a ways before making the throw, as though three drunken paces would add to the velocity.

Hold this, you said around your cigarette, pulling your hair back and handing me your bottle. I watched, rapt, as my fingers opened and closed around it. *Oh shit,* I said. *I'm drunk.* I set the bottle down, afraid I would drop it.

I'm done pretending to smoke, you said, stumbling and holding out the cigarette. *What do people do with these when they're through?*

I took it from your hand and tossed it off the roof, both of us taking quick side steps to the ledge. We watched it vanish into the narrow alley below, reappearing in a small orange burst as the ash hit the ground. From up there we could see the sharp spokes of the city, puncturing the hazy sky.

Don't you ever get sick of living here? you said.

The wind lifted our hair in hanks. *Where else would I go?*

Somewhere where there's weather. And things to see and do. Your empty bottle fell on its side, rolling on the black tar. *Sometimes I feel like, fuck San Francisco.*

On the ground below lay a splayed mop, its wrung tentacles flattened. I could feel you staring at me: that crawling sensation of being eyeballed.

You drive me around all the time, you said, your voice heavy. *I'm so completely used to the side of your face.*

You've got the booze blues, I said. *You're thinking too much.*

I'm always like that, you said.

What you meant was, you were always like that now.

Some kid turned on a boom box and poured beer over his head. *How much longer do you want to stay?* I asked. Everyone was a stranger; everyone was turned up too loud.

You motioned toward the horizon—the Transamerica pyramid like a fountain pen's nib, the piers, the ferries docking, the black, light-studded hills beyond. *I'm sick of looking at it,* you said, shouting over the music.

Why? I said, trying to hide my panic. *People come from far away to see this and we get to see it every day.*

My house is this way, you said, and then you realized you had miscalculated, swinging your arm in the opposite direction. *No, that way.* Those around us suddenly wanted to figure out where their houses were, too: how far they had to go, from there, to be home again.

Bullshit, you said, a minute late. *People come from far away to jump off our bridge.* You laughed. *People come here to die.*

I don't know if we can go yet, I said, shivering. *But I want to soon.*

Really? You think about moving too?

A tiny spark flared in me, lifted itself weakly, and died. *No,* I said; I never had. *I meant, I don't think I can drive yet. I don't think I should drive us home yet.*

You nodded, pulling—inexplicably—a purple rubber ball out of your pocket. *I think I stole this. Shit, from the toy store.* You looked up, alarmed. *It was an accident,* you said.

It's okay, I said.

You leaned over the edge. *How high will it bounce, you think?*

Not all the way back up, I said.

You let it go: it came up about one story to our three. You picked up a bottle and before I could stop you it was out of your hand. It caught the streetlight glare as it shattered: a hundred stars dying on the pavement. My insides sloshed.

You shouted, *Keep throwing things!* Your face had become serious. *Find more things.* You took off your sweater and tossed it over the side, the arms extending on the wind—an invisible person, jumping off the roof in your clothes. Some kid ran up from behind us and threw a drumstick over the side. *I still totally need this drumstick!* he shouted, hurling it over his head.

Our faces were wind-smacked. *Hey!* you yelled. *Twenty-two years!*

What? I said. *I don't—*

I'm dropping them off the side! You held out your arm and opened your hand, letting go of nothing. *Now they're gone! I'm zero years old! Today can be my birthday!*

Somebody in a fake Afro and bow tie set off one of those high-pitched fireworks. The noise made everyone squint.

Let's get married, you screamed. *Share all that money with me!*

What the fuck! I said.

Marry me and we'll move away! We'll move to the other side of the country!

Where!

You know how many places there are? you said. *All these places we've never been!* The firework died halfway through that sentence, leaving you screaming for no reason.

My ears rang so bad they ached, throbbing somewhere deep. You reached in your jeans pocket and found everything collected there: the lawyer's business card, a wad of lint, a ticket to the Conservatory of Flowers. Receipts, tissues, coins, who knows what else, because over it went, falling in a hail of junk to the abandoned stretch below.

Nora, I said, *I love you.*

You grabbed at my thin jacket, reaching into my pockets and pulling out handfuls: more receipts, my car keys, a clump of dollar bills. And another small item—as soon as I saw it, before I even understood what it was, I felt my throat catch with its familiarity. Me, mine, my head said. Don't. Those thoughts were wordless, amounting to a large exclamation point inside me as I reached out to save it and missed: the little red toy car I had bought you, sinking toward the earth, surrounded by the last scraps of cash I had in the world.

Goddamnit, I said, quietly enough that no one could hear me over the music. I turned toward the stairs to go salvage what I could, to at least find my keys. The alley was deserted. I put my beer can in a brown paper bag I found lying on the ground. My knees buckled and I leaned against the building. Suddenly I realized I had put my beer in the bag upside down: I had a paper bag full of loose beer, the can bobbing like a merry buoy. The paper gave, the bag bursting as I leaned over the pavement, my insides beginning to stage their escape.

I made it back into the apartment, and then to the bathroom. There, I unbuttoned my pants and collapsed on the toilet, confused. I had forgotten what was so urgent. Vertigo reset my vision every two seconds, my sight jerking to the left, then snapping back like a typewriter beginning a new line: six inches of that bathroom on endless loop. *Francis,* you said through the door. I let all of it go on the white rug at my feet, belatedly picking up the garbage bin and holding it to my face. The papery wads from the trash attached to my wet mouth: someone's Kleenex. I dropped the bin and it clattered. The noise brought you into the bathroom.

Oh God, you said.

It was the voice of someone tasting something bitter; it was distilled disappointment in crystal audio. Hearing you caused a sensation inside me like my diaphragm was shrinking. It was the kind of regret I really miss sometimes: hyper-present but soon forgotten—preferable to the kind that hums under the surface, refusing to die.

You don't do everything wrong, I said. *I do.* I was sticky with sweat, reeking of spilled beer. My naked lap stared up at you. *Weren't you drunker than me?* I slurred. *I could have sworn you were totally—*

I vomited again, into the sink this time, which was inches from the toilet. You smeared your hand across my forehead. I said it again—*I do everything wrong*—because I wasn't sure you had captured the statement's full impact: it included everything. *So if you want to live with me,* I said, *you're a fucking idiot.*

You knelt and put your arms around my middle. I had the most comforting thought: She'll take me home. She'll drive me home the way I've driven her before; we'll turn down her street, pull into her driveway, and walk up her steps. Our steps. The house where we live. We'll wake up next to each other. She is in control. *Thank you,* I said in advance.

Greta's here, you whispered, like we were siblings hiding from mom and dad.

My head was a hundred-pound weight. I leaned toward the sink again, gripped by a burning heave. *I can't care about this right now,* I choked.

Someone tapped shave and a haircut on the door.

Occupied, you called.

Open up, Greta said, muffled. *One of you open up, please.*

Francis, you whispered. *You've got a situation here.*

The hell I do. I wiped the sting from inside my nose. *What is there to say?*

It smelled vicious in there. Your eyes were soft.

Greta knocked again. *Frank, I need to talk to you right now.*

I forgot she calls you Frank, you whispered.

Nora, is that you in there?

You winced. *Hey, Greta. Francis is a little sick right now.*

The voice beyond the door turned sour. *I've been a little sick lately myself.*

Your eyes shot to the floor.

I don't remember the connecting scenes—between when Greta left me shaking in the hallway and when you and I headed home. It's a rare gap in my memory. I could attribute that missing piece to the booze, if I were being generous to myself. But the truth is, I would rather not recall.

I didn't have to tell you what Greta had said. Why else would she show up at my roommate's girlfriend's party—they disliked each other intensely—so confident, so certain I would listen? You knew that that kind of assurance, in her, could only

be born of necessity. You knew she had something to tell me—
something compelling enough to get my attention.

What else could it have been.

What I do remember is that as you drove us home you
were pretending not to cry.

Don't cry, Nora, I said.

Do you know my birthday, Francis?

June 15, I said.

I found your car keys, you said.

I shoved them back into my pocket. *When did you go
find them?*

You sniffed. *I have the same birthday as Wade Boggs
and Sam Giancana.*

I dried the tear trails on your cheek. *I know this
changes everything, but I still want to be with you, Nora.*

I know, you said flatly.

The sidewalks were clogged, the traffic apocalyptic,
though the clock on the dash said it was close to three. A
guy in a Groucho Marx costume darted in front of the car.
Fuck! you shouted, flattening the brake pedal. You leaned
back, eyes wide. *That asshole!*

It's okay, I said.

That fucking Groucho! you hollered, starting to laugh.
You wiped your nose with the back of your wrist.

I put my hand on your leg. *You know who was born
on my birthday?*

Yeah, you said, *I looked you up too. Thurman Munson,
for one. God, I can't believe he just ran out in front of me
like that! And Tom Jones. But you know who the best one
is? Seriously, you're so lucky.*

Who? I said.

Dino. Dean Martin!

I guess I am pretty lucky. I emitted a clenching little laugh. *I'm about the luckiest guy I know.*

Your face went dark. We turned onto your unlit street. *On the day you were born,* you said, *they opened Graceland to the public.*

Can you see the bathroom where he died? I said.

You pulled into the driveway and shut off the headlights. *That's the one thing they won't show you.*

You had left the heater on in the house and the place was scorching. *We're in the desert,* you said. *We're sub-Saharan in here.*

I blasted the air-conditioning, calling over my shoulder, *We'll make it freezing and it'll even out.*

I'm right here, you said, from behind me. I jumped. You put your arms around my middle, resting your head on my back. I held you in a backward hug, and then turned to kiss the bony part of your cheek. You didn't look me in the face. You were looking at my body.

I'll probably be a disappointment, I said.

I'm kind of a virgin, you said.

A beat passed. *Then I'll definitely be a disappointment.*

Maybe not. I have no frame of reference.

What about Greg Linderhoefer? Or that guy with the hackey sack, what was his name, from Palo Alto—

Everything but, you said.

I rested my chin on your head. The thermostat finally kicked over to cool, a frigid breeze rushing through the vent at our feet. *I anticipate freaking out,* I said.

You looked at our shoes. *Ditto.*
The Everything But Girl. We hate you, you know.
You pinched me and said, *You won't.*

I remember, from above you, my fingers grazing your
stomach. I had lifted your top, soft as tissue, laying it
on your rib cage. I said, *Your skin is so soft.* I said it with
incredulity, as though nothing had ever been that soft: as
though it were an illusion. We were still clothed. You said,
I won't turn you down, the tendons in your hand taut as
you gripped the mattress edge. I said, *I don't know if we
should.* I was afraid for a million reasons. I said, *I'm afraid
for a million reasons.* I stretched out beside you and lifted
the elastic lip of your blue panties. My wristwatch caught
against the stiff waistband of your jeans. Your hips were
moving against my forearm. You whispered something
and I stopped to hear it, saying, *What, I couldn't hear?*
You said, smiling, *I said 'Don't stop.'* I stopped, to put a
finger in my mouth. I said into your shoulder, *I want to
be inside you,* repeating it like a prayer. Everything felt
inevitable: prefabricated, like the cosmos had snatched us
by our necks and dropped us there. I said, *I just want . . .*
but couldn't finish my sentence. I thought, I wouldn't
even need to move. I would be inside you, not moving,
and I would bury my face in your neck and hide. *Are you
going to take your glasses off?* you said, smiling. I was suddenly immobile. I could no longer make my arms move,
my fingers. You said, *Don't think about anything else.* You
said, *Where are you? Stay with me.* But I could only think
about everything else. *I won't turn you down,* you said
again, as the moment slipped through our hands.

I woke up in my clothes. On the opposite wall was a seascape in a filigreed frame. Where the larger waves crested there was a concentration of pale yellow, reflecting an absent sun. But the tips of the whitecaps were hypoxic, icy blue, as though the scene were between day and dark, lit simultaneously by sun and moonlight. Your head crushed my bicep, the hard part of your jaw pressing the skin. You were half-naked in your parents' bed. I willed you to open your eyes. When you did you pawed at your puffy face and grabbed my wrist. It took you a while to tell the time on my watch.

You sat up, covering yourself with an arm. *I guess City Hall is where you go to do this, right?*

I leaned against the headboard. *You're serious.*

I'm always serious.

Tell me why you want to marry me. Give me one good reason.

You pulled your arm away, baring your body.

When you go through a tollbooth, you turn off your stereo so you don't bother the attendant.

I squinted. *Do I?* I said.

You listen to me, you said.

I can't help it, I said. *I'm captivated by what you say.*

Pretend for a moment that we don't get married. Pretend we decide—you stood up, putting on your underwear—*that this isn't a good idea; that we shouldn't be together.* You scanned the floor for clothes. *We break up and it's over, we're not friends anymore. I can't do that.*

No matter what happens, I said, *I will never not know you.*

You stepped into your pants. *That's an impossible promise.*

Maybe. No, you know what? I'm telling you, it's not.

The pitch of your voice rose. *Do you really think we'll find people we like better?*

This is totally illogical, I said.

Answer anyway.

I buried my face in a pillow. *Whose side of the bed was this? Your mom's?*

My dad's, you said.

No, I said into the pillow. *I'll never like anybody as much.*

As I lifted my face, you bent down and found your shirt, your hair falling over your eyes. You began to put the shirt over your head, your face hidden inside it as you said, *Put your shoes on.* You straightened up, smoothed your clothes, and pushed in the pockets of your jeans. *Put your shoes on if you want to marry me.*

The sun outside was cheerful, bracing. We were on Van Ness, City Hall in dead sight, when you said, *I don't know about this, Francis.*

I braked at a stop sign and closed my eyes, pausing long enough for the cars to begin honking behind us.

Go, Francis, you said. *What're you doing?*

I panicked, putting the car in park. *I don't care,* I said. *I don't care about Greta. Who knows if she's even pregnant? She could be lying. I want to marry you. Okay? People can get married when they're twenty-two.*

You glanced at the swearing drivers behind us.

She could be lying, I said. *She could be full of shit.*

I'm just saying I don't want to get married here, you said. *Because of Harvey Milk.* You pointed toward the ridged rotunda, the severe, spiked steeple. *I just remembered he died in there. And Moscone. I can't get married in there.*

A car pulled past us. *Asshole!* the driver shouted.

I smiled, relieved. I knew what I wanted, and it was what you wanted, and the day felt young. I hit the gas and flipped a U-turn in the intersection, a crescendo of horns rising like trumpets, heralding our good news.

11

I became aware of my wedding ring, silver and real on the hand holding the steering wheel, somewhere in Nevada. I could turn back now and still be able to explain, I thought. My suitcase contained no photographs, no mementos. I had brought only clothing, a toothbrush, and the meager contents of my wallet. The finer bureaucratic concerns—my birth certificate, past tax returns, account numbers—were left behind. Fuck them: they had brought me only grief. The silver pocket watch Greta had given me on our wedding day I had placed on the bureau we shared. I left no note. Carrying the suitcase, I had crept through our bedroom that morning, stepping toward my worn white car. Greta had been up early. I had come home the night before, had attempted an apology she was wise to ignore. When I left she was standing in the shower, eight to ten hours away from the moment, I imagine, that she began to worry—or, more probably, that she cursed my name, understanding what I had done.

But that time hadn't come yet; she was still at work. Somewhere after Lovelock, but before Elko, I glanced at the glimmering point of afternoon sunlight that the ring shot onto the ceiling of the car and thought, If I go back now, I can still save the situation. I could say I had stayed late at school, that I had gone to a movie by myself. I could say anything, because anything was better than this.

Two days later, I had stopped only to piss and gas up and rest my sore eyes while parked in parking lots. I was indifferent to food. My hands and arms had grown pink and sweat-slick from the burning air through the open windows. I had driven east on I-80 from Vallejo, moving beyond the pocked asphalt of the Bay Area, through California's mountainous edge, winding through cleared forest as the incline increased and receded. Directions were unnecessary. East was all I needed to know. I would keep going until the road ended. In Nevada, the ground beside the flattened spine of highway became an orange-brown sea, sunflowers sprouting beside the road, salamanders darting beneath my tires. In Utah, the dirt turned white. In Wyoming, the earth rose in ominous, pale green stalagmites, like the surface of a distant planet. And then, in Nebraska, the terrain morphed into quilt-squares of green, punctuated by oblong blue lakes.

The smoke began as formless wisps, escaping from the car like ghosts in fast-forward. When the smoke turned black, I pulled off the interstate. In Chappell, Nebraska, I lifted the hood beneath an abandoned station's stories-high

Texaco sign. A surprise tongue of flame licked my wrist before the fire retreated under the engine's maze. I held the burn in confusion before running to the trunk to get a gallon jug, dousing the engine and the wound, spilling water everywhere. I pulled my suitcase from the rear of the car and stared at the manic hum of the highway, heaving, my pants soaked.

The wooden pole of the Texaco sign looked rotten, like a dead tree. Beside it, bizarrely close to the gas station, was an ancient white farmhouse. I saw through the windowpanes, the glass wobbly with age, that it was empty. There was a small wooden sign, handwritten: WWII BOMBER CRASH SITE, TWO MILES, with an arrow pointing to a deserted field.

The two miles took me a half hour to walk in the May heat. The dirt path ran up and down small hills, curving through fields of dead grass. Tan gravel flitted into my shoes. Touching the blistering burn on my wrist, I thought about the car. I wondered if, when I returned, it would be in flames again. I imagined the whole thing enveloped, the white paint bubbling, alighting in weightless curls.

The crash site emerged when I turned a corner: ten PVC-pipe crosses in a semicircle, lashed together with metallic twine. Power lines droned overhead. There was a plaque: DURING A THUNDERSTORM B-24J #44-40758 CAUGHT FIRE, DESCENDED TO 500 FEET, AND BEGAN CIRCLING THE TOWN OF CHAPPELL, NEBRASKA, WHEN IT EXPLODED. ALL PERSONNEL ABOARD WERE KILLED INSTANTLY.

The flight had originated in Lincoln, three hundred miles away. But I pictured the airmen in their small-town homes, waiting weeks to be deployed, suppressing fears of an enemy with ready guns. I imagined their legal wills being drawn in the sweaty office of the town's only notary. And then, before their trepidation could fully mature: dying here, in an innocuous field like the ones in which they had played as children.

The plaque listed the date they fell from the sky as June 7, 1944. My birthday, less thirty-eight years. I sat down on my suitcase. There was nothing else in that field, nothing else anywhere I could see—a fence in the dead grass along the highway, some hills, cows. I breathed so deeply it stung, and emptied my shoes of rocks.

I walked the two miles back, soaked with sweat. The white car sat silent and extinguished. I considered trying to start the engine, continuing on my way. But the air still possessed the caustic smell of dangerous heat. South of the abandoned station were only dirt roads; to the north, across the highway, was a small lake and the outer edges of a town: Chappell proper, I guessed. It was about a hundred yards away. I crossed the overpass beneath an enormous sky. On the shore of the moss-green lake was a brown-brick building with a mural of a cartoon family eating at a picnic table. The words LAKE CHAPPELL were painted across it in primary-colored bubble letters. The building housed bathroom stalls and a sink, like the cement structures at rest stops that, during this frenzied drive, I had learned to watch for. I held the angry burn under the tap, the sting diminishing. I washed my hands with the pink soap from the dispenser on the wall and splashed water over my neck. The stream ran cloudy as it fell into the sink.

Outside the bathrooms was a more formal memorial to the ten men—this one made of stone, surrounded by a log-fenced parking lot. It said their names and where they had been from. Peculiar, MO, Waynesboro, MS, Cranford, NJ. I read on: I had been wrong—they weren't on their way to face the enemy in Germany or Japan. At least not yet. They were on their way to the West Coast. Maybe they weren't ever supposed to go abroad. Maybe they were going to fix tanks and hammer in rivets. Mammoth Springs, AK, Camilla, GA, Stromsburg, NE. Maybe they were going to spend the rest of the war in Portland, Seattle, San Francisco. I touched the carved stone with a grimy fingertip. Anadarko, OK, Rochester, NY, Oneonta, NY. And the last: New York, NY.

I examined the contents of my wallet: $467, withdrawn from our checking account. I had left Greta with nothing but the tips in her purse. No car fire I ever heard of was remedied with $467. I was stranded. I felt a curious absence of panic.

I walked back to the Texaco station, but didn't stop. I strode through the grove of elm trees that guarded the wraparound porch, right up to the steps of the grand white farmhouse. I leaned my suitcase against the screen door and walked around to the rear entrance.

I stopped, taking in the yellow tape with which someone had fashioned a wide X. CAUTION, it read. DO NOT ENTER. The tape, loose and faded, wafted in the occasional breeze, attached to the pillars of the back porch. The entire rear of the house had burned.

Behind the tape was a gaping hole in the wooden planks of the house—it looked as though the fire had exploded outward, ripping open the back wall, errant flames snaking up to the second story. The black exterior of the house hung in clumps, like hair pulled from a scalp. Long pieces of charred lumber, the wood grain split and corroded by flame, dangled from the level above. I ducked beneath the tape and leaned against the outer border of the flame's reach, where the paint was still white. I sniffed the wood; the smell of scorch remained. I touched a blackened board, the tip of my index finger shining with a bitter smear of gray.

I stepped into the house through the open hole, my feet crunching over black silt, into what had been the kitchen. The fire hadn't extended to the front of the house, where there was a dining area and a sun-soaked room with a faceted bay window. But the smoke had turned all the interior walls the uneven yellow of a textured al fresco. Where pictures had hung were rectangular white ghosts. The floors were littered with leaves and twigs. Birds flew just beneath the ceiling, bobbing like they were pulled on strings, bouncing up the staircase to the second story.

I figured the bedrooms were up there. I climbed the creaking stairs slowly, carefully. I knew they could crumble. I entered the room at the far end of the hall: the master bedroom. Because it sat above the kitchen—clearly the source of the blaze—it had sustained damage, including a blown-out window. The wooden window frame remained. I stepped into the room and heard the floorboards creak; I jumped back from the sound as though from a growling dog.

Beneath the singed windowsill was a scatter of papers. Before I could tell them not to, my legs moved forward on that gritty black floor and I knelt and scooped the papers up. The knees of my pants stained instantly in the soot. I held the wordless pages in my hands, their meanings obscured by smoke damage. In the stillness of the place was the remnant of frenetic terror: someone had lived here, someone had left here—quickly, and afraid.

The back of the house faced the fields beyond the back porch—toward the ten crosses in the distance, hidden behind that small hill. I looked out the window, sure that in an instant the floor would give way, and saw hundreds of shards of glass, blown as far as a dozen feet away by the blast. The sun illuminated their random constellations, hidden among the golden weeds. The house groaned again, and I clutched the gray papers to my chest as I ran down the stairs and out the front door. I gasped for breath on the porch. My suitcase was where I had left it, next to the door—as though someone had come home, so excited to arrive he had tossed the suitcase aside, running toward the open arms he had missed.

I sat on the porch steps. My burned wrist screamed. I looked down: the papers in my hands had disintegrated. I was nowhere, and it was nowhere I had ever been.

. . .

I stayed. I fashioned a bed out of my own clothing in a corner of the sunlit front room, the longest distance possible from the burned-out kitchen, figuring this area was more structurally sound. The first two days, I woke each morning to walk across the overpass, the interstate assured and purposeful beneath my feet. I sat by the lake or walked around town. There was a bar, a bank, a red-brick post office, a barbershop, a small Mexican restaurant, a mechanic, a hobby shop, a scattering of homes, a high school, and a tiny general store that sold no produce. I guessed that people had to leave town to buy fruits and vegetables, or grow their own. At the edge of Chappell, a row of enormous silos kept watch over large and mysterious machinery. Beyond the silos were fields and fields of green and yellow.

On the first Sunday, I sat in the Methodist church on Babcock Street, closing my eyes to listen to the rhythm of the speech. And then it was time to stand and sing, and I picked up the hymnal in front of me to sing five verses of a song everyone there seemed to know. *Reveal thyself before my closing eyes. Shine through the gloom, and point me to the skies.* The organist finished, the congregation closed the books and dispersed onto the lawn for punch. I walked back to the farmhouse, the hymn stuck in my head—*In life and death, O Lord, abide with me.*

I walked. I visited the crash site often, to sit in silence or sing songs aloud. *Fish and chips and vinegar, vinegar, vinegar.* I walked parallel to the interstate for ten miles, where not much was different, and walked back. I walked to town and from the bleachers watched the high school's baseball team defeat the nearby town's. *Shut him down,* the crowd would yell to the pitcher. *Put him back in that dugout!* The first few days, I ate at the bar: salted nuts, fried shrimp. The bathroom there was bizarre—two toilets side by side, no partition. On the wall above the sink was a novelty Halloween postcard featuring a gargantuan naked ass; on it was painted a jack-o'-lantern. I locked the door and washed my underarms and crotch in the sink. I walked to the edge of town, watched men manipulate the strange equipment by the silos. At night, in the burned house, I would count my money and try not to think. On the fourth day I used the payphone outside the post office to call Greta. She picked up, said nothing. We listened to each other breathe a moment, and then I hung up. I walked to the bus stop and waited. No bus ever came. I walked around the neighborhoods, waving at the old women tending to their tomatoes and begonias. Some of them waved back. At the general store I purchased a notebook and a small pack of plastic pens. I took them wherever I went—always armed, ready to document something, anything. I never wrote a word. Every time I spent money, I felt my bowels quiver. The cash was going to run out. This couldn't go on forever. I could feel the desperation creeping toward me like an advancing enemy.

On the fifth day I called Greta again. I wanted to hear her voice. I let it ring and ring, the answering machine evidently turned off. Until finally, three or five or I don't know how many minutes into the call, she answered.

Hello? Hello?

I looked over my shoulder at the deserted main street. A young woman stared back, before pushing her stroller onward.

I'm sorry, Greta.
You've lost your job.
I assumed, I said. *They called you?*
I'm surprised you're calling here.

I closed my eyes and saw the firm contour of Greta's naked hip, the way her mouth opened as she put on lipstick. I heard her lilting laugh. I thought of her fingers, years earlier, touching the welt on my neck.

I think about you all the time, I said. It was almost true—it was true with one degree of separation: I often thought about how hard it was to think of her.

Well, I said. *Okay then.* And I hung up.

My burn peeled, oozed, and settled into a borderless hillock of scar tissue. My car grew a brown hide of dust. At night, I watched raccoons and skunks through the window—scurrying about the porch, leaving with nothing. I anticipated them coming through the hole in the back wall someday, but if they did I never knew about it. Maybe they smelled me and left. They had probably explored the house long before. Too scared to spend more money on food, I ate what I found in the burned kitchen—cans of peas with seared black labels, cans of other things without labels at all. I opened them, laboriously, with a butter knife I found in a drawer. In the pantry was a box of Saltines; the fire had fused the plastic wrapping to the crackers. Plastic utensils were melted into the counter, and a deep red stain in the floor had me spooked until I noticed the broken, scorched ketchup bottle nearby. Every time I scavenged food, I ran from the kitchen as if at any moment the ceiling would come down on top of me—as though the rest of the house were safe. I realize now the whole thing could have collapsed at any moment.

A few days after I arrived, I walked into the barbershop. Inside was a man whose own hair had long since departed. *Can I work here?* I said to him, my words sudden, barely planned—after so many days of silence my own voice was unfamiliar.

He wagged a straight razor through some kind of solvent in a mason jar. *Can you, or may you?* he said, winking.

It was an unexpected relief, being spoken to like a child.

May I work here?

He looked at my clothing, his smile faltering. I shifted my feet, holding the burned place on my wrist.

I could use some help, he said.

His name was Martin. He asked me to sweep the cut hair into piles and then empty the metal dustpan into a burlap sack in a shed out back. What he did with the hair I never knew. Each day I walked from the burned house to the barbershop, rising early to cover the few miles before the sun fully awoke. The May breeze was more forgiving in the hours before noon, and sometimes I closed my eyes and listened to the distant whir of the tractors in the fields. Martin opened up shop seven days a week at nine o'clock exactly, a bell trembling in the doorjamb. When no customers came for a haircut or a shave, I swept anyway. *You'll run a broom-shaped groove into my floor, son,* Martin said, chuckling. Other times I sat in his back office and organized his desk, which was already tidy and probably had never been used anyway. My fifth day working for Martin, without looking me in the eye, he passed me a razor and a baby food jar filled with shaving cream. That night, small clumps of my beard fell into the bar's bathroom sink like miniature rodents. Sometimes I washed the shop's windows, or wiped down the vinyl barber chairs. In the evenings, staring up the staircase of the burned house, I would think of ways to keep busy at

Martin's; I refused to stand idle. Every day, Martin gave me a five-dollar bill at six o'clock and said, *Here you are, son.* He never called me anything but son. I would thank him and, calling good night over my shoulder, step into the orange dusk. Some days I would head to the pay phone beside the post office, ready to call home. And then I would change my mind, the receiver still in my hand, the moment gone.

I always brought a change of clothes with me to the barbershop. When I left, I would stop at the lake to bathe. I hid behind the willow branches that dangled above the thick skin of the water, closing my eyes and floating naked on my back. I washed my sweat-soaked clothes in the water and changed into the fresh garments, sitting on the same damp rock at the water's edge. My clothes had a green cast from the algae of the lake. I smelled faintly of mold.

Three weeks passed this way—and they passed so quickly I marvel thinking of it now. I marvel to think of that time at all, really. Every morning, I awoke in groggy misery: the familiar pain, the default terror. The existence I had grown so accustomed to. Resentments and regrets and the certainty that I wasn't good enough. And then my eyes would adjust to the light, and I would watch a small bird dart overhead, and I would snap back into the present— remembering where and who I was, remembering that I had left all of that behind. And the pain would lift. It was the most peaceful time of my life.

On the first day of June, I showed up to the lake one day and found it surrounded. *What's all this?* I asked somebody. *Fishing derby,* the man said, adjusting his ball cap. So that night I bathed beside the burned house, in the stream of a garden hose; the metallic taste of its water was like a portal to childhood.

At the barbershop, an old man named Dale was a regular. He came in almost every day, to sit in one of the boosted chairs—there were two, though Martin was the only barber—and speak slowly and carefully about the high school football team, bird watching at Lake McConaughy, the thirty miles he drove each week to the Wal-Mart in Sidney. He rocked as he spoke, nodding in time like a bobbing oil derrick. He brought his grandson each Wednesday—a small, sullen boy named Peter, no older than seven. When Martin and Dale got to talking, Peter would slink to the shed behind the shop; there, a child going off without disclosing a destination went unnoticed by adults.

One afternoon, he was in the shed when I went to empty my dustpan. Outside, the air was stiff with pollen and dust. I knocked at the shed door, and Peter's tiny voice came back muffled: *Come in.*

I entered. Light came in through the burl holes in the wood planks and a small window. The shed was about ten by six, and though I brought discarded hair there each day, I had never stopped to look around closely: two lawn chairs sat unfolded in the center, and tin Coca Cola signs were nailed to the unfinished walls. Beneath the usual gardening implements, hung on hooks, were plastic tubs, their lids open, full of cheap baseball cards, jacks, Ping-Pong balls—a sea of little boy curios, clearly forgotten: astride one ballplayer's face were hairy black corpuscles of mold.

Are you hiding? I said.

Peter shook his head no.

It's pretty dark in here. You're not scared of the dark?
No, he said.

He looked up at me expectantly, waiting to be commended for his bravery.

I wanted to commend him. But instead I emptied the hair into the sack and said nothing, keeping the door slightly ajar behind me when I left.

■ ■ ■

About a week into June, Martin turned on the radio. *Thought I'd listen for the weather report,* he said.

I glanced outside. *It's sunny every day here.*

They'll announce visibility, Martin said. *Tomorrow's gun day.*

What's gun day?

In June of '44, Dale began, *a plane on its way out west caught on fire in the sky . . .*

I set the broom against the sink. *I know the story,* I said. *I've seen the crosses.*

Martin adjusted the radio dial. *My second cousin was on that plane.*

Martin's from Stromsburg, Dale said. *About three hundred miles out.*

Vance C. Johnson, I said. *Stromsburg, Nebraska. I've seen the marker a dozen times.*

Martin looked up from the radio. *He was my second cousin. A few years older than me, only eighteen when he died.*

Stromsburg's off of I-80 too, out toward York, Dale said.

Can you do without the five dollars tomorrow, if I pack you a lunch? Martin said to me.

Dale looked at his hands.

I can, I said.

Every year on the anniversary of the crash, Martin shot the twenty-one gun salute in the fields south of the burned house. *I'd do it at the crash site, but Miller's got his livestock out there,* he said. He had asked me where I lived, and when I didn't answer fast enough he offered to pick me up the next morning outside the barbershop. I don't know what he thought, exactly, but I could guess. The nearest town was miles away, even smaller than Chappell. They were the only two towns in the county. Maybe he thought I was a hitchhiker. I'm sure whatever he thought, he knew I had come in from the highway. To get to the field we passed the abandoned Texaco station, and I cursed silently as I saw my car parked in the lot—its California license plate, its grimy exterior. But if Martin noticed it, or believed it to be mine, he said nothing.

Do you bring someone with you every year? I asked him as we parked. He had four guns secured in the truck— two handguns, a thick shotgun, a spindly rifle.

No, he said amiably. *I fire all twenty-one rounds alone.*

Also in the back of the truck was a big wooden crate full of junk—orange plastic detergent bottles, a semi-deflated basketball, a half-dozen gallon jugs of water.

Dale doesn't come with you?

Martin pulled out a triangular-folded American flag, nestled in a wooden case, from the cab of the pickup. *He's got arthur-itis. The kickback hurts the joints.* He unfolded the flag. On the starred end were two metal eyelets, and he fitted them over two nails he had hammered into the wooden cage attached to the truck bed. *We'll start with the Luger.*

I stared at the small arsenal. *Which?*

He peered at me. *Your daddy didn't teach you how to shoot?*

No, sir, I said.

He waited a moment for an explanation. When he saw that none was coming, he pointed at a thin-nosed pistol. *That one there's the Luger.*

I picked up the gun like any second it would turn on me. I held it out to him, anxious.

Good boy, he said. *Every firearm ought to be treated with respect.*

Okay, I said.

Say it—every gun's a loaded gun, Martin said, loading it. He handed it back to me.

I took it, the textured grip rough against my palm. *Every gun's a loaded gun.*

Good boy, he said again.

Wielding a deadly power wasn't something I thought I could get used to. And then I did. Because after a moment, shooting that gun just felt good. Everything I had ever felt about the idea—the associations most city kids carry—melted away. I had no idea how many bullets the thing held and didn't keep track as I fired, so I would just keep going until Martin stopped me to reload. I slipped into an unmediated state, one without running commentary, pulling the trigger again and again. It wasn't bloodlust; it wasn't Freudian. It was just something I had never done before. And I was doing it in a place I had never been, with a person I didn't know. I closed my eyes and pulled the trigger, thinking, What would I be doing right now, in my other life?

Let's count off the twenty-one, Martin said.

Taking turns, we fired ten shots each in succession, aiming toward a lanky cottonwood tree. I had the Luger and Martin shot the air rifle; sound-wise, mine made a blast and his made a crack.

How's it feel? he said. *Accurate, that one is.*

I wasn't aiming at anything, I said.

Well, he said. *The Luger is a fine gun.* He began reloading the rifle: sliding the ammunition inside it, the gun bent in half. He straightened it with a resounding snap and looked through the sight. *One more shot left,* he said. *That'll make twenty-one.* He paused, changing his mind, and stepped toward the truck bed. He set the rifle down and returned with another weapon, nearly as thick as my arm. He held it up to me. *This is a Remington 870 Wingmaster twelve-gauge pump-action shotgun,* he said, like he was introducing a friend at a party.

Holy shit, I said.

Martin squinted into the distance. *We ought to watch our language.* He held up a shell the width of my thumb. *In honor of the day.*

Something inside me ached. *I'm sorry.*

He shook his head. *You didn't mean anything by it.*

I took the shotgun in my hands. *It weighs a ton.*

Go on, he said. *You take the last shot.*

Martin, you should be the one to—

You go ahead, he said, smiling faintly. *Finish the salute.*

I lifted the shotgun, wedging the stock in the groove of my armpit, the vinyl flag flapping sluggishly against the truck's cab. I listened to myself breathe. Every second I didn't shoot I grew more apprehensive. I knew what kind of power I was holding. The sound, the force it was going to send through my body. I was scared.

You've got this, son, Martin whispered. *You've been shootin' like a pro all—*

But I cut off that last word, pulling the trigger the second I felt able. The birdshot went who knows where—we weren't close enough to any target to note a result—but what stayed behind was the cracking recoil. Martin took the gun, and I clutched at my bruised flesh.

Jumped back and bit you, did it?

I lifted my shirt over my head and looked down: blood vessels had broken in red, pointillistic bursts beneath the skin. It looked as though I had been misted in the armpit with a paint sprayer.

Martin lifted the shotgun, resting it on his shoulder so the barrel pointed skyward. He turned to the flag hanging from the truck, raised his arm, and held a hand to his temple in salute.

My shirt was on the yellowed ground, but I stood straight and saluted too. That was when I finally made the connection. *It's the seventh?* I asked him, our hands still poised at our heads. *Today's the anniversary of the crash?*

He nodded.

It's my birthday. I'm twenty-four years old today.

He lowered his arm after a moment and went into the truck, returning with three peanut butter sandwiches wrapped in wax paper. *Happy birthday,* he said, holding two of them out to me.

Then we pulled that junk out of the wood crate in the truck and shot at it. The other handgun was a gleaming .357 Magnum revolver, and I stuck with that for the rest of the day. When Martin hit the basketball it jumped an inch into the air, and then he lay down on his belly to shoot at a gigantic empty bottle of Tide. He set out those five jugs full of water with a big grin. And sure enough, when I finally did hit one—my last shot of the day, the first with any measure of accuracy—the water gushed forth in a translucent stream of victory.

Not bad at all, Martin said, patting me on the back. *You'll be sore tomorrow*—he motioned toward my arm— *in the wrist and such. Take the day off.* He held out a ten-dollar bill.

I wanted to tell him, *There's no need, you've done enough. Please, Martin, you've already been so kind.* But I said nothing. I reached out and took the money, folding it into my pocket.

I retrieved the massacred detergent bottles and plastic jugs, and when I turned to walk back I saw the brass peppering the dirt—our spent shells. Martin came out from the cab with a big plastic bucket. He set it down and began bending to pick them up, bracing himself with a hand on his knee. *Martin,* I said. *Let me do that.*

Alright, he said, settling on the tailgate.

The bucket was soon full. *How many years have you shot the salute?*

A while now. Forty or more.

Don't you have a son, a grandson, anybody to come along?

Robert lives in Lincoln, he said. He pulled his eyeglasses from his face, polishing them with a handkerchief. *And Vance lives in Des Moines.*

Do you see them often?

Christmas, he said.

Do you miss them?

Sure, he said pleasantly. *When did you see your family last?*

I looked out at the fields. *You barely know me. You don't know me from Adam and you took me out in the fields and handed me a gun.*

He waved his hand. *I can tell about people,* he said. *And you seem like a fine boy to me.*

• • •

The next morning, I woke to a creaking on the burned house's pine floor. A small boy stood over me, his figure blotting the hexagonal window's streaming sunlight. It was Peter, Dale's grandson.

You live here? he said.

I sat straight up. *Peter?*

I'm seven. How old are you?

I looked out the window, my heart in my throat.

Where's your granddad? I said, half shouting.

Ain't here. I rode my bike.

I looked out the screen door behind Peter. Scuffed handlebars leaned against the steps like plastic antlers. *I used to have a bike like that,* I told him, my pulse slowing.

His expression shifted abruptly, narrowing in sudden suspicion. *Don't you have your own house?* His face was a sunburned knot. *Don't you got a wife and kids?*

Outside, the sugary contents of a spilled drink lay in a vivid red puddle near the porch steps.

Yes, I said. I leaned back on my palms, the grit on the wood floor piercing my hands.

Where's your kids at?

At home, I said, hesitating. I pictured Greta's soft and indelible face. *With their mom.*

How old are they?

I shook my head.

They could come here and play with me, he said. *Sometimes I play store.*

What kind of store?

Groceries, he said. *You use leaves as money.* He pointed toward the highway. *Your kids ever swim in the lake?*

I glanced out the window. *No,* I said.

I thought of the bay. The wet air; the ringed white salt stains on the boulders just beyond the shore. I remembered digging for hours there as a kid, compiling whole indexes of green, smooth rocks, and pulling the legs off the ghostly white crabs, and listening to the bass thud of the roiling surf.

He smiled nervously, suddenly shy, and took a step backward. *I ain't supposed to talk to strangers,* he said, his face twisting. *You a stranger? I only seen you once or twice.*

A summer wind pelted the side of the house with dirt. I thought about how to answer. Would I let one of my students talk to me? Some homeless drifter? And yet—I knew Dale, didn't I?

No, Peter, I said finally. *I'm not a stranger.*

He brightened. *Good,* he said. *Could we go into town so you could buy me a candy bar?*

As we walked along the overpass, crossing the highway, Peter slowed his bike to match my pace.

Where does your dad work? I asked him.

I don't know, he said.

What about your mom?

She's a nurse.

Do you have any brothers and sisters?

Yeah, he said. That was the end of his sentence. I smiled.

At the general store, Peter clattered his bike to the ground—no lock necessary—and made a beeline for the candy display.

What's your favorite one? I asked him.

Look! he said.

Oh, I hate those, I said.

They hurt your teeth, Peter said, giddy.

I'm a Kit Kat man, I said.

Can I get two? he said, bracing for me to disapprove.

Sure thing, I said.

He grabbed two Look! bars.

Don't you want two different ones? I said.

He looked up, his brow knitted. *What for?* he said.

We were walking toward the checkout line when Dale came up from behind.

Pete, he barked. *Goddammit, Peter, get over here.*

What? Peter said, genuinely shocked.

What the hell is this? Dale said, looking at me.

I was out for a walk, I said, *and I ran into Peter.*

Peter looked up at me. *No you wasn't.* He turned to Dale. *He was sleeping in that burnt-up house by the gas place.*

Dale's eyes went wide.

I asked him for a candy and he said I could have two. I can have two, right?

Dale took Peter's hand, gripping it with both of his. *You don't even know his name,* he growled at the boy. *I don't even know it.*

The checkout girl stared up at us.

Look, Dale, I said. *It's not like I've never met the kid.* He stared at me coldly.

It's not like I would ever hurt—

I choked on the words midsentence. It's not like I would ever hurt a child, I had almost said.

I set the candy bars on the counter. Dale looked down at them, confused. I walked toward the door, then paused and turned around.

I'm sorry, I said. *I didn't mean to cause any harm.* I left the store and began walking toward the burned house—toward what had become my home, toward the place where I could no longer stay.

My life in Chappell had pressed a reset button. My most basic assurances—that I was a man with a wife, with bills to pay, with a job and a requisite middle-class trajectory— had ruptured. Who was I, anymore, but the owner of a small white car, with so many of Martin's dollars in his wallet? I started to run, my ankles aching with each step, each shock of pavement. The noise had quieted. The situation was reframed. The answers were in the questions I hadn't asked—and I had asked so few; my God, how long I had gone without asking anything of my days, emptily performing them as though they were inexhaustible. I bit my lip, losing my breath, thinking the thoughts I had tried to push down—*You ignore everything you don't want to see*—since I had left California: my wife, coming home to an empty house each night. The girl I had loved, so completely and utterly gone. Edmund—wherever he was, whoever he was with—robbed of a vital chunk of his trust.

I was, it had suddenly become clear, a career asker of the wrong questions. A man with limited foresight. A man with infinite hindsight. A man whose fingers fingered two quarters in his pocket.

I slowed my pace as I reached the pay phone outside the brick post office.

As Buckingham's extension rang, I spun the grimy phone book on the end of its chain tether. The air smelled like heat.

How long, I asked myself, did I want to run?

Besides the notebook, pens, a deeply discounted haircut from Martin, and those early, misguided meals, some money had gone to toothpaste and soap, a muffin, a deck of cards, a lone can of beer. Nothing that wasn't disposable, nothing I would keep. But with the money I had brought with me and the money I had earned—how I hesitate to phrase it that way—I walked to Chappell's lone mechanic's shop. He drove us in silence to the old Texaco station, lifted the hood of my car, and began to tinker. I knew the effort was useless: I would have nowhere near enough money to make whatever repair he suggested.

I saw him eye the car's stratified filth. *You say she just broke down today?*

Yeah, I said.

I'd tow her, he said, *but the tow truck's in the shop. You believe that!* He reached out to slap me on the shoulder for emphasis, but I didn't respond. *No matter,* he said, unnerved. He did some maneuvering near the engine—I couldn't tell you what he touched, where he looked, if I tried. *You say it caught fire when you were drivin'?*

Right, I said.

Well there's six flammable liquids under the hood, he said. *Did it smell real bad?*

It didn't smell good.

Was the smoke real thick and black, or was it more gray and thin?

I don't know, really. Black. Can't you tell where it was on fire?

Well, yes I can, sir . . . it ain't near any of the fluid lines. He ducked under, grimacing. *I'll tell you what happened. You got some grass or some dirt up in there, and it heated up on the engine, looks like. You say you put it out with water?*

That's right.

Well, that took care of it, looks like.

Are you fucking kidding me?

He grimaced: a response to my profanity. *Yes sir,* he said, though he was roughly thirty years older than me.

It's been fine this entire time?

Well, I don't see any other problem here, except this dent. Somebody T-bone you?

229

He jump-started the battery, charged me eighteen dollars for his time, writing up a small invoice on a pad of carbon paper, and then clattered away in the pickup. I put the brown leather suitcase into the backseat. The engine turned over without incident, as though I had imagined it all—the smoke, the fire—as though four minutes had passed instead of four weeks. I had almost three quarters of a tank left. I scraped the wipers over the windshield's layer of dust. I didn't revisit the lake, the barbershop, the hatched crosses. I rolled down my windows, turned on the radio, and made my way to I-80's on-ramp.

Hours later, I let myself think of Martin. I imagined him opening the door at nine o'clock to find me absent. I imagined him looking up and down the street for me. And I hoped he had just put the broom back in its closet, going about his business without further thought. I hoped that he forgot me that very second, that he never thought of me again. I hoped—for his sake, and for the sake of a few others—that I was easy to forget.

12

We'll need witnesses, you said, so we headed north. In your car, as I drove, you rifled through your purse. *I have my birth certificate—are you sure she has yours?*

Yeah, I said, glancing over my shoulder to change lanes.

I haven't seen your mom in a long time, you said.

Do you really want her there? Maybe we can call—I don't know, is there someone else we can call?

Why, you think she'll freak out?

My mom liked what it said about her son that his best friend was a girl. She liked how you said please and thank you. She liked how your parents sent Christmas cards and invited her to Memorial Day barbeques she never went to.

She'll be happy, I said, pretty sure it was true. Knowing that even if it wasn't, she would keep her mouth shut. And she would be happy to see me, regardless of my news. I hadn't spoken to her in months.

We pulled into her cul-de-sac, at the end of a row of identical one-story subdivision houses. It was a Monday morning but she was home—to an Avon lady, a day of work means someone sitting on your couch applying used lipstick samples. I rolled down my window and let the engine idle, staring at the wide ass of her SUV.

How long are we going to sit here? you said.

Through her open curtains I saw her enormous television. On the screen, the camera homed in on a guy with thick glasses. I could see text at the bottom of the screen—WITNESS CALLED BY THE DEFENSE, I guessed, or CROSS-EXAMINATION; all she watched were jury trials.

This is good news. It's not like we're telling her something bad, you said, yawning. *God, we're running on no sleep. We should just go in and tell her. Quick like a Band-Aid.*

I'm sorry about last night. I guess I just—

Don't be, you said quickly.

Frankie! My head snapped toward the driveway, where my mom clomped toward us in her heels. *And you brought friends,* she said.

My mom was tall and mostly thin—she carried bulges in a few isolated places but had the appearance of a healthy, trim woman. She wore a pressed pantsuit and thick makeup, her lips stained a deep berry. Her hair was a cropped confection of boyish platinum blonde, teased high on top and sleek on the sides: the overall effect was a cross between David Bowie and Dolly Parton.

Hey Mom, I said, stepping out of the car. You followed. *You're looking very corporate today.*

I've got a client in fifteen, she said, out of breath. She eyed you. *Is that little Nora? Give an old lady a hug.*

You obeyed, her shoulder pressing into your neck.

I haven't seen you since Frankie's eighteenth at the Hungry Hunter. She couldn't stop touching your hair. *God, you're pretty,* she said.

Ma, I said.

She squinted at me. *Don't you have class?*

Can we go inside? I said. *I have to tell you something.*

Her face slumped into a frown as she whipped out her cell phone. *I'm canceling.* She covered the phone with her palm. *She's cheap anyway. Joanne?* she said, bellowing into the mouthpiece, trotting toward the house, motioning for us to follow.

You leaned in, whispering. *Did she get along with Greta?*

I guess. I brought her up here like twice.

You grimaced. *In five years?*

Done, my mom said, clapping her phone shut. We positioned ourselves on the taupe leather sectional. She put the television on mute. *You have news. I can tell. Frankie, have you told her I'm clairvoyant?*

Mom's clairvoyant, I said.

Okay, news. News news news.

Nora is my girlfriend now.

She squinted. *What about—*

I dumped her, I said.

She looked at me sideways, smirking.

There's more, you said.

Nora, I blurted. *Don't.* I didn't want you to tell her what Greta had said—I couldn't bear hearing it aloud.

Oh, tell me, Mom said. *Tell me.*

That was when I noticed the tumbler—brown frosted glass, straight out of a seventies airport lounge. There was no coaster, just a series of wet circles in a little Olympic-logo pattern beneath the drink that—at twenty to noon—she had nearly finished.

What? you said. *We have to tell her if she's going to be a witness.* You turned toward my mom. *We're getting married. Today.*

Oh, can I come? Mom said. *You'll let me come, right?* I nodded toward her glass. *I'll drive.*

Oh my God, she said, rounding the coffee table, kissing me on the forehead and then settling next to you. *Oh, hi!* she said, like you had just walked in the room. *Did you already tell your dad?* she asked me.

No. We came here first.

Oh! she said again, happy to have won.

I drove my mom's car to the freeway, heading for the county clerk's office on Texas Street. The two of you rode in the backseat so she could do your makeup. I glanced at you in the rearview, your eyes closed obediently as her brushes swept across your face. She explained each item as she used it, and I dreaded her inevitable sales pitch.

Where's Jess? I said. *Does she still work at the cell phone place?*

Oh, God no, Mom said. *She works at the Chevy's in Emeryville.* She blew on your eyelids, your eyelashes fluttering. *Your sister comes home smelling like grilled beef, Francis. I have to wash her clothes separately.*

We came to a stoplight. *You look pretty,* I told your reflection.

Of course she does, Mom said. I waited for you to catch my eye in the mirror, but you just closed them again as she commanded that you purse your lips.

Do you think Jess could make it here in time? I said.

She's working a double, Mom said, dusting silver powder across your eyelids. *What time are your parents getting here?* she said to you.

You began to answer, but I had taken a wrong turn and the GPS started to freak out: *Turn. Around. Turn. Around.*

Mom, why does this thing have a British accent?

It's Australian. I changed the setting. The Australian boy sounds so cute.

Recalculating, it said, addled. *Recalculating.*

What the fuck do you need this for? You barely leave your house.

She dug around in her bag, and I knew she was fishing for her thousand-dollar camera. *You look so gorgeous, little girl. Welcome to the happiest day of your life.*

Mrs. Mason, my parents died. They're not coming.

Her hand went still, the bag's contents no longer rattling. *Frankie,* she said distractedly, *did I know about this?*

It just happened, Mom.

Don't call me Mrs. Mason, Mom told you. *I'm Jill.*

Recalculating, the Aussie said. *Make a . . . LEFT . . . onto . . . Texas Street.*

She kissed your powdered forehead. *I'm sorry, kiddo. That's just too damn much.*

We're here, I said, parking.

We stepped into the searing air and it was hard to breathe; the atmosphere was suddenly inhospitable, like we had stepped onto some distant planet.

The woman in the glass booth slipped us our license application through a slot, and even through that tiny opening I smelled her bad breath. I filled in my name and address, putting down your house. My parents' names, the state where they were born—that was easy to remember, since they had never left it. I started to hand the form to you but pulled it back.

What? you asked.

It's okay, I said. *I'll just finish it up.*

I wrote Sandra where it asked for your mother, Jack where it said "Father." I didn't know their middle names, so I made some up. Sandra Ruth Lucas, I wrote. Jack Ray Lucas. I got to the bottom of the page and saw the fee: filing the application was $75. I looked over the other costs—$36 for the ceremony, $15 for an extra witness, since we needed two and only had one. I had negative $112 in my checking. You had paid for our coffee that morning, had covered the bridge toll when we left the city. You were giggling at a pamphlet: *Getting a Clue Before You Say I Do.* Your face was thick with cosmetics, like a topographic map.

I can't pay this, I told Mom.

She peered at me, her breath sweet and sharp. *You're getting married and you don't have a spare hundred?*

I'm getting married and I don't have a spare ten, I said.

She pulled out her checkbook.

Technically, you have to do these things by appointment, so because there were two couples ahead of us, we had two hours to kill. The three of us drove to the twenty-four-hour taco place, installing ourselves in a red vinyl booth.

Are you going to call your dad? you said.

I don't know, I said nervously. I sopped up some grease with a tortilla. *He's probably on a conference call or something. We don't really need to call him, I think.*

What does he do?

He's a consultant, Mom said. *Or, wait . . . no, that's right. A consultant.*

He's not in sales? I said. *I thought he was in sales.*

Maybe we can all go out to dinner or something, you said.

Yes! Mom said. *You have to have a reception. He'll come to the reception.*

No, I said abruptly. Both of you stared at me. I made my voice as calm as possible. *We don't have to do that, Mom. It's not—*

Mom took your hand. *Oh my God,* she said, *I just figured it out. You're pregnant.*

Fuck me, I said.

I'm not, Jill, you said.

You threw me a look that nearly stopped my heart, because I knew Mom saw it—she looked between us rapidly, reading our faces. In honor of the occasion she gave me a grace period, but I prayed she wasn't keeping a tally of questions she would later lob my way.

That was how it started—*We'll need witnesses.* Maybe if we had never told my family, everything would have been okay. Another $15, and the two witnesses could have been total strangers. Another $15 and we could have gone home to our house that night, floated our livers in champagne. We might have awoken the next morning to say, *Good morning, Mr. Mason* and *Good morning, Mrs. Mason,* giddy with a simple kind of hope.

On the last day of the last week I knew you, we bounded toward a 7-Eleven to find your Something New. My mom had you by the hand, head ducked as she traversed the empty aisles. You were wearing blue underwear, so that was done; she wiggled her emerald ring over her swollen knuckle and put it on your thumb—*There,* she had said, *something borrowed.*

It was finally hitting me: you were going to marry me. All I had wanted, for almost a decade, was for you to like me back—I had aimed low and landed hugely, improbably high. *This is crazy,* I said, trying to catch up with you.

No, my mom called over her shoulder. *It's tradition; you guys should start out with all your bases covered!*

This, you said. *I want this.* You held it out to me: a Dr. Pepper–flavored lip balm.

I took it to the counter and pulled out a card I knew would be declined.

It's a dollar twenty-nine, the girl said. *You don't have any cash?* But she ran the card through, and I watched in disbelief as the receipt began to print. I signed it, knowing full well that, including fees, I had just bought you a thirty-seven-dollar chapstick. But we ran out of there beaming, headed toward the next thing.

Though all civil ceremonies were supposed to take place in the small antechamber off the main lobby, ours was the last of the day and Mom begged. So we stood facing each other beneath the grand, mammary dome of the building, listening to the whir of the floor buffer down the hall. You wore jeans and a cable-knit sweater. I was in gray work pants and the faded black sweatshirt I had worn since high school—the same clothes I had worn the night before. Our sneakers matched. The official began her call-and-response routine, bowing toward each of us when it was our turn to speak. *Marriage is a promise that takes a lifetime to fulfill,* she said; I guess she was embellishing the boilerplate. She was smiling, and I knew it was because we looked young and giddy. She had a wedding ring of her own.

Who gives their blessings to this union? she said.

I do, my mom said.

I do, said the witness we had paid for, smiling stiffly, hands clasped at his crotch.

Who has the rings? the woman said.

There were none, so we mimed them, slipping nothing over each other's fingers.

Mazel tov, she said, using my back to sign her name on the license.

We drove back to Mom's and she told us to go ahead of her to Chevy's—to include my sister in the festivities, she had set up an impromptu reception there without asking either of us. Mom said we should drive alone: *Pretend there's tin cans on the back,* she said, pointing to my car.

I can't believe we're going to Chevy's, I said, after we dropped Mom off at home.

I don't mind. I want to see your sister. And your dad.

I pulled into the parking lot of a supermarket near the air force base. *Listen, Nora, I don't want to call him.*

You're worried he'll be mad?

239

My wife, I thought, looking at you. That's my wife.
He's not . . . you don't know what he's like.
What do you mean?
I struggled for the words. *He's an inconsistent man.*
You frowned. *I'm confused.*
I don't want him to be—I don't know.
How bad can he be? you said. *Your mom is so lovely.*
I shook my head. *I don't know.*
Say yes, you said.
I sighed. *What do I say? 'Hey Dad, come pay for my wedding reception?'*

Your eyes lit up. *I should call him! I should call and say, 'Mr. Mason, this is your daughter-in-law.'*

Yeah, right. I imagined him, gruff and distracted, a golf cart or chattering caddy audible in the background. *No, wait, that could work,* I said. I remember thinking, Maybe he'll be nice to you.

You took two quarters out of your purse and grabbed my father's business card from my hand, heading toward the pay phone not far from where I had parked. I watched you hold the receiver between your neck and shoulder as you dialed. There was something on your ass. I squinted, looked down at the passenger seat: you had sat, somewhere, in gum. *Oh shit,* I said.

When I looked back up, you were speaking into the phone. Your face was pinched, worried. *Oh shit,* I said again. Why had I let you do this? This was the guy who called Jess a whore when he found out she had pierced her belly button, who rescinded a donation to my middle school after finding out my male science teacher had a ponytail. I rolled down the window but all I could hear was the drone of the air force planes, the nasal whine as they took off or landed. You were nodding into the phone, smiling. Oh, thank God, I thought, remembering the dad who took me to Rockland Park on our bikes, how we rode damn near to Lake Berryessa. I had forgotten about the dad that showed up now and again to congratulate me for things, slip me a twenty or a gift card or a beer. That was who you had called. It was going to be okay.

You came back and opened the passenger door.

What'd he say?

He didn't, you said. *He's playing squash with a client, so I talked to his secretary. She said she'd tell him.*

That we got married, or to come to dinner?

What is this on my seat? What is this on my ass!

Gum, I said. *What did you tell her?*

I told her everything, you said, picking at the thick green wad. *I have to change.*

We can't make it to the city and back in time.

I want to get you home so bad, you said suddenly. *I can't wait to get you home.* You leaned in, natural as anything.

We'll go buy you something to wear, I said, my eyes closing as you put your hand up my shirt, whimpering in my ear.

In the Solano Mall there were a few elderly couples power-walking, some moms with strollers. *Here,* you said, pointing to a shop. It was a cheap jewelry store for teenagers, fully stocked with ill-made prom gear—badly sewn evening gloves, useless tiny purses, sub-CZ faux-diamond studs. *I just realized I need to look cute,* you said, grabbing some four-dollar pearl earrings, a thin strand of beads. In the Mervyn's you zeroed in on a strapless white dress. It smelled like overheated polyester in there, like scorched carpet fibers and unchanged diaper. You grabbed your size in the white dress and barreled toward the dressing room. It was Tuesday afternoon in a low-traffic department store: there was nobody around, nobody working the fitting rooms. You grinned, motioning toward the handicapped cubicle.

You can't be serious.

Can't I?

Can't you what? Get arrested for lewd conduct?

But when you went in, I followed you.

You had barely locked the door before I had you pinned against the mirrored wall. We attacked the buckles and zippers that impeded us. When I lifted you, you were light. I shut my eyes to avoid my reflection in the mirror behind you, but then I didn't have to; you took my glasses off and I couldn't see. You gripped the back of my T-shirt in little fists, preparing yourself. *Are you sure?* I whispered, hesitating. But before you could answer I had decided for you, the hangers on the hooks above us rattling. It was happening, despite every one of my failures. *Are you okay?* I said, my chin pressed against your jaw. From the way your face wrenched, from the sounds that you made, I knew the answer.

Did I do alright? I said.

It took a long time for you to open your eyes.

The dress fit so well you wore it out of the store. I paid for it at the counter—you had to lean funny so the guy could scan the tag still attached to your hip, all three of us laughing—and we left. *I suppose these shoes will do,* you said, pointing at your Chuck Taylor's. *I think it works,* I said. I couldn't breathe right. You had folded the gum-tacked jeans neatly before leaving them on the fitting room floor.

. . .

Listen, my mom said over the mariachi music, *I talked to Jess and it sounds like she can keep the ice cream cake in the freezer until it's time.*

Okay, Mom. Good work.

You leaned into me, my arm around you. *Ice cream cake,* you said. You looked like a cat in the sun.

Your dad will probably bring Carolyn along, Mom said, sipping her margarita. *If he can make it, I mean.*

I don't care if he shows up, I said.

Jess is taking her break as soon as everybody gets here, Mom said. *Did I tell you she's looking at Cal for next year?*

For what? What does she want to do?

Ask her, Mom said. *She's your sister, Frankie.*

I felt a presence draw near me, but before I could turn around I was in a half nelson. *Hey, Mister Matrimony,* Jess said. *Congratulations.* She offered you her hand and you clasped it, beaming.

Jess turned to me, suddenly serious. *Hey, can you make sure my seat isn't by Dad?*

You laughed, thinking this was a joke.

Francis, someone bellowed. And there he was, trailed by my stepmother, Carolyn—a stubby, rounded brunette who knew how to cook only tuna casserole and adored Barbara Streisand.

I gotta get back, Jess said, scurrying toward the kitchen.

Stand up, he said. *Shake your old man's hand.* I stood, and you did too.

Fiery little redhead, he said.

I watched your smile go from genuine to fake.

Jess arranged for the little band of waiters to come by with their sombreros and Spanish guitars, wishing us a happy birthday. *We don't have any wedding songs,* she said. Then they brought out a bottle of Cuervo.

I'm still a little queasy from last night, you whispered.

Seconded, I said.

What were you guys for Halloween? Mom said.

Hasty, my dad shouted.

We weren't anything, you said. *We went to this awful party and got really drunk.*

Shut up, I thought.

Well, there you have it, Dad said. *It was either that or the other explanation.*

She's not pregnant, Steven, Mom said. *Have some class.*

Nora, you know he wants to be a teacher? Dad said, turning to you. *This area isn't kind to the poverty-stricken. Hope you like living small.*

Your face hardened. *I own a home,* you said. *In San Francisco.*

Every fork stilled. My father had a one-bedroom condo in Vacaville, near the state prison for the criminally insane. My mother only owned her house because her parents had willed it to her—before that, just after the divorce, she had been forty-four and living in a studio apartment. You might as well have said you were descended from royalty.

Another piece of the puzzle falls into place, my father said. He looked at me and raised his glass, bitterness clouding his expression.

They cleared the ice cream cake and Jess pulled up a chair. All of us watched the waiter set down the bill.

Steve, Carolyn said—the first time she had spoken all evening—*let's get this.*

Isn't it customary, he said, *for the father of the bride to cover this kind of thing?*

Steven, Mom said. She shook her head.

Where is your family? Jess asked. *I didn't notice until now.*

Hey, I said. *Who wants to look at our marriage certificate?*

I'm talking, Francis, Dad said. *I asked a question.*

Steven, take a hint, Mom said.

I'm sure my father would love to pay for my wedding, you said.

I remember thinking, Please don't.

But he and my mother are both dead.

My father nodded solemnly. I was momentarily relieved—even an asshole like him could respect something that big. How could you hear something like that and press on? He couldn't. He had been shut up, he would be quiet now.

So that's how you own the house, then, he said.

I stood up and pulled out your chair like a gentleman. You held my arm as we walked toward the door.

Wait, Jess yelled, running after us. *Hang on, Frankie.*

God, he just gets worse every time, I said, shaking my head.

Here. She handed me a folded piece of paper.

I opened it. *Is he fucking serious with this?*

It's five grand, dude, she said. *Who cares what he is, just take it.*

I put the check in my pocket.

Remember when he used to not be like that? Jess said.

We faced the bay, stretching out in the dark. I made out the restaurant, across the way in Berkeley, where we had gone to the prom.

Not really, I said, giving her a hug. *You're going to Cal?*

Are you joking? She smoothed her apron. *I'd never get in.*

We said our good-byes. On our way back to San Francisco I stopped at an ATM, depositing the check before he could call in a stop payment.

■ ■ ■

When we had almost reached the Bay Bridge I asked if you were tired.

Yes, you said. *Extremely.*

We're almost home.

You looked at me lovingly. *You know, I think you'll be a good teacher,* you said. *I think you have the kindness for it.*

I don't know, I said. *I hope so.*

You sat up abruptly. *We should go to Colma.*

Now? I said.

I want to tell them, you said. *I have to tell them.*

The cemetery gate was closed, but we managed to wrench it against its chains enough to squeeze through. We walked until we reached the small hill, illuminating the stones with the flashlight on my car keys. As we knelt by their grave it was hard to see your face.

Hi Mom and Dad. You sounded cheerful.

Do you want me to give you a minute? I said.

In the darkness, I could feel you waiting.

Hi Jack, I said, hoarse. *Hi, Sandy.*

We got married, you said. *I wish you could have been there.*

My parents would have chased you away pretty quick, I said. *They were fucking ghastly tonight.*

Don't say that, you said. Even in the dark I could see how the grass had stained your white dress. When you spoke again it was inevitable: *Be glad that you have a family.*

I guess, I said. *Sometimes it's hard.*

Can we change the subject? you said.

Calm down. Jesus. There was a pause. I knew it scared you—how quickly, how easily I had slipped into anger. It was one of those moments you feel slithering from your grasp—the tone shifts, and you know you won't be able to wrest it back. No, I remember thinking. Stop. Don't.

Why are you talking to me like that? you asked.

I'm not talking to you like anything, I lied.

You know, sometimes I feel like you don't even like me, you said.

I looked into your narrowed eyes. *I do like you,* I said. *You know that already.*

You started to speak. *You're really*—you paused, shaking your head—*you're kind, and then you're fucking cruel, Francis.* You plucked blades of grass. *I wanted to visit my parents' grave on my wedding day and you couldn't just let me do that.*

How am I stopping you? I drove you here, we're sitting here right now.

You're mocking this, you said.

Let's just start over, I said. *Can't we just start over?*

You're mocking me, you said.

Greta, what do you—

What did you just call me?

I heard it in my head, loud as a bullhorn. *I didn't— I'm sorry.*

You breathed heavily. *How stupid do you have to be, to get a girl pregnant?*

My insides turned to ice. I clenched my fist, wishing for something to punch. *I suppose earlier you took some precaution you didn't mention?* The tone of my voice was toxic.

Your lip trembled. *I'm sorry.*

You should be, I snapped.

Talk to them. Show some respect. Please, for me.

You want me to talk to them?

Yes, you said.

I knocked on the damp earth, not yet marked with a headstone. *Hello? Anybody home?*

The déjà vu of that moment—every fight I had ever had that went nowhere—created an immediate response that rose inside me. You had been carrying anger around, not bothering to tell me about it. It was like a lie. And I knew about lies. I had been a liar, a deceiver, a willing participant in my own moral debasement, for as long as I could speak. And like any liar, the thing I hated most was being called on my falsehoods. I felt, in the haze of the evening, that you were telling me in so many words that I didn't really love you. The pure and uncomplicated feeling I had for you was the only truth I had known for years, and it counted for nothing.

Don't, you said. Now you were crying. I could hear it in your voice.

Can anybody hear me? My mouth hovered above the dirt. *Just wanted to say thanks.*

Francis, stop. Your hand lurched forward, as though you could block the words before they hit the air.

Thanks for dying, I said, *so I could finally fuck your daughter.*

Without looking at you, I stood up, brushed the grass from my knees, and trudged toward the car. When I realized it was *your* car—we had taken *your* car that morning, that morning when we had gone to get married—I set the keys on the hood. I stood there a moment, and then did the only thing that would show you how indignant I was. I started walking.

I want to tell you what it was like after that.

I waited for you to come to me. It was what I was used to. That night, I got to my apartment after walking for three hours and then flagging down a cab in Daly City; my roommate had to pay the fare. The next day I started to sort things for the move into your house. I went to class, to my student-teaching engagements. If you needed some time, fine. We were *married*, I thought. That was week one. The second week, I started calling. I put a letter in your mailbox—did you get that? Your car was always gone. The third week I stopped leaving my apartment. By week four, I had undergone the lovelorn makeover: drastic weight loss, facial bags from a sleep deficit that was alternately narcotic and pulverizing.

I went back to Greta somewhere around the fifth week, half alive, to prepare stoically for domestic life, suburbia, fatherhood. I felt certain that she knew where I had been, what I had been doing—that she had intuited at least the flavor of my absence, if not its particulars. And yet she said nothing. So neither did I. I didn't tell her about the funeral or the wedding, or what you and I had done in the dank dressing room—though not for the reason you think. It wasn't that I was afraid of her reaction. It was that I feared if I told her, she would swallow her own anguish to comfort me in my time of loss. I may not have loved Greta with much integrity, much honor. But I did love her too much for that.

That week, she and I went out to dinner. I took her to an Italian restaurant and she held my hand in the parking lot after, and we were almost to the car and I was thinking, I'm forgiven. I had been waiting for a punishment, a day of reckoning, and I felt the last of that anxiety lift. She was pregnant. She was scared. I'm forgiven, I thought again. And with that thought the atmosphere shifted—she tightened, winced in such a way that I actually wondered if she had *heard me thinking*, if my posture had changed in some way she was able to read for what it was—and as we reached the car she turned, looked me square in the face, and said, *Don't do me any favors. I don't need you to. If you want to go, go.*

I held her gaze, let go of her hand. I thought of ways to turn it back on her, or play dumb—*Is that what you want, Greta? Why are you saying this now, Greta?* But her expression stopped me.

If you want to leave, do it, she said.

My mind cleared. Her face seemed to absorb the ambient light around us, her hair picking up in the wind. She looked radiant and livid. Every particle of me felt sharp and true—like I was a blade, like I was an instrument of death.

I don't want to leave, I said, meaning it.

About a month after Greta lost the baby, the annulment papers arrived. The documents were accompanied by stationery from the lawyer I had met at your house. I signed and returned them, wondering if I should have withheld consent. Maybe it would have forced you to talk to me in person, though even if you had I suppose it wouldn't have mattered. You didn't think of this, of me, as a mere mistake. The document cited California Family Law statute §2210(c) as justification for nullity: *Party,* it read, *was of unsound mind.*

13

Eight hours after leaving Chappell, I took a rural turnoff boasting the holy trinity: Gas, Food, Lodging.

How much? I asked the kid behind the counter. I felt haggard, and in the motel lobby's gilt-framed mirror, I looked it, too.

Forty, he said.

The smell inside my car had thickened: my filthy body, clothing steeped in lake water. It was imperative that I clean myself properly, with hot running water. It was imperative that I be presentable.

Forty, the kid said again. *Only smoking rooms left.*

I counted out the five-dollar bills.

The room was half the size of any motel room I had ever seen, the walls yellowed by cigarette smoke like stained teeth. I threw my bundle of putrid clothes into the bathtub, went outside, and drove to a drive-through window. I took my six sad tacos back to the room, eating in front of the wall-mounted television. I watched three episodes of a program about a detective team who seemed never to get it right the first time. When I could no longer stand the noise, I put the TV on mute and rinsed my clothes until the water ran clear. I parboiled myself beneath the scalding shower stream and shampooed my hair three times. I fell onto the bed gasping, rolled my neck until it released several violent cracks, and in a haze not unlike a head rush, slept.

I dreamed Greta and I were in Chappell, repairing the back of that burned house. But every time I gave her a nail, she requested another. I was handing them to her in quick succession—I couldn't offer them fast enough. I heard no hammering; they just disappeared, sucked into that black maw.

I woke up sweaty, the night sky showing through the rough tweed curtains. The slick polyester coverlet slipped across my body with each ragged breath. The alarm clock read 4:45 AM. It was time. Despite the season the air outside was cool, and as I pulled back onto I-80 a chill overtook me. I reached under the seat for the black hooded sweatshirt I had worn since high school, but it was missing. There came a sudden vision: the sweatshirt, balled on the motel armchair where I had tossed it the evening before. It was gone. I couldn't make myself turn around to get it. There was no hope if momentum was lost. There was nowhere to go but forward.

At Iowa's eastern border, I sped across a wide silver bridge that spanned the Mississippi. Past Illinois, where, in a disorienting loop, I circled what signs indicated to be Chicago; it looked dismal. Then Indiana, which was over quickly. Ohio took longer, Pennsylvania longer still. Predawn in those mountains, there was nothing to see by. No towns, no lights along the highway. I could finally open my eyes completely after squinting my face sore in the daylight. As dawn broke, what I saw of New Jersey was green and tall, its high, verdant cliffs rising beside the highway. The signs became more insistent in the gray of the small hours, and then it was midmorning and I was leaning forward, gripping the wheel, navigating sudden freeways and trying to figure out which level of the George Washington Bridge to use. I was scared. I thought, Sing a song.

I crested a hill peppered with stacked residential streets, entered the tunnel-like lower level of the bridge, and left the continent behind. I strained my neck, looking for a city to appear. It did. It looked too dense, as though it were a solid mass with vertical points; I didn't know how the life down inside could exist or breathe. I started to sing my students' favorite song, "John Jacob Jingleheimer Schmidt," tentatively, uncertainly. *His name is my name too. Whenever I go out, the people always shout.* The water below looked shimmering and unclean. New York was a thin outcropping of urban landscape surrounded by water—an idea I was used to. I was breathless, the song repeating.

I began to whistle, turning the air-conditioning on and then off—I was either too hot or too cold. I felt as though all my life I had been too something. Nearly out of gas, I took an expressway stemming from the bridge's exit ramp and watched the landscape morph into brown cubes. Exiting, I read the street signs aloud, checking them against the directions I had written down. *Broadway,* I said. *One Hundred and Seventy-Eighth Street.* On the sidewalk, trash bags rose in mounded pyramids. I paused at a stoplight, scanning. Mothers walked with their children, rolltop metal covers enclosed storefronts like sardine tin lids. *One Hundred and Eighty-One.* I parked on a residential street, parallel to Broadway and laden with thin trees, in front of a synagogue. I stepped out of the car and walked to a building less than a block away.

Approaching that building, scrap of paper in hand, with an icy stab I remembered something. My breath snagged in my throat. The motel where I stopped had required an address at check-in. I had given them the one in Vallejo—my and Greta's address—without hesitation. As people pushed past me into the tan-brick building, I ran a finger over the names on the buzzer panel, imagining my lost sweatshirt being shoved into a mailer by that teenaged concierge. I pressed a button, picturing that envelope being stamped by a postal meter, being shipped back to California, bouncing in the cargo hold of an airplane. A voice came through the intercom—*Hello? Hello?*—and my solar plexus compressed as though I had been punched. *Hello,* I choked, but the intercom must not have worked because the voice continued. *Hello?* it said, and then, resigned, *Hello.* There was a pause. Then, a zapping reverberation opened the building's inner door. Reeling, I entered the lobby: a step toward my thwarted destiny, my unlived life. My fingers depressed the elevator button. Through the porthole on the elevator door I watched each floor slowly pass, thinking about how I had destroyed my life in the name not of this girl's existence but the fucking *memory* of her existence, not because I loved her—though

I did—but because I had lost her. The indefensible things I had done in the name of my former certainty, the people I had hurt—that kind of humiliation defied description. I thought too of the humiliation I had left in my wake, picturing Greta as she examined that envelope's return address, some nowhere place in some nowhere midwestern state. And then opening it, recognizing its contents, her eyes adjusting to the glare of my final disgrace.

The hallway smelled of garlic, of toxic solvents and mop water. I lifted my hand to knock but the door opened, a person standing there backlit by a sunny window. Only the simplest thoughts surfaced: you were thinner than I remembered, and taller, and your hair had changed.

Nora, I said. A useless thing to say, a placeholder. A simple way to begin again.

...

You love to worry, you told me once, shaking your head. It was high school, we were rushing back to Alameda to retrieve my noisome truck, convinced it was going to be towed—I had left it in a big abandoned lot on the naval base so we could take your car. I don't remember now why we had to take yours; maybe your air conditioner worked better. Something like that. *You love to worry, so you do things that worry you,* you said. More than you touching me, more than the feel of your body beneath mine years later, that subtle judgment was an aphrodisiac—the sense that you were looking at me closely. I was lulled by the revelation that I was a man of pattern, a creature of inviolable temperament—that I did things a certain way, that there was a center to me, a consistency. *You do so love to worry,* you said, and it was true—I had long worried that I was *no one in particular*, an absence that negotiated the world not by action but by reaction. That you thought otherwise, seeing in me a quality, an individual texture—that, Nora, is what made me love you most. As though I could look deep inside you and see not you, but a reflection of myself. As though you could tell me, on a daily basis, who I was.

The day after we first slept in my bed, unable to drag ourselves from our talk, you asked me a hundred questions. Your hand was on my forearm, the pads of your fingers cold. *Tell me all the bones you've broken,* you said.

My collarbone, my ankle, my nose.

Tell me all the scars you have, you said.

I looked down at my hands, counting. *This one from a burn in the kitchen. This one from chicken pox.* I pointed to a knee, skinned on my first cycling foray without training wheels.

How do you think the world will end?

I frowned. *I don't think it will.*

You paused, somber. *Tell me the most pain you've ever been in.*

I guess the collarbone, I said.

No, you said. *The worst you've ever felt.*

I couldn't think of anything.

You must be able to think of something, you said.

So I tried again, and what I thought of was the reverse; I thought about how that moment—you, lying in my bed—was my *happiest* time. And I thought about how you, in the same moment, were riddled with pain. It weakened you. It distorted your gait, fogged your vision, fucked up your speech. It was like a fist around your central nervous system, every firing synapse filtered through a sustained hurt. I thought about how we were smack in the middle of the worst time in *your* life, and I felt the situation get pale and undermined, beating back a flickering doubt. I did things that worried me and then I worried, yes. But I suppressed the questions I ought to have asked, letting your imploring eyes and naked legs file down that sharp thing within me, dulling it into an approximated peace.

That pain you carried was something I better understood years later, when I saw the body on that beach; I was slapped back by duality—there was sorrow, but there was also an insinuation of relief. Long before my conscious mind entered the equation, a part of me wished you dead. And I believed you were. If Buckingham or anyone else didn't, it didn't change the simple truth: I could bear your death better than I could your abandonment.

That day, you asked one more question before we went out looking for signs. As you spoke, your head was propped on your arm, your legs curled beneath you. *What is your greatest fear?*

I knew immediately. It was that someday I too would be forced to face the pain you were facing then.

But I lied. It was my first lie to you, and I added it to the others I'd told, accruing like bricks in a wall, like layers of gauze over a wound. My lies were always miscalculations: every one I hid behind revealed more than the truth would have.

That I won't be strong enough, I answered, *to live the way I ought to.*

. . .

In Chappell, I had remembered how to do it. Two years earlier, the policeman had called your apartment to notify you of your parents' death. I had been on your couch, you were making French toast; the phone rang. He had taken off his hat like a gentleman to tell you he was sorry and you asked him, *How did you know where I live?* He explained to you how easy it had been. He said, *It was actually pretty easy.* He explained to you how people, out there in the world, were no longer difficult to find.

The light behind you slid away as you stepped into the hall. Your face came into focus. You held a vice grip on your breath. I asked a sudden question of myself: What do you expect from this?

Francis, you said.

I rejected a stream of words, none of which worked.

You studied me. *Can I ask you a question?*

I wish you wouldn't, I said.

I'm glad to see you, you said. As you said it your hand went to your mouth, as though you had violated a self-imposed order.

I thought you were dead, I said.

I was thinking of calling you, you said. *To catch up.* You sighed, a kind of retraction. *I think about calling you,* you said, correcting yourself.

What do you expect from this? I asked myself again. Why are you here? And then I knew. I wanted to say the two words that could go at least an inch toward my redemption.

I came here because I needed to tell you—
You cut me off. *How did you find me?*

That day in Chappell, standing at the pay phone in the yellow dust, the operator's voice had been clinical, pinched. *L-U-C-A-S,* I had enunciated. *New York City. Yes, thank you.* I had left Nebraska with a number and an address; there were more Nora Lucases in New York than I expected but only one who had opted to put "Ms." in front of her name. I wondered if you had known I would look for you someday. I wondered if you had wanted to force me to see how proud you were of your autonomy.

But I had called Buckingham first. I had said, without greeting, *I'm calling about the woman.* He said, *Pardon?* And I said, *I'm calling about the woman my class found on the beach.* It felt incorrect to say it; that had been someone else's life.

I thought you were going to come talk to me.

I was unwell, I said. *I think—I doubt I need to tell you that.*

Her name was Mary, he said.

Mary, I said.

I hear you're out of a job, he said.

What was her last name?

I'd have to look at my files, he said, before hanging up.

A nothing name; the name of a stranger.

With your address on the dashboard I drove. Two useless years, my life in shambles. Consult the directory, a call made with loose change, three thousand miles. All this wasted time.

You stood in your doorway, awaiting my answer.

It was actually pretty easy, I said.

You had lived there almost a year and a half, had sold your car ages ago. You rarely went to California anymore. It was hard to get out there very often. *I don't fly,* you said. *It's one of my things.*

I hate to fly, too, I said.

We were still standing in the hallway. I was acclimating to the ideas. That old car of yours was gone because you had sold it. This was where you lived now. You had this apartment, to which you returned each night; you had this apartment that you called Home.

Actually, I said, *I really hate flying. I feel like I have to hold perfectly still or I'll anger fate and the plane will crash.*

What if you have to pee? you said.

I wait, I said.

You have to take control of your destiny, you said, smiling faintly.

We still hadn't gone inside, as if there were a line you wanted to avoid crossing. You motioned behind me, and we went down the stairs and out to the street. I toured your neighborhood with you as though we were normal people, out for a stroll in the middle of a sunstroked day. With every step it became more natural, a feeling not unlike a heart rate slowing, cold fingers warming. At the bottom of your street we went into a wine shop that was bigger than your old apartment. You picked up a bottle from Spain and said, *This looks good. Though I guess we should stick to wines from California.* We were quiet. Your lame joke was an offering. The bottle fell from your hand—for a wrenching second we watched it fall, certain it would break. *I am always so goddamn clumsy,* you said. You retrieved it, placing it back on the shelf.

With my cash I bought two bottles and we went back to your place: it, too, was bigger than your old apartment. Up to then, we had kept it light: *Do you like this neighborhood? It gets so much hotter here, and then way, way colder.* But at your front door you busied yourself with the keys as you said, *You can take a shower if you want.*

I did, as thoroughly as I could without being in there for too long. I borrowed your toothbrush, spitting faint trails of blood into the sink. I brushed twice, three times, and returned in your Giants T-shirt and a pair of pink pajama pants. You looked up from the kitchen table.

It's like seeing a ghost, you said.

Do you want to hug me?

Yes, you said, not moving. Waiting.

I closed my eyes. *What I said. It was horrible.*

Which time? you said—immediately, without a second of lag time.

I was glad. Anger was better than indifference. Though I didn't answer, you stepped forward and everything dissipated, like a vapor clearing, like dust wiped clean. It was like living a moment out of order: time had gone into reverse and we would find ourselves beneath the Golden Gate, before attending that drab funeral, then greeting your parents, alive and well, and finally shrinking back into children, and then babies, and then nothing. Your arms felt thin on my back.

You smell just like you, I said.

Open the wine, you said. *I'll order dinner.*

We had sushi, strange and wonderful—a lobster roll with banana, shrimp with coconut. After six weeks of cold, unmarked cans, I could have cried.

I watched you examine my face. *Let's just ask our questions now,* you said.

I nodded. *Why do you live in New York?*

You speared gyoza with your chopsticks. *San Francisco felt ruined. Now tell me your story.*

I don't know how to begin, I said.

Do you still live in San Francisco?

No, I said.

Do you still live in California?

No.

Where do you live?

I swallowed. There were people talking in the court-yard outside, children's jump ropes slapping the concrete. You continued.

Are you a teacher?

No.

You pushed away your food. *Was the baby a boy or a girl?*

No, I said.

You winced, and went quiet.

Do you think we were ever really in love? you said finally.

I looked you in the eye for the first time. *Of course,* I said.

I changed, my clothes washed and dried in the basement of your building, and we went out. You showed me how to ride the subway, and despite the briefness of our trip the rocking train nearly lulled me to sleep. We went to a narrow, deafening bar at the top of a hill, where there was a sign posted: NO DANCING ALLOWED. The staff seemed to know you.

Where are we again? I said.

Washington Heights, you said.

No, I mean, this is New York? We're in New York City?

You spoke to the bartender. *We'd like two Manhattans, please.* You slapped the counter like you were in a Western. The guy pulled out martini glasses and dropped in two maraschino cherries. He frowned. *I'm out of bitters,* he said, dumping the cherries back into the jar. You ordered us two Belgian beers, and we sat on a zebra-print bench.

It's too loud in here to talk, you said.

That's probably for the best, I shouted.

You pointed to a TV over the bar. *We'll watch the game. Yankees–Twins.*

You rested your head against my shoulder. I set my beer on a spool-shaped table and put my arm around you, pulling you close. *Have you been to any ball games out here?* I said. But you didn't hear me. *Nora,* I said. You didn't answer, didn't stir. I leaned down and spoke into your hair. *I'm sorry.* I inhaled, strands suctioning to my nostrils. *I'm sorry,* I said again.

You sat up and turned around. *I know a place we could go.*

It was a high, pebbly rock wall overlooking a river, and we stayed there for a long time, staring at the toxic-green orbs illuminating the bridge I had crossed. At a liquor store, you had bought condoms—I watched you motion to where they hung behind the counter, expressionless—and two Colt 45s, and we drank from the massive bottles in plain sight of the street. Our legs hung over the edge of the wall as we faced the broad forested edge of New Jersey across the river. Through a thicket of branches the cars passed under our shoes.

Are you happy? I asked you.

I'm happier than before, you said.

How do you get happier? What do you have to do?

It's something you have to make. You looked out at the water. *It's something you have to invent, and then re-invent.*

I want to work for it, I said. *I want to be happy.*

You have to stop wanting all the time, you said. *That's part of it.*

We were quiet.

What's that road down there? I said.

The West Side Highway. It goes along the river, all the way down the island.

I'll drive you wherever you want to go, I blurted.

You pointed at the bottle in my hand.

I'm fine, I said. *I promise.*

We walked the few blocks. *Ignore the stench,* I said as we approached my car.

You motioned for me to get in first, because you remembered: the driver-side door didn't open.

I can't believe you remember that, I said.

I remember, you said.

Blocks later we approached the on-ramp, heading south. *I have no idea where I'm going. I need you to tell me.*

For most of it you just keep going forward, you said.

A few minutes later we were picking up speed. The river seemed too close to the edge of the road, like any second it could sweep us away.

What's the name of this river?

The Hudson, you said, running a hand through your

hair. When you pulled your hand away a few strands stayed laced in your fingers. You began to roll the window down to drop them outside and I stopped you.

Don't, I said.

You looked at me. *What?*

Leave it in the car.

You did, watching the hair fall. To you, it was a strange request. To me, it was a minor guarantee: at least I would have something of you.

I pressed on, the numbers getting smaller: we passed Fourteenth Street. *I think we're about to hit the end,* I said.

It goes past the numbered streets, you said, sitting up. *After that they're named.*

I took a breath. *Greta got pregnant again. She was pregnant when I left.*

You looked away.

She's due in less than four months, I said gravely, uncertain you had heard.

You exploded with ugly laughter. I froze.

Canal, you said, pointing. It was coming up on our left. *Take Canal Street.*

I turned onto a street clogged with people, cars, and signs. Where you lived, almost everything was in Spanish, but here everything was covered in red Chinese script. *This is like San Francisco, sprouted,* I said. *Or San Francisco is like this, stunted.*

I never compare them, you said. *I never think about San Francisco anymore.*

Some inner part of me bruised. We stopped at a light and waited for it to turn green. When we moved again, we dodged in and out of the lane to overtake the slow, monolithic buses. You were smiling strangely, beautifully, like some kind of deranged saint.

Go over the bridge, you said. A massive stone archway loomed and I sped through it, ascending. At midspan you craned your neck. *Now look to your right. Not yet . . . not yet . . . okay, now.*

I obeyed. And framed by the window I saw another bridge, darker in color and lit with globe lights, the whole thing enshrouded in a web of cables. The picture was whole, the dimensions distinct: the bridge in the background, and in the foreground, your serene countenance. Everything was in that face. The lost happiness. The pain of these two years. Whatever the new pains might be. And the peace you had made with all of it.

I've seen this in pictures, I said, my eyes oscillating between the road ahead and the view beside us.

Look in your rearview, you said.

I glanced up and saw a massive collection of shining buildings, leaning at a diagonal in my mirror.

It's beautiful, I said.

You sank into the seat. *Now you've seen what you came to see.*

When we got back to your neighborhood, it took twenty minutes to find a parking spot six blocks from your apartment. Inside, there was no discussion. In your bedroom you put on a cotton nightgown and I removed my shoes and shirt. I brushed my teeth again, returning to find the air conditioner blasting and you beneath the massive comforter, your head protruding from the top as though it had swallowed you. You had your back to me, and I moved into the familiar position we had once held, tightening my arm around your middle. But you pulled out of my grip and told me to turn over. I faced the other way, stung, until I felt your arm close over my side and I understood that you were going to hold me instead.

Do you think we were really in love? I said.

You rubbed your feet together for warmth. *It doesn't matter anymore,* you said.

We made cursory love. You put your hands on the clothed parts of me—gripping the waistband of the pants I didn't fully remove, smoothing palms over my crewneck. You pointed your face away as though you were withholding sight of it, gently pulling my fingers from your clit to replace them with your own. *You don't know,* I was saying, breathless, *how much I missed you.* I willed you to look at me, feeling like an intruder. Sex, for me, had always been an exercise in isolation, a pleasant but dissociative task. Afterward, I usually felt a sense of confirmation; I was alone in the world, even in this. Watching you come, in profile, I knew you were elsewhere, and I understood that we had made a parallel discovery: regardless of the partner, fucking and loneliness were two sides of one coin.

After, you asked me what you needed to know, and I obliged you. You sat up against the wall and extended your legs, your feet cool against my stomach.

The church, I told you, had been small. We were married on a warm day in April. One of my cousins arrived in denim shorts and a tank top, and Greta fretted about it; it made her feel judged. The woman who rented us the restaurant for the reception kept pestering my mother, telling her more had arrived than were paid for. It was a dry wedding, since my in-laws were covering the bill. But I went with my father to a liquor store up the street, and we each drank a tall boy on the walk back, hiding them when cars passed. He told me he was sorry I was living in the suburbs, where we had moved a month before. He told me that marriage would be harder than I expected. I thanked him. I was close to finishing my credential, and I remember as I took a long pull from my beer he said, *You're going to be a good teacher.* I thanked him again. He said, *You'll be one of the good guys now.*

You cut in, and asked me, *Is that why you wanted to be a teacher?*

But I continued on. To my parents' credit, I told you, they kept quiet about my previous wedding. Somewhere along the way they had evidently sprouted a sense of decorum. That night, the gifts piled in Greta's parents' living room rattled me. It was overwhelming, and incredulous, being so loved.

Were you happy on that day? you asked me.

I had felt, I told you, like if I just focused on the happiness *around* me, things would stay okay. If I just stayed in that moment, I would never think again about what I had lost. But I remember when that ease began to dissolve. Greta's mother came toward me at the reception, short and squat in her sequined sweater. She put her hand on my elbow and told me how thankful she was. Greta was elsewhere, changing out of her veil maybe, or chatting with her giddy friends. Her mother looked up at me with Greta's same eyes, beaming, and told me how lucky she was to have such a kind man for a son-in-law. As she spoke I felt the joy leak from me. All I could hear was what I wasn't.

A flash of white light illuminated the air shaft beyond your window, and rain, from nowhere, pelted the brick building. A swollen, belching thunderclap startled me so badly I jumped, and it felt like the images around us scrambled. I shut my eyes, disoriented, and opened them again. And then the shapes of the room ordered themselves in the dim light, and the silent minutes ticked by. The rain vanished as suddenly as it had come. Both of us lay on our backs beneath the blanket, and I heard your breathing slow and deepen. That was when I spoke.

I wanted to be a teacher to learn how to not be my father.

You're not him, you said. Your eyes were still closed.

I don't know what to do next, I said.

You linked our arms like we were about to step on a dance floor. Your voice was gentle.

Yes you do, you said.

In the light of morning I awoke on my stomach, the blanket on the floor. I could hear the shower, so I got up and knocked on the bathroom door. *You can come in,* you said. Your shower curtain was clear. It was the first time I had ever seen you naked, in full light and all at once.

I watched you look away before you spoke. *So what time are you leaving?*

I steadied myself against the sink. *I don't know,* I said. *I'm not sure yet.*

I saw what was different about you, then. Your body had become leaner, its edges more sharply defined. You had hardened. You were grown. I sat on the closed toilet seat, watching you soap your hair with your arms above your head. The way you had your hands raised, I thought—of all things—about when you helped me move into my first apartment. On the ceiling of my bedroom were glow-in-the-dark plastic stars someone had left, and you stood on a chair to rip them down. Your arms were raised over your head like they were right then in the shower, as you pried the stars from the ceiling, bending your fingernails back once, then twice, cursing both times and sucking your fingertips. *Leave them if it hurts you so bad,* I said. You did. And after that I slept beneath an incomplete galaxy, staring from the mattress on my floor at the gaps you had left behind.

I took in your slick hair, the horizontal line of your mouth. Your face was pink from the water's heat. *It's so good to see you,* I said. In my head the words sounded stupid, oversimplified to absurdity. But as I spoke them they felt like the truest ones I could have chosen.

Your eyes were eerily blue against the white of the tiles. I approached the shower and we both leaned forward. We kissed through the clear vinyl, and then I handed you your towel. *Good to see you too,* you said. As you dried yourself I straightened my side of the bed—the same side that had been mine in my bed, and in your parents' bed, those years before. You were still in the bathroom as I dressed, gathered my things, and left.

I ran the six blocks to where I had parked, panting. But when I arrived at the spot where my car had been, it was gone. I circled the block, convinced I had made a mistake.

Hey! somebody shouted. An old man was sitting on a plastic lawn chair, perched on the dog-shit-riddled sidewalk. *You drive a little white hatchback?*

What? I said.

They towed it a while ago.

Was it in front of a hydrant or something? Did it have a ticket on it?

Wasn't the sheriff's department. Somebody else. You make your car payments?

Everything stilled. *Fuck,* I said.

You gotta pay those on time, he said. *They'll find you. They have a sensor they scan with. A little ray gun.*

I shook my head. He was saying something about VINs, parking lots in Newark, retrieval fees. *It don't matter where you go,* he said. *They'll find you any goddamn where.*

I scanned the street, bent over from running.

Call the police, he said. *They'll tell you where to get it.*

Where's the nearest airport?

How's that?

Airport. Where's the airport?

LaGuardia, he said.

Which subway goes there?

There's a bus that—

I don't know how to ride the buses here, I said. *Tell me how to get to an airport on the subway.*

He blinked, frowning. *Walk over to One Hundred Eighty-First,* he said softly. *Take the A train that says Far Rockaway, to JFK. You have to call the police, son.*

I took off at a run, finding the station. I boarded the train and sat on the bench, watching my fellow passengers:

people in the same car didn't look at one another. But as we passed another train running alongside us in the tunnel, many in that train stared openly at me. The distance, the sheets of metal between us—it freed up reservations. We all fixed our eyes on each other, knowing we would never meet again.

I made it to the airport after an hour or so. I scanned the dozen screens, disoriented, out of my depth. I didn't have much money left, but I knew I could cover the one-way fare.

14

Maybe you don't remember everything, the way I do. But I keep these memories for the two of us. If you ever want them, you can have them.

Do you remember that time we got drunk and pissed on the church? I don't remember how it came to that—we weren't far from my parents' house. This was high school, so they would have still been married, living in the apartment near San Francisco State. They wouldn't have cared that we were drunk; I doubt they would even have noticed, but there we were: you, squatting outdoors at two in the morning, as I stood hovering above a stream that soaked the church's little rose garden, both of us laughing without sound.

You never wanted me. That's what I've been trying to say.

Without ever having jumped off a bridge, I think I know what it feels like. It's a betrayal of our first contract with the world: that there will always be ground beneath us. At first it's like when you expect a few more inches of sidewalk before the curb, and then that moment of vertiginous suspension when the next step doesn't materialize. And then nothing for a second, before the piercing wind. They say you have four seconds between the bridge and the bay. Maybe that isn't enough time to make it to fear. Maybe one stays firmly in confusion. Maybe one makes it to panic, but by then it doesn't matter. And so in that fourth second before the water breaks whichever bone it touches first, perhaps there's something like peace. We're all looking for certainty. In those four seconds, certainty is all there is.

I heard you're out of a job, Buckingham had said, his words half-drowned by a nearby tractor—how ubiquitous that sound was in Nebraska. I asked him for her name, and when he said it, I wanted to feel something. But there was so little left to feel. *Mary,* I said back, inventing the missing details: Mary lived alone in a sunny apartment. She walked along the piers on the weekend, drank with her friends in the North Beach bars. Mary had parents who loved her, and who became alarmed by her sudden absence—why didn't she call on Sunday night? She always called then.

If that was how Mary died—the four-second fall—then she knew that everything I just invented about the sea's calm embrace is bullshit. She knew that as you fall there's only the impulse to climb back up, against time. That in the final moment, you're reduced: you are only your fear.

What I've done can be reduced, too. My students saw something horrible and I did nothing to help them. I hit a child who showed signs of abuse. I left my pregnant wife;

I lied to her, easy as breathing. And all of those events felt like accidents, aberrations—like betrayals of another of our fundamental contracts with the world: that we're free, and that we choose who we become.

Or maybe Mary had a husband. Maybe she came home each night to a man who couldn't give her what she wanted, even if what she wanted was simple: to have her love returned. Maybe Mary had seen the only thing she ever wanted taken from her, the way Greta had. Maybe Mary had destroyed the only thing she ever wanted, the way I had. Maybe Mary fell from the bridge accidentally. Maybe she was a hiker who slipped on a cliff in the headlands. Maybe she was mugged, murdered, and dumped into the bay. I didn't ask. It isn't my story to know.

The story for me to know is the one I made, crafted from the raw materials of failure. I pulled at the tethers of my life, resisting them like a child. I built that story with every word I used to wound, every lie I erected. The story for me to know is the same as the question I'm forced to ask: What did they know?

What did they know—those two kids who you and I used to be. What did they know about love? And what anything meant, and how to live. What did those two people who raised me know, those people whose own stains filtered down into the fabric of me? I want to know what those two dozen students, the ones whose faces adhere to my conscience, were thinking as they watched—as I had, as we all eventually do—an adult drop low enough in their regard that adulthood itself was diminished. Though I think they're the only ones about whose knowledge I'm certain: they knew nothing. I was supposed to teach them.

The pilot came over the intercom a few minutes ago to say that we're about to descend. It's night outside—it's been a long stretch of darkness beneath us, but soon we'll start to see some lights. People are shifting in their seats, antsy for arrival, getting ready to land, stand, and go.

At the airport, I called my wife to tell her I wanted to come home. You know what she said? Not *How dare you* or *You son of a bitch.*

She said, *Why?*

And I said, *Because I love you.*

If she were still alive, Greta said, *would you be saying this to me?*

The announcements had come over the loudspeakers, the terminals abuzz with arrivals and departures. People milled behind me. I considered her question.

No, I said.

You loved her more than me.

Not more, I said. *Just differently.*

Different how, she said. I heard the genuine curiosity in her voice.

There are people you can't help but love, I told her, *and there are people who you choose to love. You wake up every day and you decide to love them.*

And I'm the latter.

Yes, I said. *And the latter counts for more.*

She was silent. I thought I had wounded her. And then she spoke.

Thank you, Francis, she said, *for being honest just this once.*

I used to tell myself, in moments when I felt bad about things I had done, that guilt is useless. *It's a dead scene,* I said to you once. It was a few years before they died, and you were feeling bad about a fight with your mom. *Guilt serves no purpose,* I said. *You have to let it go.* But the only thing I've found to be useless, if you want the truth, is disappointment. Guilt, at least in theory, helps one avoid repeat failures. Disappointment just kills a piece of you. Disappointment tamps down hope. I don't want to be disappointed anymore.

That night we pissed on the church, you cried after. I walked you to the bus stop and saw you wipe tears from your neck. I asked what was the matter and you said, *I can't believe I just did that.*

I laughed. *No one could see us.*

That's not a reason to do something. You were hunched beneath the bus stop shelter. *I never do things like that.*

I remember speaking before thinking. *Almost everything important that people do,* I said, *is something they think they would never do.*

I can feel us beginning to lose altitude haltingly—sink, then tilt. They've asked us to buckle up for the landing. Any minute they'll knock on this door and discover me: my hands gripping the edge of the sink, the mirror fogged from my breath. My glasses folded on the toilet lid. I made myself get up and walk. I've been looking in this mirror, trying to see what you saw. I want to know if what you said is true. I want to know what my purest self looks like.

I suppose when we land I'll call Jess for a ride. Emeryville is just one town over from the airport. I can see the city in my mind: the two bridges, the twinkling hills. The only place I've ever loved. Jess will double-park at the terminal in Dad's old car, leaning over to unlock the passenger door.

She'll drive north to my sad freeway town, pulling up to the little house on the little court, and from the porch I'll wave good night. And maybe Greta will let me inside, and maybe she will refuse. She will say the things she needs to say, and I will listen. I will change. And what remains of who I was, what I felt for you, will get packed up into some out-of-the-way corner of me—some place where it won't get in the way, where I can open it up and thumb through it now and again. It will atrophy quietly in that abandoned place. It will wither and go stale. But it will not die.

You never wanted me, Nora, and cutting the cord to the brief time when you thought you did is something I will never master. I know myself. I will carry this pain as though it has meaning, balancing an unwieldy hope for a future—extending outward, bright before us—that will never arrive. And I will keep on biding the meantime, answering these questions you never asked, telling you this story you already know.

ACKNOWLEDGMENTS

Sincere thanks to the following big-hearted people: Maureen Gallagher, G. V. Cooper, Christine Mayall, Ken MacLennan, Sahar Mozaffar, Diane Berl, Rick Kleine, Maureen Mitchell-Wise, Daniel Anker, Richard Wright, Bruce Wilson, Shennan Hutton, Amanda Davis, Micheline Aharonian Marcom, Cornelia Nixon, Mary LaChappelle, Brian Morton, Victoria Redel, Rob Spillman, Michelle Wildgen, Brian DeLeeuw, Nicole Haroutunian, Sara Weiss, Nicki Pombier-Berger, Julie Stevenson, Dan Degnan, Adrian Kinloch, Jessica Winter, Heather M., Nat "Ace" Jacobs, Beth Fitzer, Elizabeth Dunn, Stephanie Palumbo, Erin Kirkham, and Deborah Way.

Heaps of praise and thanks to the brilliant (and aptly named) Meg Storey, and the rest of the good people at Tin House Books; and to Sarah Burnes, the most patient and generous agent anyone could hope for.

Thank you to Amy Hempel, for her keen eye and kind advice. Thank you to Paola Peroni, for her super-human support and steadfast friendship. Thank you to Alex Banner, for everything.

Warm thanks to the Kimura, Rund, Christie, Fowler, Ratliff, Donahue, and Arnold families—especially my parents, and *especially* especially Cody and Meggie.

Finally, with tremendous admiration and love, thank you to Adam Ratliff (and little Warren), without whom life would be like a broken pencil: pointless.